I0586959

ELUSIVE HEARTS

AN UNEXPECTED ROMANCE - BOOK ONE

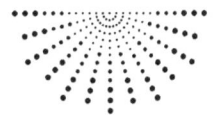

ROSIE CHAPEL

ULFIRE PTY LTD

First printing: 2022
ISBN: 978-0-6454794-0-9 (e book)
ISBN: 978-0-6451985-9-1 (paperback)

Ulfire Pty. Ltd.
P.O. Box 1481
South Perth
WA 6951
Australia

www.rosiechapel.com

Cover Design: Holly Perret: The Swoonies Romance Art

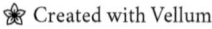 Created with Vellum

ACKNOWLEDGMENTS

To…

My husband – the inspiration for every one of my heroes.

My long-suffering and stalwart proofreaders, Janet and Melanie.

Graham from Fading Street Publishing Services for his editing expertise.

Holly Perret of The Swoonies Romance Art for this sublime cover.

Prof. D Kennedy for on his assistance regarding historical accuracy.

My amazingly supportive readers for coming on this journey with me. I truly appreciate your loyalty.

Thank you!

Dare to dream!

Elusive
HEARTS

A Regency Romance

ROSIE CHAPEL

PROLOGUE

APRIL 1818

*S*apphira Beresford loved this time of the year. Winter's gloom forgotten under sunny skies. The mild air was perfumed with heady blossoms, myriad colours festooned the trees, and flowers carpeted the parks. More exciting, *this* spring, in fact this very day, she was getting married.

She stood by the open window and stared out over the beautiful vista, her thoughts meandering like the path weaving its drunken way to the orchards.

At two and twenty, Sapphira was among the last of her friends to wed, in the main because her betrothed had only recently reached his majority. A detail stipulated to in the formal arrangement drawn up between their respective families two decades previously.

Jeremy FitzAllen, an earl no less, was quite dreamy really. Slightly taller than she — an important trait when you are reasonably tall yourself — with fair hair, and velvety brown eyes.

They had been friends all their lives and Sapphira could not recall a time when Jeremy wasn't there. Was she in love with him? A question she mused on frequently, without ever coming to a satisfactory answer. They liked each other; he was an agreeable companion and treated her with respect. There was no indication he was cruel or boorish or would ignore her the minute they signed the register.

What more could she ask for? Mutual kindness, consideration, and gentle affection. To Sapphira it felt like love, ignoring the obscure restlessness teasing at her subconscious.

Turning away from the pretty view across the gardens, she looked at her gown. It was a vision in the palest blue, elegant and not too fussy — she detested clothes adorned with bows, and lace, and ribbon.

Walking over to where it hung on the door of the armoire, she stroked her fingers over the silk. Underneath, a costly indulgence as it was unlikely they would last the day, a pair of low-heeled shoes in matching blue silk — the criss-cross pattern over the toe woven in a darker hue — and trimmed with a jewel encrusted buckle. She had to admit they were perfect.

A prickle of something akin to unease ran down her spine. Of late, Jeremy had been distracted, distant. She had ascribed it to pre-wedding jitters and when challenged, Jeremy had laughed and told her she was imagining things.

"He is correct, my girl. Pull yourself together," she admonished herself.

Alice, her personal maid, came through the door carrying a pile of delicate undergarments, effectively diverting Sapphira's doubts.

The arduous task of dressing for her wedding began.

The congregation at the church was abuzz. *Where was Lord Jeremy?* His parents were here, as was his older brother and his family but of Lord FitzAllen, Earl of Brunswick, there was no sign. Fans were opened or hats lifted the better to mask concerned mutterings.

The clatter of horses drawing a carriage produced an immediate silence. With bated breath they waited. *Was this the tardy gentleman?*

Sapphira and her father, the Earl of Templeton, appeared, silhouetted in the arched doorway. A collective gasp, then a sigh rippled through the church.

"Papa, something's wrong. Look at their expressions," Sapphira murmured. Everyone was staring at her as though she had grown an extra head. Her gaze travelled around the church, coming to a dead stop when she realised that where her betrothed ought to be waiting was conspicuously empty.

Her father patted her hand. "Nothing to fret about, my dear." He motioned to the vicar, who hurried towards them.

"Where is Lord Brunswick?" Sapphira hissed in undertones.

"We thought you were he," the vicar replied, less than coherently. "What I mean is, we supposed the carriage that just arrived to be bearing him, not you," he qualified.

Sapphira fidgeted. That same curious foreboding reared its ugly head. *What if...?* A sneaking suspicion pestered and pestered until she allowed it to form. He would not be so crass as to actually leave her at the altar, would he? Surely, he was simply late.

Her heart raced. A hot flush surged through her followed by a chill, icier than a December frost. The vicar was speaking again, but his words were distorted, and sounded as though they were coming from a great distance. She crumpled onto one of the stone benches set against the walls of the ornate porch. The cold from the unyielding slab seeping through her finery.

"Sapphi, Sapphi," her father's voice penetrated the whooshing in her ears. A fan was wafted in front of her nose, the snap of air welcome.

Closing her eyes, she forced the turbulence in her head to settle and strove to salvage her composure. "I cannot believe he would treat me thus," she croaked.

"Come, poppet, let us go home. You look in need of a stiff brandy," her father coaxed.

Despite the humiliation of her current situation, Sapphira felt a grin twitch at her lips. Papa's answer to all troubles was a stiff brandy. "A moment," she begged.

He was troubled by her pallor but acquiesced. "Whatever you need, my dear."

Sapphira rose from the bench, straightened her shoulders, brushed non-existent fluff off her skirts, and strode purposefully down the nave to the chancel steps.

She braved the multitude of guests. A wild giggle threatened to spill over at the sea of horrified faces, which resembled some of the satirical engravings found in London print shops. Oddly, this helped calm her.

"My lords, ladies, and gentleman," Sapphira began. "Today was intended to be a day of celebration. A day of joy and good cheer. Regrettably, Lord Brunswick has seen fit to abandon me without a word of explanation and has doubtless absconded to goodness knows where."

She ignored her mother's stunned exclamation and the flurry of whispers.

"I refuse to wallow in self-pity and allow this day to be wasted. Please join me at The Towers where a sumptuous wedding breakfast awaits. One I suggest ought to be renamed the Severance Luncheon." Her green eyes gleamed at the quickly stifled mirth this remark engendered. She dipped a low curtsy. "I look forward to seeing you there."

With that, she swept out of the church and into the sunlight, noticing as she passed the family pew that there was no sign of her sister, Gisela. Her mother might be a trifle feather-brained, but she wasn't blind. Why had she not queried Gisela's absence?

Sapphira's mind went into overdrive. Her betrothed *and* her sister missing. This could not be a coincidence. Snatches of conversation, puzzling comments, strange moods, and unanswered questions popped into her head.

A series of seemingly unconnected threads merged to create a very large knot. Worse, was her mother a party to their disappearance? *No!* Shock and mortification morphed into white hot fury.

Lord Templeton intercepted his daughter as she erupted from the dim interior, spewing dire threats and gesticulating erratically. Unhurriedly, he hooked her arm around his, slowed her pace, and led her to the waiting carriage.

Reaction set in and Sapphira's legs began to tremble so badly she worried they would not hold her. She clung to her father. "P-papa, what do I... why did... I cannot..." she pleaded.

"Hush, sweetheart, wait until we get home. Fret not, there is probably a simple explanation." He mollified, while battling to quell the anger that his daughter had been dealt this blow. He could not *wait* to hear the FitzAllens' justification for so embarrassing a debacle.

"I know what the explanation is," she choked. "The wastrel has run off with Gisela."

Her father spluttered a denial. "No, no, no, my dear. Nothing so drastic, Likely he is nursing a hangover and forgot the time."

"*Forgot the time*? Papa, do you think me addled? He has a

whole household to get him ready and remind him this is his wedding day and get him to the church on time. Neither should he need reminding. 'Tis not as though this was sprung on him yesterday," Sapphira retorted. "Moreover, Gisela is not in church. Did Mama not think that peculiar?"

At a nod from the earl, the groom clicked the horses and the splendid carriage, polished to within an inch of its life, rolled away.

Sapphira sat in the library, quite alone save her thoughts, which were not particularly illuminating. She had spent hours chatting with her friends, family, and the various guests who had travelled to The Towers nestled in rural Kent, some from a great distance, to witness a wedding.

Her face ached from keeping a cheerful smile in place, when all she wanted to do was throw a tantrum of epic proportions.

Now most of the guests were wending their way home, save those staying at The Towers who had retired to their rooms for a rest before the evening's entertainment began. The earl was determined none would find his hospitality lacking in any way, regardless of the circumstances.

Sapphira wanted no part of it, conceding she had little choice but to show her face.

A peace, of sorts, descended over the sprawling house.

Not ready to discuss the fiasco with her parents, Sapphira had excused herself and slipped into the quiet library. Here, surrounded by her beloved books, the tension began to drain away.

Upon their return to The Towers, Sapphira had combed the house from top to bottom, even pestering the domestic staff. Gisela was nowhere to be found but, in her sister's bedchamber, Sapphira uncovered a brief note.

By the time you read this, we shall be on our way to Gretna Green. Any attempt to follow us, in hope you can change our minds will be futile. We are in love and have been for years. Unable to face the prospect of knowing we could never be together, this was our only recourse.

Please do not think badly of us.
Gisela

As explanations went, it was sorely inadequate. Sapphira's main complaint being why they left it until her wedding day to flee.

"Mayhap today was their first opportunity. Everyone was either at or heading to the church. Easier to slip away." Her best friend, Hester, had posited.

"More likely she could not bear the idea I might be married first," Sapphira countered uncharitably.

Gisela, younger by four years, was the darling of her doting mother who ensured she was the centre of attention. To be fair, she was breathtakingly beautiful. Petite in stature, her delicate features were more vibrant than Sapphira's, who felt like a pale copy in comparison.

Well-versed in the medley of ladylike pursuits a nobleman's daughter was expected to master, Gisela also knew how to turn on the charm when it suited her. In fact, the epitome of refinement.

Sapphira, on the other hand, hated such decorous pastimes and had shown woeful incompetence in most — despite everyone's best endeavours. Growing up away from the city and all its constraints, she was perhaps more... uninhibited than her peers.

While others were learning deportment, Sapphira was running wild with the children of the estate workers. Instead of becoming proficient in embroidery, or drawing, or painting, she had — to her father's delight and her mother's horror — persuaded one of the stewards, a retired soldier, to teach her archery and fencing. She possessed a tolerable singing voice and could play the piano after a fashion.

Her greatest love was books for which she had developed a passion at an early age and was currently working her way through The Towers' extensive library. The ancient world fascinated her, and she often daydreamed about visiting the ruins scattered around the Mediterranean, accepting it was wishful thinking.

Until today, it had not occurred to Sapphira that Jeremy might prefer a genteel bride; a wife who would slot seamlessly into the parlours of the *ton*, not cause them to whisper judgementally behind their fans.

A wife like Gisela.

She forced herself to examine their relationship with an objective eye. She believed they were friends. She had trusted him. Yes, they had disagreed on occasion, in fact, their explosive arguments were legendary, but they blew over as quickly as they began.

Despite theirs being an arranged marriage, Jeremy had done the gentlemanly thing and courted her, with no sign his heart lay elsewhere.

It kept coming back to why he... *they*... had waited until today? If the idea of being married to her had been so abhorrent, their families could have come to a suitable arrangement. Clearly, all they had to do was swap sisters.

Sapphira was at a loss. Yes, Gisela was prone to be a trifle empty-headed, rather vain, and often selfish, but Sapphira loved her anyway. She thought it was reciprocated. The same went for Jeremy; if he did not love her, she presumed he cared for her.

Apparently not.

A headache niggling, she pushed herself out of the chair and traipsed across the dimly lit hall to the drawing room. The conversation with her parents could no longer be delayed.

CHAPTER ONE

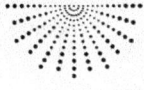

MAY 1818

*G*ripping the polished wooden railing of the great ship for support, Sapphira stared out over the vast ocean. She had been on board *The Trident* for nearly three weeks and the captain assured his few passengers, they were less than two days from their destination.

The winds had been favourable and the sea not too choppy, making the journey less arduous than it might have been. The sun sparkled on the water and an occasional seagull wheeled overhead, a sure sign they were approaching land.

Turning, she rested on her elbows to study the crew busy at their miscellaneous tasks. The smooth running of the ship fascinated her. It had taken a day or so to become accustomed to the sheer volume of equipment tucked around the main deck, and to duck every time she went below but, before long, it became second nature.

Then there was the constant swaying, and the creak of the sails and masts. The cramped quarters — and hers were spacious compared with those of the crew, and the somewhat repetitive menu. In truth, Sapphira genuinely enjoyed the plain fare they were served. It might be simple, but it was beautifully cooked and, she had to admit, far less stodgy than the meals she normally ate.

Sapphira felt the privations were worth it for the chance to witness the night sky in all its glory. Crystal clear and laden with stars… so many stars. An insatiable star gazer, she thought the skies above the Templeton estate to be impressive, but the celestial display repeated night after night, took her breath away.

She never tired of it and — to the consternation of her fellow travellers, not to mention the bemusement of the crew — often did not retire to her cabin until the pearly light of the encroaching dawn pushed back the darkness.

The captain, however, understood what drove her to stand for hours all alone, buffeted by the wind, for it was also his solace. He did not know why this young woman travelled on his ship, but he had watched her change while aboard.

Initially, painfully reserved — not unexpected given she was surrounded by brawny sailors — slowly, Miss Beresford, as she had begged to be addressed, had relaxed. Throughout the voyage, he had begun to see hints of what he suspected was an innate vivacity.

She reminded him of his daughter, and he found himself feeling similarly protective, to the point of issuing a gently couched warning about the port city where they were due to dock.

"Thank you, Captain Richards." She had smiled her gratitude, but he noticed it did not reach her eyes. "Thankfully, my companions have visited before and are familiar with the more questionable districts. I doubt we will stay any longer than necessary. Lord Dynham is eager to get to the site, something about recently excavated buildings. He has organised rooms close by, owned by a family friend." Sapphira shrugged, more in amusement than incomprehension.

Lord Archer and Lady Hester Dynham, an unorthodox couple, spent several months of each year touring ancient ruins. Their generous invitation, issued shortly after that awful day, for Sapphira to join them was accepted with alacrity. It provided the ideal opportunity to vanish for a while and saved the haranguing her poor ears were receiving from *well-intentioned* commiserators.

Never in her wildest dreams did Sapphira imagine she might actually get to see the ruins she had read about so avidly. Yet here they were, almost within her grasp.

Their destination... Pompeii.

An entourage of carriages rumbled up a dusty avenue. Either side, rows of tall, thin pines, swaying gently in the sea breeze, offered cool shade to the weary travellers. At this point, Sapphira, desperate for a proper bath, would have happily flung herself into the Mediterranean, fully clothed, for the joy of feeling clean.

The trio's chatter had dwindled as the day wore on, reduced to desultory remarks about the countryside they were passing through. Content to admire the spectacular scenery, Sapphira turned her mind to envisioning their host for the next couple of months.

All Archer and Hester had told her was that this Leofwin Colleville, Marquis of Osmund, lived in Italy because it suited his health. That Hester had known him for years. That he had inherited the villa from his great aunt, and that he spent his days pottering around the ruins of Pompeii. Not much at all, in fact.

To stop from dozing off, Sapphira began to create a picture of their host. Leofwin... he sounded like a character from Chaucer's Canterbury tales, or a medieval knight. He would be an academic, a little bent with age, with grizzled features, and sporting a shock of white hair. Doubtless a bit crabby and hard of hearing, always rambling on about some auspicious find or area of interest — one of those salt of the earth types.

She grinned to herself as the image solidified in her head.

The avenue opened onto a sweeping half-moon shaped frontage. At first glance the term villa seemed a misnomer, for it resembled the crumbling farmhouses they had seen dotted around the countryside.

Sapphira hopped out of the coach before she could be assisted down by their driver. Stretching aching muscles, and relieved that the constant rattling of the coach was silenced, she breathed in a lungful of the fragrant air.

Facing her, under a pan-tiled roof was a rambling building, the expanse of what she assumed to be local stone, alleviated by arched windows and the massive front door, each one trimmed in pale-red brick. Above, at random intervals and framed by wooden shutters, several smaller, square windows. The muted palate seemed to mirror the hues of the landscape.

In between the windows on the ground level, enormous terracotta pots overflowed with sage and rosemary. To Sapphira's right, in the dappled shelter of an unfamiliar tree, four sturdy wooden chairs surrounded a circular table whose surface resembled a random mosaic of brightly coloured tile fragments.

The scene, oozing rustic charm, was elegant yet restful, and foreign yet unexpectedly familiar. A place where one could unwind after a long day. Hester and Archer joined her, as three people burst through the enormous front door, gabbling unintelligibly… to Sapphira's ears at least.

"Ahhh, Nuncio, Amalia, and this *cannot* be Mariella?" Hester's cry was drowned in a delighted chorus as she was greeted with an exuberance that would not be tolerated in the rarefied world of the *ton*. Laughing merrily, Hester was swept into the house, the four chattering in the same language.

"I had no idea Hester spoke Italian," a startled Sapphira said to Archer as they followed in their wake, while their modest retinue began the laborious task of unloading the carriages.

"It is easier than having an interpreter or resorting to a kind of sign language while speaking in monosyllables," Archer explained. "Moreover, we considered it impolite to expect everyone to speak English, this is their land, not ours. We are the interlopers; it is up to us to make the effort."

"Oh, I agree wholeheartedly," replied Sapphira. "'Tis a beautiful language, very lyrical even when people argue. Do you remember that verbal altercation in the street outside our lodgings? Those two men were bellowing what had to be appalling insults, but it sounded like poetry... well, almost." She twinkled.

Archer chuckled at the simile, and ushered Sapphira through the doorway into a surprisingly spacious atrium. The villa's interior was open plan; rooms flowed into one another, delineated by graceful archways rather than doors. Pastel decor, minimal furniture, and whitewashed walls, along with lofty, open-beamed ceilings added to the sense of airiness.

Straight ahead, Sapphira's gaze was captured by what she could only describe as an exedra or partial loggia.

"Oh," she squeaked.

Slender columns, encircled with some kind of clinging vine and supporting a dome-vaulted plaster ceiling, drew the eye to the glittering turquoise expanse of the Mediterranean.

"Do you think Lord Osmund would mind?" she asked, her feet taking her across the cool tiled floor before Archer could answer. The tiles led seamlessly to an oblong shaped terrace, which was bordered by a knee-high, classically carved, stone balustrade; the stone cap, wide enough to sit on. The façade of the house jutted out beyond the columns, protecting the interior from the weather.

Sapphira sighed in delight when she glimpsed the frescos depicting lush gardens adorning the internal walls on either side. To see a modern replica of something she had read about in one of her father's massive volumes on the architecture of Ancient Rome, in the flesh so to speak was wondrous.

As she reached the balustrade, Sapphira released another squeak, aware she sounded a trifle unbalanced but unable to prevent it. A series of stairs, chiselled out of the hillside, curved down from where she stood. Beneath her, two more villas, built into the slope, terrace-style.

"Archer." She spun around to face Lord Dynham who had followed her. "Are these all part of the same property?"

"Indeed, they are. When Osmund inherited the place, only this level was habitable. Those two," he flicked his hand towards the lower buildings, "were dilapidated. He took his time refurbishing them and, as you can see, replicated designs from antiquity. I rather think he enjoyed the challenge of recreating an ancient Roman villa, even employing traditional techniques. Mind, I imagine, given the number of experts who work at Pompeii, he had all the advice he needed."

"How marvellous, and what a view. I would never tire of sitting here and admiring it. It is changing constantly, that water, the most incredible blue." She sank onto the broad railing and, shading her eyes with one hand, stared out over the bay, watching endless spangles of sunlight dance on the waves. *Goodness it was heavenly.*

Lost in thought, Sapphira didn't register the thud of a new footfall, nor did she hear the murmur of voices behind her. Nothing until the sound of a warning cough. Flushing, she leapt up and turned.

Her eyes widened and her mouth formed a perfect O.

"La—Miss Sapphira Beresford, may I introduce Lord Osmund?"

Sapphira gawped, there was no polite way to describe her expression. A handsome, tanned, and dark-haired, nothing like the image in her head gentleman, bowed. "Welcome to the Villa dei Fiori, Miss Sapphira Beresford."

Gathering herself, Sapphira stammered, "Th-thank you f-for your generous invitation, Lord Osmund." Belatedly, remembering to curtsy. "Y-your home is sublime."

"Thank you, Miss Beresford. I am glad you approve."

His tone was grave, but Sapphira had the impression levity lurked behind his bland response.

"Please come with me. I shall show you to your rooms. Hester has been stolen away by my staff so 'tis probable we shall not see hide nor hair of her until dinner." He shook his head good-humouredly at Sapphira's badly disguised astonishment. "We do not stand on ceremony here. We seldom have guests, and I have become quite adept at domestic tasks."

Instead of going back through the house, he shepherded them to the level below. Sapphira noticed he used a cane and had a pronounced limp, but the steps did not seem to hinder him unduly. Doubtless he was used to them.

Entering by a set of double doors, they came to another atrium, mirroring the one in the main house, off which ran two corridors.

Taking the corridor on the right, Lord Osmund opened the first door they came to, and ushered Sapphira into a sun-drenched room.

"Your suite where I hope you will be comfortable," he said. "I daresay you would like to freshen up after your ride from Naples. If there is anything you require, Luisa, your maid for the duration, will see it is supplied. Please join us on the terrace below when you are ready. Drinks will be served before dinner."

"Thank you, my lord," she replied with a shy smile. "You are most considerate."

"I like my guests to feel at home." He bowed slightly, adding, "The Dynhams' rooms are along the opposite corridor."

The voices of the two men faded as they walked away. Sapphira pushed the door closed and leant on it, corralling her wayward brain.

"So much for wizened and elderly," she grumbled to the room. "I could teach lessons in how to conjure up mythical creatures." Her thoughts went off on a tangent. "I wonder how he injured his leg?"

Unable to answer her own question, she turned her attention to the room.

Painted in a pastel lemon wash, the walls were unadorned save a simple illustration of a garden by the sea — perhaps it was Lord Osmund's — which evoked long hot summer days.

Here too, the furnishings were functional rather than ostentatious but the bed, with its crisp white sheets and layers of coverlets, looked inviting.

Through the inevitable arch, a sizeable dressing room, complete with bath and, miracle of miracles, a water closet — rare even in the exalted mansions of the *ton*.

Sapphira marvelled at the modern amenities her host had integrated into his home.

Three windows, their shutters open, overlooked the bay.

It was idyllic.

Her luggage had been delivered to the room but had yet to be opened. Mindful of her host's comment, Sapphira unbuckled the broad straps around her trunk, unlocked it and began the tedious job of arranging her clothes.

She had been frugal in her packing, thankful she had limited herself to four riding habits in fine wool, four cotton day dresses in pastel shades, and two silk evening gowns, as she hung them in the capacious armoire.

Save a pair of shoes in the palest tan leather — chosen because they matched everything — and a pair of satin house slippers, her footwear consisted of robust flat-soled boots, which she lined up under the gowns. She tucked her collection of lightweight shawls, delicate undergarments and the several pairs of gloves into the chest of drawers.

Finally, broad-brimmed bonnets were slung over convenient hooks by the door.

Placing her other accoutrements on the dressing table, Sapphira did a slow circle, checking everything, pleased with what she saw. "I am also quite capable," she told the room and swiped her hands together, before shoving the trunk into a corner, out of the way.

"Now to freshen up."

CHAPTER TWO

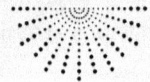

*I*t is remarkable how a thorough wash and a change of
clothes lifts one's spirits, Sapphira thought as she
thanked Luisa who had arrived promptly to assist.

Taking her time, she descended to the lowest level of the
villa, mesmerised once again by the stunning vista
before her.

In the early evening light, the dazzling colours were
morphing into softer hues but were no less beautiful. In fact,
Sapphira deemed them more so.

An open door led to another terrace, much wider than
the one on the uppermost tier. Underfoot, an expanse of
terracotta, blue, and cream tiles in a geometric pattern.
Above her head, a wooden pergola, its lattice work inter-
woven with a profusion of flowers and trailing greenery.

At the rear of the pergola in great square planters, like
benign sentinels, a line of what appeared to be fruit trees,
perhaps lemons — Sapphira made a mental note to ask her
host. In the centre, surrounded by six wrought iron chairs
with colourful cushions, a well-scrubbed wooden table on
which stood a silver platter bearing crystal decanters and

four glasses. Three candelabra shed a mellow glow across the space.

The breeze had dropped. The rays of the dying sun shot streaks of flaming cerise through the darkening sky, catching the underside of the odd cloud with its fire, and turning the glassy sea molten.

She appeared to be the first one down and hesitated on the threshold.

"Good evening, Miss Beresford," a deep voice spoke from the far side, and a figure detached itself from the shadows. "Would you care for a drink?"

"Thank you, yes please," Sapphira replied politely and edged closer.

"I do not bite." Lord Osmund chuckled at her reticence and opened a hand towards the chairs.

Sapphira slid into the nearest seat and accepted the proffered glass. She took a sip and wrinkled her nose. Given the subtle blush of the drink, she was anticipating a light wine, and the effervescence was unexpected. Not dissimilar to the champagne she had tasted occasionally, she found it much more palatable.

"This is lovely." She lifted the glass in indication.

"An Italian speciality," he said gravely. "I have grown fond of it over the years."

Sapphira took another sip, willing her brain to come up with a witty comment or pithy observation. She was not usually lost for words.

"How was your journey?" Lord Osmund broke the awkward silence.

Sapphira embarked on a lengthy account of their travels from the moment they left London to arriving at his home that afternoon.

Hiding his amusement, her host topped up her glass, which loosened her tongue further.

Conscious her mouth was running away with her, Sapphira was helpless to curb her babble, relieved when Hester and Archer joined them, and she could take a breath.

"Thank goodness, I have been regaling Lord Osmund with tales of our voyage, and fear his poor ears deserve a more interesting topic of conversation." Sapphira gave a wry smile.

"Not at all, I was enjoying your description," he countered gallantly.

Sapphira swallowed a snort, covering it with a cough and sent Hester a look of appeal.

Used to reading her friend's expressions, Hester asked a question about the current excavations and there the conversation remained for the rest of the evening.

With what Sapphira would come to recognise as one of Lord Osmund's numerous idiosyncrasies, he suggested dinner be served where they sat.

"I prefer to take my meals here. The climate lends itself to dining outside, and eating under the stars appeases my internal muse," the marquis clarified. "I have no artistic talent to speak of, but I recognise beauty in all its forms. This," he swung his arm in an arc, "begs to be revered at every opportunity." His gaze fixed on a point somewhere over the bay, Lord Osmund's austere features softened.

"Why, you are becoming quite the poet in your old age," Hester teased.

Sapphira stared, but the moment had gone. Lord Osmund's face hardened again, and she pondered its cause.

Their host was a bit of a mystery.

Leofwin Colleville was intrigued by the young woman who had accompanied his friends. He had received Hester's letter, begging him not to be perturbed by a third guest whom she believed required a spell out of England, only three days prior to their arrival.

While he understood the need to avoid the unpredictable English weather, Hester's words badgered him. *Requiring a spell out of England*; a perplexing phrase, leaving one to speculate whether the person in question was running away, from something or someone.

When Archer introduced her as Miss Beresford, Leofwin was positive his friend was about to say lady, before correcting himself quickly. Sitting at an angle to her, he leant back in his chair to study this Miss Beresford as the shadows lengthened, aware she would be blind to his perusal.

Her blonde hair was swept up into an intricate bun, a few ringlets framing her face. He thought her eyes were green, but although the candlelight made them sparkle, it was too dark to discern their hue. Her countenance, which until now had seemed withdrawn, became animated as she talked about a book she had been reading on the voyage. Her fingers describing invisible arcs as she emphasised a point.

Her skin appeared almost dewy in the glow of the moonrise and, for a split-second, Leofwin itched to stroke the graceful column of her neck. He shook it off, inwardly chastising himself for so ridiculous a lapse. What use had he for women? *None.*

Except for Hester, whom he had known almost the whole of his life, he found the women outside his immediate family to be grasping, shrill, and selfish, or shrinking violets who couldn't say boo to a goose, or too caught up in their own beauty to consider the lesser mortals who bowed to their every whim. Frivolous martinets the lot of them.

No, Vesuvius was more likely to erupt again, before he, Leofwin Colleville, would bear anything other than a tenuous camaraderie for a member of the gentle sex.

Fate smiled to herself. *Challenge accepted.*

The following day, for Sapphira's benefit, Leofwin gave his visitors a comprehensive tour of his property. This included the stables adjacent to the main villa, and the shoreline — accessible via a short flight of steps directly off the terrace where they had eaten dinner the previous evening.

It was certainly extensive.

The impressive stable complex accommodated several horses, as well as the coaches which had borne the new arrivals from Naples — now parked alongside Lord Osmund's own carriage and a small cart. Archer mentioned that two of the horses were his, generously cared for in their owner's absence by Lord Osmund.

Four stablehands, busy doing their respective chores, greeted them with beams of delight and the same unintelligible chatter Sapphira had heard from Nuncio and his family.

She made a mental note to try to learn something of their language during her stay — although they seemed able to understand each other with mimes and hand signals.

Beyond the stables, fruit trees grew in abundance, on the cusp of blossoming. A large and flourishing vegetable patch. A fenced area, which housed a small flock of goats was also where the horses grazed.

The grounds abutting the buildings were scrupulously tended and formally planted, but towards the outer reaches of his land, Leofwin had allowed parts to grow wild.

A faint flush of colour could be seen on some of the trees,

prompting Sapphira to ask their host whether he knew the varieties.

"My aunt itemised every plant in the garden, she was meticulous in that regard. According to her list, they are a mixture of magnolia, crab-apple, crape myrtle... a recent introduction, I understand... and jacaranda, although in truth, I do not know one from the other." He smiled apologetically.

"Goodness what exotic names, and how fascinating. Would you consider me impertinent if I begged to examine them?" she replied, her interest in plants vying with her reticence. Sapphira loved growing things, whether they be flora or fauna. Her mother despaired of her daughter's preference for tending to herbs or talking with the gardeners, or taking the dogs for long walks, or assuming the care of rejected calves or lambs, over more ladylike pastimes.

"I would consider you... unusual," he prevaricated, "but be at liberty to explore to your heart's content."

"What of the climbing plant covering the pergola?" she persisted, recalling the sinuous, vine-like branches laden with buds but devoid of leaves. 'Tis most interesting and, I surmise, foreign to the cooler English clime."

"Wisteria is its name and its flowers, which I believe are on the cusp of blooming, resemble a soft purple waterfall. Interestingly the blossoms come before the leaves sprout."

That explained the lack of greenery.

"The vine on the upper terrace," he continued, anticipating her next question, "is jasmine, also due to blossom any day. I confess the delicate fragrance has become synonymous with home. Aunt Maud might have neglected some of her property, but her passion for flowers never waned, and is reflected in the name of the villa."

"Villa dei Fiori." Sapphira turned that over in her mind.

"Fiori, fiori... ha... Villa of the Flowers?" She made a wild guess.

"Correct, your quick understanding of the language does you credit." Leofwin bowed slightly.

"I am picking up a word here and there," she demurred. "Thank you, Lord Osmund. I too have an appreciation for plants." Ignoring Hester who rolled her eyes at her friend's massive understatement. "To study such stunning specimens is a boon unanticipated," she finished primly.

"I am pleased my paltry garden kindles your enthusiasm," he rejoined.

"Goodness you two are being starchy," Hester interjected. "I cannot think why, you have not met prior to yesterday. "Osmund, are you being deliberately stuffy?" She pinned her friend with a shrewd gaze.

"Not in my nature," he countered with a sly smile.

"Pooh, you were born stuffy," Hester teased. "Come now." She hooked her arm through his. "Do be a gentleman and organise a drink. I am fair parched from all this walking." She fanned her face dramatically. Lord Osmund's face relaxed from its habitual gravity.

"Minx." He grinned.

Sapphira watched the pair teasing each other as they strolled back to the house. Hester and Lord Osmund behaved as though they were brother and sister, something she commented on to Archer.

"They are closer than most siblings," he replied. "Growing up, their two families all but lived in each other's houses. It created a strong bond, which continued into adulthood. A rare blessing." Archer had no need to elaborate. Friendships between unrelated men and women, while not unheard of, were uncommon.

"'Tis rather nice," Sapphira said, watching Hester and Leofwin laughing at something one of them had said.

"It is, moreover, I know Osmund would protect Hester with his life, should the occasion arise."

"A fine recommendation," Sapphira nodded. Their conversation petered out as they reached the house, whereupon Lord Osmund rang for cool lemonade and a platter of biscuits.

"If you are agreeable and feel rested, tomorrow we shall go to the site," their host proposed, while they enjoyed the selection of refreshments.

"How far is it?" Sapphira asked.

"Maybe forty minutes by carriage, slightly less on horseback."

"Oh, might we be able to ride there?" Forgetting herself in her eagerness.

Lord Osmund chuckled. "You *are* keen. I take it you are a proficient horsewoman?"

"She could put most men to shame," Hester interjected drily.

"I consider myself reasonably accomplished," A hint of hauteur in Sapphira's tone.

"Are you happy to ride?" He directed his question to Hester and Archer, already knowing their answer.

"Of course, by far the most convenient method of transport, and the quicker we get to the site, the longer we can stay," Archer spoke for both.

"I am struggling to quell a bubbling excitement," Sapphira confessed. "For so long I have yearned to see Roman remains in situ, and here I am, half an hour's horse ride from my fantasy becoming reality."

"I hope they live up to your expectations."

"Oh, they couldn't not," she sighed, her expression dreamy.

"Please do not envisage a pristine ruin. Pompeii is dirty,

dusty, and precarious. It is easy to turn an ankle if you are not vigilant. Much of the site is still buried."

Lord Osmund's tone was equable, but Sapphira perceived a mild reproof. She studied him contemplatively.

"I am cognisant of the inherent risks associated with ruins. We do have the odd one in England, you know," her tone cooled considerably, while the colour in her cheeks heightened. "I believe I possess a sufficiency of wit *not* to trip over the first cobblestone, or fall down an unmarked hole, or have a fit of the vapours should a body be unearthed."

Hester glanced at her husband, sending a silent message. These two seemed determined to rub each other up the wrong way. Archer canted his head in understanding and fought a smile. He saw no reason to interfere, and they were quite entertaining.

"Forgive me, Miss Beresford. My intent was not to question your competency, only to give you fair warning. It is rare to meet a lady familiar with the peculiarities of sites under active excavation." Lord Osmund placated.

"No, 'tis I who ought to apologise. I reacted without thought," Sapphira conceded, gruffly. What was it about this man that goaded her so? He was politeness itself, yet she felt he was scrutinising her every move and every word, willing her to make a faux pas. Why? Save her description of the journey the previous evening, they had exchanged less than two dozen words and, until this moment, she had behaved impeccably.

Unbidden, the distance between here, and her, until recently, untroubled life in England, in both miles and comfort, seemed immense. Homesickness washed over her, and her flushed cheeks paled.

CHAPTER THREE

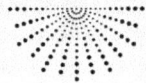

*B*y rights she ought to be settling into married life with Jeremy, not swanning around Italy.

Had he come to his senses, or was he basking in newly wedded bliss? Did Gisela feel at all contrite? Sapphira doubted it.

Her erstwhile suitor and her sister had not returned by the time Sapphira departed less than a fortnight after her aborted wedding. Of practical mind, she rarely dwelt on it. What was done could not be undone, nothing was achieved by weeping and wailing. Only, at night when all was quiet and sleep elusive, did her insecurities pester.

When Hester had suggested she accompany them, Sapphira had declined. Was it not better to face Society, head held high, than turn tail and flee?

"What utter nonsense, since when do *you* care what Society thinks?" Hester had retorted. "You know you want to travel. Now is the perfect opportunity. Just think, two months in Italy. The chance to explore, nay assist in, the excavations at Pompeii, perhaps even venture further afield. Sapphira, seize the moment."

Archer had added his encouragement and, under their joint pleas, Sapphira capitulated.

Her parents took some persuading, genuinely concerned about their older daughter's state of mind. After all, who jumps on a ship and sails halfway around Europe to mend a broken heart?

When it became obvious Sapphira was not to be dissuaded from what they referred to as her madcap scheme, they gave their blessing, relieved she would be travelling with Lord and Lady Dynham.

"I am sorry, Lord Osmund. I had no call to be discourteous when you have been nothing but generous. Mayhap I have not yet recovered from the voyage. I am not usually so fractious."

Leofwin, a little perturbed when Sapphira's face paled, dismissed her apology with a warm smile and a wave of his hand. "Do not think on it, Miss Beresford. Even the hardiest of travellers find the long sea voyage arduous. In a day or so, you will feel restored and ready for anything. Perhaps we ought to delay our visit to Pompeii?" He made it a question and encompassed all three of his guests.

"Oh, please, not on my account," Sapphira begged. "A good night's sleep will set me to rights. Truly," she added. "The mere idea of seeing Pompeii is enough to revitalise the weakest of souls." She smiled then, and it was like the sun breaching the horizon to scatter the dark of night. Her face glowed and her eyes sparkled.

Leofwin blinked, momentarily dazzled. *No, this would not do.*

Sapphira was up with the dawn the following day, eager to get to Pompeii. She chose a well-worn outfit, adjusted to allow her to ride astride. It might be frowned upon among high society, but she was in Italy, and had decided the rules could be bent for once. In her mind, comfort trumped fashion.

When planning their trip, Hester confided that her modiste had done something similar for several of her outfits, the cut of the skirt cleverly disguised so as not to offend. "No one knows us there and the locals do not care how you sit on a horse," she said when the pair discussed it prior to departing England.

"It is something I have done since our first visit to Italy and never regretted it. The last thing any of the people working at the ruins care about is what you are wearing. In all honesty, we could arrive in breeches, and no one would bat an eyelid."

"That would be interesting and likely very freeing." Sapphira had mused. "Do we dare?"

"Hmmm… can you imagine Archer's face?" Hester had pulled a comical grimace and the two friends chuckled, their conversation moving onto what other garments were necessary as opposed to desired on their journey.

Hester had proved a fount of knowledge regarding their luggage, suggesting Sapphira limit herself to absolute essentials, and to travel in attire which could be thrown away at the end of the voyage.

Glad of the tips, Sapphira had applied them, impressed by how little she needed. Granted, it *was* a trifle challenging aboard ship, but she managed.

This morning, clad in a forest green riding habit, she felt she presented a picture of practicality rather than frivolity.

Her host's behaviour continued to perplex. One minute he was aloof and remote, the next congenial — but only with her. With Hester and Archer, he was never anything other than open and friendly.

Sapphira could not think what she had done in so short a time to cause affront. Perhaps it was because she was a stranger, and had been foisted on him, so to speak, at the last minute. No doubt he had been looking forward to cosy chats with the Dynhams, and now he had to include an unexpected third.

Determined not to read too much into the situation, she maintained a cheerful demeanour when in his presence. Hopefully when he got to know her a little better, their exchanges would become less strained.

A hearty breakfast consumed, Lord Osmund led his guests to the stables and soon, waved off by an excitable Mariella, the four were trotting along a well-tended, if dusty road, chattering about the day ahead.

Sapphira was captivated by the humpbacked peak which dominated the otherwise gently undulating landscape to their left. Inexorably, her gaze was drawn to its slopes.

In the morning sunlight, the mountain evoked a sleeping giant — huge but harmless, yet the catastrophic eruption of AD79 had buried everything in its shadow.

"Vesuvius looks so benign," she remarked, as they rode. "Hard to believe the destruction it unleashed."

"And still grumbles," Lord Osmund said. "The last time just over twenty years ago."

"Oh," Sapphira shot the peak an apprehensive glance.

"I think we are fine today. She is quiet."

"She?" Sapphira raised a brow.

"*She* seems to fit, *he* doesn't. I never thought about it until I heard those working at Pompeii referring to Vesuvius as a she..." he grinned at Sapphira's incredulous expression. "Such things are not unusual, many inanimate objects are categorised as feminine, ships being a case in point regardless of their assigned name, even grand buildings. Something about their beauty, their aesthetic. Perhaps it's best not to ask and just accept."

"Perhaps you are correct. Although rather than based on their beauty, I posit the origin was far less esoteric. More likely the image of an erupting mountain reminded some gentleman of his wife in a towering rage, or a ship of her intransigence, etcetera, and so it began," she replied in bland tones.

Lord Osmund twisted in his saddle to stare at Sapphira. Her riposte was comical, intelligent, and unexpected. Her dry sense of humour, had she but known it, echoed his.

She returned his gaze steadily, then dropped a slow wink.

Unable to restrain his mirth at her sauce, Leofwin roared with laughter.

Sapphira was entranced, the deep, mellifluous sound reverberated around them and vibrated through her. She did not recognise it then, but this was the moment she lost her heart.

It seemed an invisible barrier had been levelled. The conversation flowed more easily and the tension, particularly between Sapphira and the marquis, relaxed.

Before they knew it, they were trotting up the track to Pompeii. There was no indication of a settlement in the vicinity, naught but a handful of farms and the odd villa.

"How in the world did anyone know this was here?" Sapphira asked as they approached the ruins.

"In the late fifteen hundreds, a man called Domenico Fontana was digging a water course and found them by accident," Leofwin replied. "According to the information, I have gleaned, it is believed he uncovered a considerable amount, all of which was subsequently reburied.

"They lay undisturbed for another hundred and fifty years or so, until a surveyor sent by the King of Naples discovered what Fontana had originally unearthed, and this was after excavations at Herculaneum had begun, although they too were almost immediately halted. He instigated a systematic investigation and, *voila.*" He swung his arm out, encompassing the scene in front of them.

"Incredible," Sapphira said, imagining the elation experienced by those who found this long-forgotten town. "I am agog to see the ruins. To be fortunate enough to walk where people of the distant past walked, to see their homes, be afforded a glimpse of their lives, is a privilege."

Once again, she surprised Leofwin. Every time Sapphira spoke, she shattered another of the preconceived notions he had created regarding his visitor. To find anyone knowledgeable about or sensitive to the preservation and conservation of ancient history in whatever form was unusual. Many who purported to be interested turned out to be treasure hunters, destroying more than they saved.

Hester and Archer were an exception. From their first visit, the couple had demonstrated an understanding of and empathy for these unique sites. Exploration quickly evolved into assistance and, eventually, they had become expert in the recovery and recognition of relics.

He had anticipated that this Miss Beresford would be a flighty chit with nothing but air between her ears. She was proving to be the antithesis of his presumption, and he could not decide whether this was annoying or gratifying.

Sapphira, blessedly ignorant of her host's ambivalence, was holding her breath as the horses clip-clopped along the hard-packed earthen track leading into the site which was veiled from view by a tangle of shrubbery and a line of Cupressus trees.

"This track has only been opened recently," Lord Osmund explained as they breached the wall of greenery. "The original path skirts the outside of the amphitheatre to the Porta Sarno from where we had to circle back. Some bright spark was either smart enough or lazy enough to forge a new entryway."

"It makes it very much easier," Archer said.

Hints of grey could be discerned through the leaves, but nothing could have prepared Sapphira for her first sight of Pompeii.

She gaped, slack jawed.

To her right, a colossal, curved building of grey stone surged upwards from the ground, punctuated by soaring arches, leading the eye to an upper level along which she spied more arches. Aware it would be of circular design, Sapphira had not anticipated such gargantuan dimensions. Possessed with an overwhelming urge to touch the ancient edifice, she slid off Minerva, her dapple-grey mare, dropped the reins, and walked closer.

A double staircase, supported by three more pairs of arches — each pair increasing in size in direct correlation to the angle of the steps — led to the smaller in scale upper level. They were steep, looked rather narrow and were certainly a deeper tread than was typical nowadays, but that wasn't about to prevent Sapphira from climbing them.

Before any of the other three could open their mouths, she was up the steps with the agility of a cat.

Dismounting with far more grace, Hester retrieved Minerva's reins and glanced at Leofwin who was staring after his guest in consternation.

"Fret not, Leo. Sapphira is sure-footed as a goat. A few

stairs or an odd wall will not impede her. That is not to say her skirts will not suffer," she placated.

"I intended to give her a brief outline of the site and warn her of the dangers. Some of the ruins are unstable." Leofwin frowned.

"Sapphira," Hester yodelled.

A head popped over the wall and a hand fluttered in acknowledgement before both disappeared.

Hester gave a tolerant shake of her head. "She will come down when she's ready. How about we go in? I am impatient to see it completely excavated."

"It is a stunning example," Leofwin remarked. He unhooked a sizeable knapsack from his saddle, and the trio sauntered to what had been the gate through which the participants entered.

On the uppermost level, Sapphira surveyed the amphitheatre. Even in its partially ruined state it was spectacular. Glad of her bonnet, which protected her eyes from the sun's glare, she let her gaze roam. Row upon row of stone seats circled the central arena, above the low wall separating the spectators from the combatants. Here and there, plants thrived in the cracks.

Turning, she admired the sprawling site from her elevated vantage point. Figures, in miniature from this height, were busy at their respective tasks, their voices carrying on the breeze.

She clasped her hands against her chest, still not quite believing she was here, actually standing on history. Roman history. History which had been buried for centuries. She wished her father could see this. He would be equally rapt.

Sapphira saw the others enter the arena through the arch below and to her left. Hester looked up and beckoned her to join them. Grudgingly, Sapphira retraced her steps, descending cautiously, and hurried to catch up. If she thought the amphitheatre impressive from above, at ground level, it was nothing short of stupendous.

Reading Hester's expression correctly, Sapphira said, "Lord Osmund, might you be so kind as to share your knowledge regarding this incredible structure?"

Hester hid a grin at Sapphira's dulcet tones, knowing her friend had done her own research during the voyage.

Documented evidence of the current excavations was not easy to come by, although academics and enthusiasts were beginning to chronicle their discoveries as well as those previously unearthed.

Determined to find something, Sapphira had combed through several London book shops in the days prior to their departure, finally tracking down a volume of recently translated treatises by the famed scholar, Johann Winckelmann. A man whose understanding of antiquities, specifically Greek and Roman had yet to be rivalled, more than fifty years later.

CHAPTER FOUR

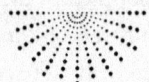

*A*stute enough *not* to mention this to her host, Sapphira waited expectantly.

Lord Osmund studied her suspiciously, but her request sounded genuine. Inwardly shrugging, he provided a thorough account of the excavations, expounding on gladiatorial combat, and how the seating was arranged to reflect Roman society.

"Regrettably, the frescos which once adorned the interior are missing, either destroyed during the eruption, damaged or removed when initially uncovered, or in the hands of private collectors," he concluded.

"Such a shame," Sapphira, who had hung on every word, lamented. "It is one thing to remove artefacts at risk of being stolen and store them in a safer place, but to steal for gain is atrocious. Thank you, my lord. Your description was riveting. Might you grant me a little time to explore this level?"

"Of course. I shall be across the way." He indicated the building just visible beyond the entrance. "Archer," he nodded to the earl who said something to Hester before accompanying his friend.

Hester looped her arm through Sapphira's, and they meandered around the ruin. Taking their time, they peered along the tunnel which circled the base of the amphitheatre, sat in several of the seats to see what view the different ranks of spectators saw, and climbed up to the top.

Perching on the upper wall, Sapphira drew a deep breath.

"If I died now, I would die happy," she murmured.

"Goodness how maudlin," Hester teased.

"Beg pardon, I do not mean to sound maudlin," Sapphira countered. "'Tis that just to be here, *inside* this beautiful monument. To hear Lord Osmund relate the details of those who fought and died, those who watched, nay cheered the gladiators, brings their world into ours." She sighed. "I cannot imagine anything surpassing this moment."

Hester studied her friend. "You do not think anything could better this?" she quizzed.

"Mayhap if I am fortunate enough to find an artefact," Sapphira mused, "otherwise, no."

"I shall remind you of this conversation," Hester replied cryptically. "Come, we ought to locate the men. Once they become engrossed in excavations, they forget everything and everyone around them." She smiled with the blithe forbearance of a wife who had long accepted her husband's foibles and loved him the more for them.

About to descend the stairs, they spotted the two men chatting with several others just outside what appeared to be a square, in the process of being excavated, made up of several smaller buildings.

"Possibly an insula," Hester elaborated.

"Hmmm... housing?" Sapphira, recalling her reading, essayed.

"Yes, although they are not certain and are concentrating on plots which require special attention. Where artefacts in their many guises are being brought to light," she enlightened at Sapphira's enquiring expression.

"To save them from thieves?"

"In the main. Also, they have discovered the weather can wreak havoc on the frescos which have been exposed to the elements. Preservation is key and I think in some cases they have decided to rebury them."

Sapphira pulled a face. "Perhaps they would be better leaving the whole site buried. Yes, it is a wonder to behold, but at what expense? It is a fine line between unearthing the past in order to carry out a detailed survey and destroying it."

"Yet here you are. You even declared yourself eager to participate if permitted."

Sapphira paused to marshal her thoughts. An unease of mind had been pestering since she climbed the steps of the amphitheatre.

"I know, and until I set foot on this site, I had no qualms about the notion, but what if by excavating the ruin, we lose it? It is not simply buildings, and frescos, and mosaics and artefacts. People died here. In the thousands. Their remains no doubt litter the ground beneath where we are standing. Are we not violating the dead by desecrating their rest? Are we not as culpable as the treasure hunters? Is there any genuine justification for revealing these ruins?"

Hester considered this; it was a question she had asked herself when first she walked around the site. "I accept the premise, but counter that your argument is extreme. The discovery was made over a hundred years ago, we cannot undo it. By documenting and preserving the site instead of leaving it to decay, are we not honouring the dead? Conserving their heritage for future generations. Providing valuable evidence for people who study the past.

"Is it not better to do that and ensure it is protected, than leave it to be stripped by unscrupulous relic hunters? You need to trust those who are working tirelessly, here at Pompeii and at Herculaneum. Think of them as custodians of history, silent testimony to the past."

Hester's interpretation allayed Sapphira's disquiet. "Thank you for putting it into perspective for me." She smiled. "I admit the chance to be involved even peripherally is thrilling. I just..."

"I understand your misgivings. I was similarly unsettled, but the genuine antiquarians are considerate of everything they uncover. There is no disrespect, or negligence. They treat each artefact, whatever it may be, with the utmost care. If someone with less experience finds something they are unsure of, they call for their supervisor. All recognise the enormity and delicacy of their task."

They reached Archer and Leofwin. Overhearing the last of their conversation, Archer asked whether ought was awry.

"Usual reservations," Hester replied. "Perhaps a topic we might revisit during dinner this evening."

"Forgive me. I am a guest here, and less educated than a novice in this discipline. Pay me no mind." Sapphira blushed furiously. "I came to help. Please might you be so kind as to show me what you are working on."

Lord Osmund studied Sapphira without speaking. Part of him... all right... *most* of him wanted to cling to his supposition that this Miss Beresford was nothing more than a featherhead, but it was becoming harder by the minute. Patently, her discussion with Hester had been insightful.

Now why did that irk him so much? *Because you want to catch her out, find something to support your assumptions,* the rational portion of his brain chided. He ignored it but *did* swallow the churlish rejoinder hovering on the tip of his tongue.

"This way. Be careful where you put your feet. We cannot afford any broken bones." He struck out at a fine pace, along a narrow path beyond the amphitheatre. His bad leg in no way hampering him.

The other three followed in his wake, the ladies almost running to keep up.

"Anyone would think he is trying to prove something," Hester grumbled.

"To whom?" Sapphira asked, not really paying attention.

"You," Archer interjected.

Sapphira stopped dead. "Whatever for?"

"I have no idea, but I have noticed you two are painfully polite with each other."

"We are strangers, is that not to be expected?"

"'Tis unusual, is all. You are generally open and friendly. As is Leo."

"Leo," Sapphira repeated. The diminutive fitted her host. She had visited the menagerie at the Tower of London, which housed lions among other exotic animals, and knew these majestic beasts were associated with the name Leo. Although the collection was admirable, Sapphira was not a proponent of keeping wild animals captive. They ought to be roaming free not prowling around a fabricated compound which bore little resemblance to their natural habitat.

Lions… there was a hint of the same ferocity in Lord Osmund, albeit well controlled; an untamed aura, yet she surmised he would protect those he cared for with his life. Perhaps he had always had it, perhaps it was as a result of his time at war. No doubt he had witnessed appalling atrocities, enough to turn the mildest of men into a raging savage.

"Sorry," she said, realising she had missed a question. "I was daydreaming."

"No need to apologise." Lord Osmund's mouth quirked, whether in annoyance or amusement Sapphira couldn't tell. "I was checking to be certain you meant it when you said you should like to assist."

"Oh, could I?" In her eagerness, she forgot his coolness of earlier.

"Of course, under supervision. Archer, Hester," he motioned for the couple to join a group of people working in a large space.

Sapphira peered through the opening but could not fathom its function.

"An insula," Lord Osmund clarified. "The homes of the less wealthy. Not as dramatic as the larger villas, but they contain a plethora of information about the inhabitants of this city."

"I imagine they must," Sapphira said. "One minute they are cooking a meal or chatting with friends, the next fleeing for their lives. No chance to gather their precious belongings. Left for us to discover centuries later."

"Quite," he replied. "This way."

Sapphira barely had time to say goodbye to her friends as Lord Osmund took off again, negotiating the occasional pile of debris or crumbled wall with aplomb.

Underfoot, the ancient road was visible. Lower than the roughly cleared paths at either side, large flat grey stones ran in an unwavering line ahead of them. Two equidistant grooves marred the smooth surface, presumably worn by the constant rotation of carts' wheels as they traversed the city.

Curious, Sapphira plied her host with questions about its construction, which he answered patiently and, shortly thereafter, they left the broad street and came into a vast open square.

With a flourish, Lord Osmund said, "The Forum."

Sapphira stared, awestruck by what had been accomplished. There was much left to be done, but the main structures had been revealed, along with arches and pillars, so many pillars. Across the square she spied more buildings. She could almost see the locals hurrying about their business, ignorant of the looming catastrophe.

"Gracious, this is incredible," she murmured. "How long did the excavations take?"

"Between when they were originally discovered and now, several years. That said, there is much more left to uncover than has been unearthed. It will take decades."

"Pompeii was a sizeable town then?"

"It was a port, so yes. To give you an idea, the amphitheatre seated around twenty thousand, which was probably more or less the population of the town. The experts estimate it stood between ten and twenty thousand at the time of the eruption. Many left after the earthquake of AD62 and, propitiously for them, had not returned."

"What about Herculaneum? Was that a similar size?"

"No, no, much smaller, about a quarter of Pompeii's population, around five thousand so it is believed."

"Was it not also a port?"

"More a small coastal town with a wharf."

"Shall we be afforded the chance to see those ruins?" she ventured, hopefully.

"I wish it was possible, but what was uncovered has either been reburied, or is only accessible by tunnels or with great difficulty. The biggest problem is the settlement of Resina atop the site. It was only rediscovered because someone needed a well, the digging of which revealed some impressive marble statues. The rest as they say…" he did not need to finish his sentence.

"There are murmurings a formal investigation of the site might be under consideration, but it depends on King Ferdinand. Regrettably, during those initial excavations many of the artefacts were plundered, in the main, for the ruler of the time, sculptures, bronzes, mosaics, frescos. Doubtless, they are scattered to the four winds now. Worse, the structures were damaged in the process." Leofwin did not bother to hide his disgust at this practice.

"I imagine such disrespect is hard to stomach. To see only the monetary value of something from the past instead of its historical significance is a travesty."

Lord Osmund stopped mid-stride and twisted to stare at Sapphira. She spoke with perception and empathy... again.

"Have you been down the tunnels?" she asked, oblivious to his scrutiny.

"It has been my great fortune to do so, once."

"Might you be so kind as to share what you witnessed? Mayhap one evening?" Sapphira could not disguise the yearning in her voice.

"It would be my pleasure. I daresay Archer and Hester might be interested in hearing my observations." Without so much as a blink, he brought their discussion back to the Forum. "In front of us is the Temple of Jupiter. To our left, hmmm... it is designated a holitorium, a vegetable market," he clarified at Sapphira's baffled expression, "but we are not certain. Perhaps a definitive answer will present itself when excavations are completed."

"What was this? Do you know?" Sapphira surveyed the structures to their right. Where the Forum and the Via dell'Abbondanza met, an incomplete yet elegant colonnade graced the entrance to what had once been an extensive building.

"At this stage they are reserving their judgement, but that inscription," he pointed to the entablature on top of the colonnade, "and another around the far side, just off the main street, attribute it to a woman called Eumachia. Apparently, she was a priestess of Venus *and* the owner of a business connected to the wool trade. There are some, however, who postulate this inscription suggests it is a dedication related to the cult worship of Augustus."

"Intriguing, mayhap it was both," Sapphira hypothesised, unaware this was also under consideration.

She moved closer, her attention caught by the almost intact border of intricate scrollwork, surrounding the portico. It depicted flowers, trailing vines, and acanthus leaves, among which were scattered all manner of tiny creatures such as birds, snails, and rabbits, mice, and snakes, even minuscule peacocks. The carvings stood proud of the background, creating the illusion of varying depths.

Sapphira was awestruck by the extraordinary realism.

"This is superb," she breathed reverently, tracing the delicate carvings. "It is so lifelike, I would not be surprised if the leaves fluttered in the breeze, or the creatures scampered off seeking their next adventure. Such skill."

"I agree, I am constantly re-evaluating my presumptions regarding their expertise. Their frescos and mosaics are similarly magnificent."

"I am anxious to see some… if that is possible."

Their interaction while still formal had become less stilted. Sapphira's enthusiasm was contagious, and it would be a hard-hearted person indeed who chose to quash her zest.

"Of course, and if there are buildings you wish to see the inside of as we pass, let me know. It is better not to enter alone as many of the areas are unstable or are subject to falling debris."

"Thank you for the warning. I shall take heed." Sapphira offered a tentative smile and was rewarded with a genial nod. It was a slow thaw, but it was better than nothing. With a relieved and inward sigh, she followed Lord Osmund's lead.

CHAPTER FIVE

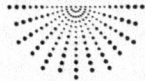

*T*he rest of the morning passed in a blur. The seemingly endless list of instructions thrown at Sapphira from every angle made her head whirl, but she listened politely, interjecting a yes or no where she hoped it was appropriate.

Basically, it boiled down to — watch where you put your feet, treat everything as an artefact until otherwise advised, pay attention to your supervisor, if you are told to leave an area do so immediately or suffer the consequences.

Finally, and most important, even though Pompeii was laid out in a grid, the streets could be disorienting because they all looked similar, making it easy to lose your bearings. Worse many were only half excavated, adding to the confusion.

Satisfied his charge was cognisant of the rules, Leofwin demonstrated a few of the techniques employed throughout the site. How to mark out a section to be unearthed. How to scrape away the layers of dirt, exposing but not damaging whatever was hidden beneath. How to draw every layer, marking the location of every item. How to pack and store the finds.

While not complicated, it required Sapphira's full concentration, and by the time he had finished it was nearing luncheon.

Sapphira's stomach rumbled, making her blush.

"Time to find the Dynhams." Leofwin pretended he had not heard. "We can resume once we have eaten."

"Where do we buy food?" Sapphira asked, trying to keep up with his long stride. "I have not seen any kind of dining establishment."

Leofwin gave a bark of scornful laughter. "There *are* no dining establishments," he derided. "Food must be brought to site by each individual."

She thought she heard him mutter something under his breath and her enjoyment of the day vanished.

In the blink of an eye the chill was back.

Schooling her features, Sapphira said nothing more, but stayed a pace or two behind him as they wound their way back to the insula where Hester and Archer were working.

One look at her friend's mulish expression told Hester not to ask. Instead, she launched into a description of what they had achieved that morning, while they found a suitable place to sit nearby.

Sheltered from the sun by a portion of wall and an over-hanging bush, they made themselves comfortable on the scrubby grass. Hester's advice regarding the type of attire to bring on this journey was well-founded. Delicate silks would be spoilt in an instant.

Sapphira was astonished to see the marquis retrieve a loaf of bread, a jar of olive oil, some local cheese, and a selection of dried fruit from his satchel, but made no comment.

He unfolded a large square of chequered material on which he placed the food neatly. Next, a bottle of wine and four goblets appeared.

Hester and Archer didn't bat an eyelid, an indication to Sapphira that this picnic-style of eating was part of their routine when at Pompeii. She was embarrassed, in the main because she had forgotten to ask about food, but also for not offering to help carry it. That said, since no one had thought to apprise her, she could not be held accountable.

Archer uncorked the wine and, after filling the goblets, handed them out. Sapphira sipped hers slowly. The day was warm, and she was hungry. Too much wine and she would either fall asleep or worse, it would loosen her tongue, and she did not want to be rude.

Her fit of pique was mollified when, later that afternoon, she was permitted, *finally*, to join the throng of people painstakingly uncovering the ancient city of Pompeii.

Lord Osmund left her in the care of Signore Fiorani, one of the senior antiquarians. An affable gentleman who matched the image Sapphira had conjured up in her head of her host. So close, in fact, she had to stifle a giggle when they were introduced.

Signore Fiorani was a walking repository of information, and the afternoon flew by.

Sapphira was ecstatic when encouraged to clear a square of ground inside an insula. She did not find anything of value, save the odd tessera — the tiny tiles used to create mosaics — but that did not matter. Being invited to assist was enough.

"You will return, *domani?*" he asked when Hester came to find her at the end of the day.

"*Domani…* hmmm is that tomorrow?"

He nodded.

"Yes, *sì*, *grazie*, I would like to very much," she replied shyly, dipping a curtsy.

"I look forward to it, Miss Beresford." His lilting accent curled round his words, making them sound like a song.

Sapphira blushed. "As do I, Signore. You were very patient with me this afternoon. I hope I did not disrupt your work."

"On the contrary, you have... as you English say... the touch." He tapped his head. "Soon you will be the expert. Now go with the lovely Lady Dynham. *A domani.*"

"*A domani,*" Sapphira replied, trusting this was the correct response. His delighted smile, affirmation enough.

"Thank you for looking after her, Signore Fiorani," Hester interjected, "I know she is in good hands with you." Given Sapphira's lack of chaperone, her inference was obvious.

"Ahh, the safe hands I think you mean," he chuckled. "*Grazie*, my lady." He swept a flourishing bow.

"Go on with you, you old rogue." Hester patted him on the arm, and the two women took their leave, the elderly Italian's mirth following them along the ancient street. Archer and Lord Osmund were waiting just ahead and the four strolled to the amphitheatre in the hazy light of the May afternoon.

Still smarting from her host's gibe, Sapphira was quiet on the ride home and, rather than joining in with the chatter, enjoyed the scenery. When they arrived at the villa, she handed Minerva's reins over to one of the grooms, thanked him, and made haste to her bedchamber. She plonked down on the edge of her bed and mulled over the day.

Save Lord Osmund's snub, it had been riveting, and she cherished the honour of being involved, even peripherally, in the excavations. Hopefully, Leofwin's irritable attitude would lessen as the days went by.

She decided that the best thing to do was grin and bear it. She could not leave, she had nowhere else to go and, other than the people in this villa, oh... and Signore Fiorani, did not know another soul in the whole of this beautiful country. She would behave as her mother would expect. Be demure, speak when spoken to, and remain polite and reserved at all times. Rise above his grumpiness.

Decision made, she luxuriated in a refreshing wash, and changed into a gown of pale lilac. As soon as the sun dipped below the horizon the temperature dropped. If they were eating on the verandah again, she would need a wrap.

Foraging through the drawers, she found one of her favourites and slung it around her shoulders. Slipping her feet into soft leather slippers, she ventured down to the lowest level.

Leofwin knew he had hurt Sapphira the instant the words left his mouth, but it was too late, he could not retract them. The happiness in her face had flickered out and he wanted to kick himself for being snide.

How on earth was she expected to know the availability of anything? She had only been here two days, and the countryside around his villa and Pompeii possessed none of the amenities offered in Naples.

The minute they were on amiable terms his behaviour became surly and it was unfair. Thus far, Miss Beresford had done nothing to warrant it.

"Time to act like the gentleman you think you are," he grumbled to himself. It was not forever. By the end of the summer, she would be naught but a distant memory, studiously ignoring the uproarious laughter at the back of his mind at such naïveté.

He had to admit, there was something tormentingly elusive about this Miss Beresford. Her image materialised before his eyes. Tall, willowy, her blonde hair glimmering in the moonlight. His body responded... *what the deuce? No, I am not attracted to Miss Beresford.*

He had no time for women, or romance, or any of that inanity. He was content in his life, surrounded by his books and his ruins. He had no need of any added complications.

As if to underscore this reasoning, his leg twinged, and he rubbed the maligned limb to ease the ache. Stripping out of his clothes, he dropped them in the linen basket and splashed water over his torso, rinsing away the accumulated dust of the day.

After drying off, he reached for a large round pot, removed the lid, and scooped out a sizeable dollop. Slathering the ointment over his right thigh, he massaged it in thoroughly, breathing in the faintly exotic fragrance. The salve was something his doctor had recommended, a treatment administered twice daily when he was in the hospital. Apparently, it helped keep the skin supple, and decreased the likelihood of infection while his wounds healed.

That was six years ago, and the ravaged flesh had long since knitted into gnarled scars, but he found the balm soothing and it seemed to alleviate the discomfort. It was probably all in his mind, but he couldn't break the habit. It irked him that he required the assistance of a cane to walk but, as the same doctor had said, at least he still had his leg. For a time, there was a fear of amputation.

The injury had become a useful excuse by which to avoid the endless social whirl so beloved by the *ton*. He had disliked it when whole and hearty, now he hated it with a passion. Twittering women who cooed and gushed their pity, or worse, used his limp to their advantage. Catching his cane, then clinging to his arm to ensure he did not take a tumble — which he found comical, given he was quite able to walk without any aids.

Their wilful manoeuvres, calculated to trap him into a possible union, caused him to retreat from Society, his world contracting to a handful of trusted friends. Then his aunt died, bequeathing him this property and he had leapt at the opportunity to leave behind the artificial world of London's elite.

It was a decision he never regretted.

Life here was tranquil. The milder climate suited his leg, which ached when it was cold and damp. He had his own space and was answerable to no one. His wealth allowed him to potter about ruins, or work on the property to his heart's content. No nagging wife hassling him to attend balls, or soirees, or house parties in the country.

His mother's letters provided him with all the news from England, including whatever scandal was keeping the gossips titillated. She *did* feel moved to bemoan, frequently, the fact the family title would likely fall into abeyance if he did not produce an heir. A grievance he ignored given his younger brother, Wolfstan, would inherit.

Occasionally, he missed his family, to whom he was close. The oldest of three siblings, he had grown up in a loving home.

His sister, Lunete, three years his junior, was married with two children.

Reading between the lines of his brother's last letter, Leofwin figured out that twenty-five-year-old Wolf, while relishing bachelorhood, had joined a covert organisation run by Major Withers... who had been Leofwin's commanding officer in the war. The idea of his sibling knuckling down to serious work, never failed to raise a smirk.

No, he had no need to return. Not until he had no choice and even then, it was not essential.

Wiping his hands on a washcloth, Leofwin pulled on a pair of dark tan breeches and an ageing cotton shirt. For propriety's sake, he added a waistcoat but forewent a cravat. He opted for house shoes over hessians — they were more comfortable, and dinner was not a formal meal.

Flexing his leg, Leofwin grabbed the hated cane and, putting all thoughts of the war and its consequences out of his mind, headed for the terrace.

Dinner proved to be unexpectedly convivial. With Sapphira and Leofwin determined to mask their vague animosity, the lurking tension dissipated.

As the evening wore on, what was contrived became natural, and the four embarked on an animated discussion about Pompeii.

Sapphira's niggling concerns regarding the removal of artefacts as opposed to protecting them in situ were addressed with enough corroborating evidence for the former to satisfy even the most sceptical.

Staring up at the moon, which hung in ethereal splendour far, far above her head, Sapphira decided it would be judicious for her to find her bed. She had been tempted into at least two glasses of wine too many and being someone who seldom indulged in *one*, they had gone straight to her head.

"It appears the fresh air has caught up with me and I do not wish to oversleep on the morrow." She got to her feet, swaying ever-so slightly. "Oh my…"

Leofwin bit down on a guffaw.

"What?" she demanded rudely.

"Nothing. I agree, the fresh air will do it every time," he replied gravely, but his eyes twinkled with amusement.

Was he teasing her? Undoubtedly, but it was too hard to argue, and her tongue had a propensity to run away with her on the odd occasion she over-imbibed. "Goodnight, my lord," she said, haughtily. "Thank you for an... enlightening day." She contrived to make a dignified exit, ruined when she stumbled over air. She would have fallen if not for Leofwin's lightning reflexes.

He caught her elbow and hauled her upright. His breath brushed her ear when he murmured, "Watch those flag-stones, they can trip the unwary."

Sapphira jerked back. His face was bland but there was a subtle undertone in his voice, and he held onto her arm longer than necessary. "Th-thank you," she tried to dip a curtsy, but her legs refused to hold her. "Oh my," she repeated and fled.

Leofwin watched her go, his forehead puckering in puzzlement.

Hester saw it and looked at her husband. They shared a knowing smile, straightening their faces before Leofwin noticed.

The trio chatted a little longer, but all were tired, and shortly thereafter the villa fell quiet.

CHAPTER SIX

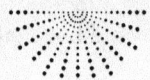

*N*ot wanting to dedicate every day to the ruins, Leofwin had arranged a few excursions around the vicinity.

It was mostly rural — farms interspersed with vineyards — but Sapphira, especially, was captivated by the similarities and differences compared with the English countryside.

Invariably, these pleasant sojourns included an impromptu meal with one or another of Leofwin's acquaintances.

Sapphira loved the rustic ambience of sitting under blossom or vine cloaked trellises, at long wooden tables overflowing with a plenitude of food, and accompanied by wines made within a stone's throw, creating veritable feasts for the taste buds.

It was a blessing they used the carriage for these outings, for Sapphira would have struggled to stay upright on a horse after some of their repasts.

Another favourite expedition was the weekly market in the hamlet adjacent to Pompeii. Mostly offering a prodigious array of foodstuffs, the canny stallholders — realising they had an audience for their local arts and crafts — began to offer small pieces of beautiful pottery, wood carvings and embroidered linens — all locally made, of course.

Hester and Sapphira were known to spend hours pottering around, chatting with the stall holders; Hester fluently, Sapphira in a peculiar mix of English and Italian.

Wholly uninterested in the delights of shopping, Leofwin and Archer gravitated towards the inevitable coterie of apparently bored husbands gathered at the periphery of the stalls, where they were easily persuaded into a debate and a drink or two.

On the days they travelled to Pompeii, they left the villa in the cool of the early morning, applied themselves to whatever they were asked to do, ate lunch in the same shady spot where they had eaten the first day, and rode home as the afternoon began to wane.

Sapphira made it her business to get to know all with whom she came into regular contact, by name and, if they had any, something about their families. It gave them something to talk about while they worked and created a camaraderie of sorts.

She had also, to Hester's chagrin, befriended the medley of stray cats and dogs who wandered the site at leisure, ignoring the exclamations of concern from her fellow excavators that they were ridden with fleas and diseases. To her, they looked to be in good condition, and she had yet to spy a flea.

"I know you with waifs and strays," Hester chided, wagging her finger. "This is not England; you do not know what deadly pestilence they might carry."

"I am very careful and always rinse my hands if, inadvertently, I touch one of them," Sapphira assured. "I am not petting them, merely treating them kindly. It does not harm."

"'Tis more they rub up against your skirts, transferring goodness knows what into your clothes."

"Tsk, do not fret, we are more likely to be struck down by some ancient ailment, which has been trapped underground since Vesuvius erupted." Sapphira replied with an impish grin.

Hester gave up; the more she pressed the issue, the more likely her friend would encourage the local wildlife.

Sapphira and Leofwin seemed more relaxed in each other's company, although Hester observed to Archer that her friend was less effusive than was customary. He ascribed it to shyness, speculating that Sapphira would come out of her shell eventually.

Hester was not so sure. She believed it all stemmed from the aborted wedding. Sapphira had not spoken about that fateful day, not once, and Hester was concerned she had bottled up her humiliation.

In her opinion, Sapphira was too composed, her normal ebullience quashed under a prim veneer, which would likely explode given the right provocation, but it was not her place to pry. When Sapphira was ready to talk, Hester would be there with a sympathetic ear, praying discourse would occur before detonation.

During the second weekend of their visit, Leofwin proposed they take one of the carriages and spend a day at Hercula-neum. There would be little visible above ground, but the protracted spell of good weather meant there was a reasonable chance they might be granted access to the underground theatre.

Signore Fiorani, who belonged to a small group of people tasked with monitoring the site to ensure its stability, had agreed to give them a guided tour.

Sapphira was both excited and nervous. She possessed a healthy ambivalence to enclosed spaces and, although desperate to explore, feared she would make a fool of herself once they descended into the darkness.

She kept her concerns to herself. No reason to give Lord Osmund yet another excuse to question her competence.

It was another glorious morning, warmer than of late, heralding the approach of summer.

They rode with the top down, and Sapphira tipped her head back to gaze up at the puffy white clouds floating lazily in a cerulean sky.

Around them, olive groves and vineyards were interspersed with fields and pasture, creating a patchwork quilt of verdant hues.

There was no doubt about it. Italy was perfection.

They trundled into Resina, an unassuming little settlement, and a replica of every other little settlement scattered along this coastline. There was not the slightest indication it concealed relics of monumental and world-wide significance. Signore Fiorani met them at an open wooden door, tucked away along a narrow street.

Alighting from the carriage, they greeted the genial Italian who responded in kind and ushered them indoors.

"I am glad to see you have dressed accordingly," he

nodded at the warm wraps the two ladies had slung around their shoulders. "It is cold beneath the surface." After locking the door behind them, he turned down a passageway. "Be careful as you walk, the ground can be slippery. Do not try to hurry, the ruins will not vanish," he advised as they were swallowed into the gloom.

Sapphira was relieved to see it was not completely dark. Signore Fiorani explained that the light came from the access shafts dug during the initial excavations decades earlier.

"We have reached the first steps," he advised. "From here the daylight, she begins to leave us. Do not fear, dear ladies." He looked at Hester and Sapphira. "We have *la fiamma*."

Sapphira was about to question what he meant, when there was a hiss and a torch flared to life, illuminating a small tinderbox on a stone shelf.

Signore Fiorani caught her glance. "The members of our team check the site daily. 'Tis our policy to be prepared. There are similar boxes below."

Sapphira couldn't decide whether that was comforting or alarming, but she smiled in what she hoped was a reassured manner.

He nodded. "*Andiamo.*"

This one Sapphira knew. *You wanted to explore*, she strove to bolster her flagging spirits. *Perhaps next time you will be satisfied with reading about discoveries instead of becoming part of them.*

Holding his torch aloft, Signore Fiorani led the way down a set of steep steps hewn from the rock. As they descended, the atmosphere grew cool and damp. Moisture clung to the walls, seeping through even the tiniest fissure in the layers of lava. The air, although fresh, was tinged with a faint odour, reminiscent of pond weed.

Just when Sapphira was beginning to think the stairs would go on for ever, they came to a halt. Signore Fiorani angled his torch to shed its glow on another, propped in a wall sconce. Lighting it, he handed this second one to Leofwin.

"We are at the upper level of the theatre. See." Signore Fiorani raised his torch and swung his arm in a slow sweep. The flickering flame highlighted what appeared to be a curved tunnel with a low arched ceiling.

"From here we go again down. These are narrow steps."

With Signore Fiorani leading the way and Leofwin bringing up the rear, the torches provided reasonable light. Either side of them, seats ran in semi-circular rows only to disappear into the compacted lava.

Here and there, green slime clung to the walls, covering the traces of murals. Pieces of statuary, fragments of decorative plaster, and slabs of broken marble littered the area.

They fanned out along the tiers, the better to admire the ancient theatre.

Almost two millennia since its burial, so pristine was the interior that, to Sapphira, rather than the theatre slowly being brought back to life from the mass of grey rock, it looked like a new construction. Ready for the artisans to come in and paint the frescos, create the mosaics, or place the sculptures.

The leaping shadows caused by the guttering torches brought to mind a troupe of dancers preparing for their role, and evoked an aura of anticipation, as though the audience were on the edge of their seats, waiting to be entertained. Sapphira had read some of the Greek plays; to see one being enacted, in antiquity, must have been riveting.

"As you can see, much has been damaged or looted, but there is hope the king will view our petition favourably and authorise a systematic excavation. It will be a massive undertaking. We need to remove all the compacted earth, while addressing the not inconsequential issue of the settlement above, but to continue working underground is dangerous. We do not want any more people to lose their lives to Vesuvius, nor do we wish to rebury all this." Signore Fiorani made an encompassing gesture. "It is too important."

"Do you believe it essential to reveal what has survived in this subterranean tomb? For surely the enterprise will be astronomical both in cost and manpower." Sapphira asked.

"You think it sagacious to shelve the project, half explored with tunnels and shafts, leaving it vulnerable to the elements and robbers?" Leofwin glared.

"I think it a fair question, especially given that less than ten miles away you have a vast and easily accessible site, which is providing a wealth of information about the world of ancient Rome. Shafts can be filled in, and tunnels blocked." She replied, seemingly unmoved by his tone, but there was a glint in her eyes.

"And miss out on what this site might tell us?" His lip curled into a sneer. "In one breath you profess to be interested in preserving history, but in the next, you criticise the very plans to do so."

Bristling with righteous indignation, Leofwin forgot his own instructions and Signore Fiorani's caution. He had twisted around to emphasise his point and pivoted backwards without checking.

Sapphira, realising he was about step onto an incomplete stair, shot forward to grasp his arm. "Lord Osm—"

"Miss Beresford," he admonished, and shook off her fingers at the same moment as his foot slipped off the damaged tread.

To a chorus of startled gasps, Leofwin landed, ignominiously, on his backside. Thankfully, he only fell as far as the next step — given where they were congregated, it could have been much worse.

Sapphira bit her lip to stop her mirth from spilling over at the litany of oaths which spewed from his mouth, immediately followed by a hasty, if brusque, apology.

The closest to him, she offered to pull him into his feet.

"Thank you, but I can manage." A blatantly incorrect claim.

"Oh, do not be so obdurate. Are you afraid I shall drop you?" She gave him a sly smile. "I am quite strong you know... for a woman."

He gave her a sharp glance and, ungraciously, accepted her hand.

Bracing herself on the concrete seat, Sapphira hauled him upright. "Be careful my lord," she exhorted *sotto voce* as their eyes met. "Theatre stairways can trip the unwary."

Rendered speechless by her word play on his own advice, Leofwin gaped.

Sapphira waved her hand at his trousers. "You might like to brush the dust off your breeches. No telling what you just sat in." With a bright smile, she asked Signore Fiorani how far the current excavations extended beyond where they stood, completely ignoring her host.

Hester and Archer exchanged a look but kept their counsel.

Leofwin, his dignity partially restored, sat on one of the seats to recover his breath. He had jarred his leg but not as badly as he had dented his pride.

One could be eased with a decent massage, the other... that might take a little longer.

While he regained his equilibrium, Leofwin watched Sapphira who was engrossed in conversation with Signore Fiorani. A strange sensation settled over him, one he could not identify. If he liked Miss Beresford, he *might* consider it to be jealousy at her sunny smile and relaxed manner, neither of which she displayed when talking with him.

And whose fault is that? You were the one to instigate this nonsense. Perhaps swallow your pride and be nice... radical I know, but... he quashed his inner voice, before it made even more sense.

He closed his eyes.

"Are you hurt?" Archer's worried question broke into his reverie.

"No, thank you, Dynham. My leg took a knock, but otherwise I am fine."

"Sure?" Archer was not convinced.

"Quite sure." Leofwin's smile of reassurance included Hester who was studying him worriedly.

"Perhaps it is time we returned to the surface," Hester said.

"Trust me, I am fine. A little bruised, but naught to be concerned about. This might be your only opportunity to see the theatre, and I have no wish to shorten the brief time we have."

Hester, mindful that he was prone to downplay things, scanned his face for signs he was concealing discomfort.

"Hester," he said gently. "I appreciate your concern. I shall sit here a moment, while you explore."

Satisfied, Hester patted his hand. Linking arms with her husband, the pair continued down the steps. Their chatter floated on the dead air, blending with the voices of Sapphira and Signore Fiorani. Even so far underground, the acoustics were as distinct as when first the actors took to the stage.

Signore Fiorani's lilting accent and absorbing commentary proved an insufficient distraction for Sapphira who had begun to contemplate whether the gloomy cavern was shrinking.

She gripped the rim of her bonnet, then, feeling the delicate weave give under the pressure, forced her fingers to relax, only to wind the ribbon around her hand, alternately flexing and releasing her clutch, slowly ruining the satin.

Sapphira knew it was irrational, but she had never been able to rid herself of her aversion to dark, enclosed spaces. A phobia first triggered when a children's game had ended up with her locked inside an old trunk in the attics of The Towers. To this day, she could not credit how gullible she had been.

Her nails bit into the soft skin of her palm. Her heart was beating too fast, making her feel faint. Gritting her teeth, she made a valiant attempt to steady her breathing. There was absolutely no possibility she was prepared to make an idiot of herself in front of Lord Osmund.

Her words came back to her... *I will not have a fit of the vapours...* yes, that was in relation to seeing a skeleton, but it was the same basic principle.

Unwilling to cause offence or appear ungrateful, Sapphira tried to bank down her growing terror.

CHAPTER SEVEN

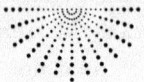

*L*eofwin's gaze wandered back to Sapphira. Her svelte figure was encased in a pastel green day dress; her shawl, in a darker hue, hugged around her shoulders.

She had removed her bonnet, which she twirled absently between her fingers as she talked. The torchlight made her blonde hair glow. He could not deny Miss Beresford was a striking woman.

Unconsciously, he tuned into her discussion with Signore Fiorani, and heard something in her voice. Outwardly, Sapphira appeared composed, but something induced Leofwin to give her a second glance.

Her face had taken on a sickly hue in the gloom, and her hands were now bunched into fists, crushing the ribbon of her bonnet. When she wasn't speaking, her jaw was clenched. Miss Beresford was not comfortable.

Leofwin frowned. His guest had shown no disinclination to visit the site or fear of entering the darkened passageways. Her enthusiasm seemed in no way feigned. He scrutinised her more closely. She was fighting a mounting alarm; of that he was certain.

A person succumbing to panic at this depth was to be prevented at all costs. Not generally sympathetic to weaknesses in others, Leofwin found he respected Sapphira for her mettle and wanted to give her a way to retreat without drawing attention to her predicament.

Perhaps I could use my embarrassment to beneficial effect? If I complained of feeling sore, Hester would want to hurry me above ground. He pondered the idea while observing Sapphira. Despite her sterling efforts to disguise it, the tension in her body was increasing.

He twisted on the chill stone and gave a low whistle.

It was barely a movement of air but, with ears sharpened by time on the battlefield, Archer heard him and swung around.

Leofwin motioned for them to join him. "I do not wish to curtail your enjoyment of this incredible place, but my leg is causing me some discomfort. I do believe I ought to return to the surface in case it seizes up."

Hester, as he predicted, became a mother hen, clucking over him.

Archer sent him a frown, confused as to why his friend was exaggerating his plight.

Leofwin shook his head and mouthed... *Later.*

"Sapphira," Hester called softly.

Sapphira peered over her shoulder. "Yes?"

"Do you mind if we make our way back up? Osmund's leg is bothering him, and it tends to cramp, which might hinder his ability to climb all those stairs. I know this cuts short our expedition, but mayhap we can return another day."

"I do not mind at all," Sapphira, deliverance from her

dilemma at hand, heard the unadulterated relief lacing her swift reply.

Careful not to rush Leofwin, the party ascended the numerous steps, exiting through the wooden door into the dazzling sunlight.

Blinking back a sudden rush of tears, Sapphira gulped in a lungful of fresh air.

"Miss Beresford, is something amiss?" Lord Osmund, who had been keeping an eye on her, enquired solicitously.

"I am fine, thank you. The transition from darkness to bright sunshine has made my eyes water." She replied in an unexpectedly husky voice.

"It affects me similarly. Here." He handed her a clean and neatly folded handkerchief.

Still blinking, Sapphira thanked him again and pressed the soft cotton to her eyes, breathing slowly, salvaging what remained of her poise. The world righted itself and the awful dizziness subsided. Honestly, she was hopeless.

She summoned up a wobbly smile. "You are very kind. How is your leg?"

"No lasting damage," he grinned, and when she tried to return his kerchief, told her to keep it. "I have plenty, and they are far more practical than those tiny scraps of lace you ladies use."

She felt she ought to be aggrieved, but he was correct. For some reason, this struck her as funny, and, slightly giddy with relief, couldn't prevent a peal of laughter. The golden sound rippled along the quiet street, making more than one person glance in their direction.

Caught off guard, Leofwin was entranced.

The visitors expressed their heartfelt gratitude to Signore

Fiorani, for giving up his precious free time to show them the subterranean theatre.

"It was my pleasure to share this so important discovery. Perhaps before you depart for England, you might again have the chance to come to Herculaneum." He smiled. After a quiet word with Leofwin who enlightened his friend as to what he believed had been about to happen, Signore Fiorani nodded understandingly and took his leave. "I look forward to seeing you next week." He bowed and strode away.

"Does he have far to travel?" Sapphira worried. "Ought we to have offered him a ride home?"

"Do not fret, he lives close to Pompeii, but his brother resides in Resina. He will no doubt have left his horse there." Hester smiled.

"He was so kind to have given us a tour, but I was beginning to feel a trifle claustrophobic. Lord Osmund, your aching leg saved me from making a fool of myself." She smiled across the carriage at Leofwin. "I was thinking of a way to leave surreptitiously without spoiling everyone else's morning."

"Glad to be of service," Leofwin replied, his face the picture of innocence.

Hester narrowed her gaze; something was not quite right here. She opened her mouth to ask what, when something in Archer's expression made her close it again. She would worm it out of one or both men eventually.

While they trundled back to the villa, the conversation, as was becoming their habit, revolved around the ruins.

"I realise that even the smallest artefact is important, but it would be splendid if something like a mosaic, or a fresco, or an amphora complete with its contents was to be unearthed while we are here," Sapphira mused, her agitation almost forgotten. "Although, I confess to being jubilant when someone finds a piece of broken tile, or a minuscule shard of pottery."

"One can only hope." The sound of Sapphira's merriment continued to echo in Leofwin's mind, and his dry response was in refuge to his chaotic thoughts. Miss Sapphira Beresford was taking up residence in his head, and however hard he quelled her image, her voice, her fragrance, she refused to be banished. It was unutterably frustrating.

"I accept 'tis unlikely, but I am allowed to dream." She ignored his laconic tone and, tilting back her head, closed her eyes, letting the sun play over her lids, mildly irked when Lord Osmund's face with its sardonic smile drifted through her mind. *It would not do.*

The remainder of the weekend was uneventful. Sapphira spent much of it among the proliferation of trees and plants thriving in riotous abandon around the villa.

She began to draw the varieties in her journal — a gift from her father who had implored her to record her travels so he could read them on her return — and pestered the garden staff to tell her the names of each specimen.

Those they did not know, she wheedled out of Leofwin, with the subtlety of a brick.

To his surprise, he found he enjoyed the exercise, especially given Sapphira soaked up information like arid ground soaked up rain.

A handful of plants on the periphery of the property proved difficult to identify.

"Hauling your aunt's tomes up here seems a trifle drastic, not to mention weighty. Perhaps we could take a small cutting." Sapphira motioned to the shrubs growing along the gentle slope where they currently stood. "That will allow us to check them against the illustrations at our leisure."

"A fine plan," Leofwin agreed, retrieving a sharp paring knife from his satchel. Meticulously, he removed a suitable sample from each of the unknown plants, handing them to Sapphira who fashioned a little pouch out of the apron kindly lent by Amalia.

They ambled back to the villa chattering about this and that, their initial wariness eradicated almost without either realising.

Heads together, the pair perused the compendia left by Leofwin's aunt, determined to identify every last specimen. Sapphira added them to her journal, each sketch with enough detail that she would remember the original plant from which it came.

Sapphira forgot to be troubled by Leofwin's reticence and, in turn, Leofwin forgot to be reserved.

By Monday, a tacit truce had sprung up between them, although neither would have admitted one was necessary.

Their camaraderie lasted throughout the following week and into the next. Hester and Archer breathed a sigh of relief. Finally, the two seemed to be in accord.

They might have predicted it was too good to last.

"I cannot believe we have been here a month. I keep pinching myself to ensure this is not simply a marvellous dream." Sapphira remarked one evening at dinner. "I do not want to think about returning to the real world."

"And what would you know about the *real* world?" Leofwin scoffed. A persistent twinge in his leg and a lurking headache, combined with a hot day and a glass or two of wine, had left him testy.

"Just because I have not witnessed the horrors of war, does not mean I am insensible to its repercussions, or ignorant of the issues facing society," she rejoined, refusing to rise to the bait.

"Humph."

"Humph? What do you mean *humph*?" Sapphira demanded.

"My dear, Miss Beresford, do I need to spell it out?"

"I rather think you do."

"You are not of the servant class, as your presence here among the nobility attests. Thus, I doubt you would recognise hardship, or the desperate straits of others if they slapped you in the face. I'll hazard your life to date has not been marred by upset of any kind."

"To which class do you presume I belong?" Disregarding his last sentence, her question was delivered in the politest of tones, her expression suggesting she was only mildly interested.

Leofwin ran his gaze over her. His lazy, almost insolent appraisal stirred an indefinable emotion in Sapphira, one she quashed immediately.

"Merchant. Accustomed to a modicum of luxury but lacking the refinement of the elite," he replied pompously.

Hester took a fortifying sip of her wine. *So much for an accord.* This was not going to end well.

The effrontery of the man. Sapphira endeavoured to maintain her rapidly evaporating calm, for although Lord

Osmund was behaving like an arrogant buffoon, he was also her host.

Out of the blue, she found his supercilious condescension comical rather than insulting.

Her lips twitching, she stood and dipped a low curtsy. "Goodness, your lordship, do please scatter some of your wisdom at my sadly uneducated feet." She put her hands together as though in prayer and batted her eyes winsomely.

"Sapphi,"

She ignored Hester's entreaty, and Archer's badly muffled snort.

"Since we met less than a month ago, I am prepared to let your sweeping statement slide. You know absolutely nothing about me. I could be a criminal as easily as I could be a princess."

"Certainly, I could be persuaded into accepting the former rather than the latter," Leofwin grunted, aware he was being unconscionably rude but unable to curb his tongue.

"*Leo*," Archer hissed. This was getting out of hand.

"Fret not, Archer," Sapphira winked. "Just because one bears a title does not mean one is possessed of gentility. There are those in the servant class who have more breeding in their little finger than some of the so-called elite."

Leofwin glared. "Are you questioning my civility?"

"Who? *Me*? Of course not, my lord, but if the cap fits…" she smiled sweetly. "Now, while I am partial to lively banter, I hear my bed calling. Thank you for a lovely day and a *most* entertaining evening. Goodnight." She included all three in her parting and was gone in a swish of silk.

"Leo, what is wrong? This is not like you at all." Hester reproached gently. "I thought you two had set aside your differences. This last week or so has been convivial. What caused that little outburst?"

Leofwin had the grace to look chastened. He steepled his fingers together and considered his answer.

"In truth I do not know. I am not myself this evening, but that is no excuse for acting like a petulant child. Miss Beresford..." he paused, trying to articulate what it was about his guest. "...perplexes me. She is at once demure and effusive, placid yet spirited.

"I sense a woman fighting to control a natural exuberance, but I do not know why. She is quick to contradict or challenge if she disagrees. I acknowledge I am not the most perceptive of people, but I cannot dismiss the impression she is hiding something, and it leaves me on edge."

Another thought struck him, "Who runs away from England? Why? Is she dodging the Runners?"

"Put down your glass and pick up your common sense," Hester advised. "Do you think for one moment Archer and I would harbour a crook? I will concede she is not who you assume her to be, but it is her story. If you want to hear it, I suggest you start behaving like a gentleman and less like a fatuous dunderhead."

"Fatuous dunderhead? Lady Dynham you wound me."

Hester chuckled. "I sincerely doubt it. Seriously, Leo, give her a chance. Sapphi is one of the loveliest people I know. She is kind-hearted and generous to a fault. Yes, she owns a temper, but it usually takes a lot to rile her up. Stop expecting the worst from everyone you meet, and you might realise most of us have no hidden agenda. Not every woman you come across is a grasping harpy."

"Sapphi?" Leofwin rolled the diminutive around in his head. "I like it. It suits her."

"Well, if you treat her nicely, she might grant you permission to use it." Hester said with a sly grin.

CHAPTER EIGHT

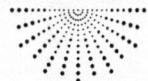

On the cusp of another weekend, Hester excused herself from the day's plans. Plagued by a touch of nausea, the thought of being jolted on horseback, even for half an hour was too much for her recalcitrant stomach and aching head.

"You three go, I shall have a quiet day in the garden and doubtless will feel myself again by this evening," she assured them.

Archer, who had never known his wife to be unwell — not once in the decade since they met — was loath to leave her, and her pallor alarmed him. "I prefer to stay here with Hester."

"Archer, no, please you must go. I should hate it if you missed something earth-shattering." Hester protested, secretly relieved. In truth, she felt wretched.

Archer took her hand. "My love, the ruins will be there tomorrow, do not fret." His smile although tender brooked no argument.

This meant Sapphira had no chaperone, a fact she had no

intention of mentioning when her friend was already under the weather.

"A day of relaxation. I shall attend to my woefully neglected letters," she beamed.

"An unorthodox situation requires an unorthodox solution." Leofwin, sensing her disappointment, intervened. "Are you a stickler for the rules?" He addressed his question to Sapphira.

"Errr… why?" She waited, curious now.

"Hester and Archer trust me, and I would rather die than break their trust. Unless they are addled, that makes me a dependable escort. Would you be comfortable riding to Pompeii with me?"

"Errr…" Sapphira couldn't seem to make her brain and her mouth connect. His suggestion was tempting… *dare I?*

"Consider my suggestion logically. When you are there, rarely is Hester, or any of the other female volunteers for that matter, within sight. With all due respect, the men among whom you work every day are not in the slightest interested in you as a woman. They view you as nothing more than a colleague. Your reputation is in no danger, Miss Beresford. You have my word."

Sapphira couldn't decide whether she ought to feel slighted or flattered. She went with the latter. "How lovely. To be accepted as one of them is an honour indeed. If Hester and Archer consent, I should be glad to accompany you." Her tone was prim, but her eyes sparkled. Time was ticking by. A day away from Pompeii was a day lost.

Leofwin looked at the Dynhams who glanced at each other, silent communication passing between them.

"If the pair of you promise not to argue, we see no reason why not," Archer answered for both.

"I promise," Sapphira vowed.

"As do I," Leofwin affirmed.

"Go then, enjoy yourself. Sapphi, the sun is fierce, remember to take your bonnet." Hester counselled.

With a grin, Sapphira headed off to prepare for the day.

Sapphira's apprehension at being alone with Lord Osmund was banished as quickly as it had arisen. Her host went out of his way to behave in an exemplary manner and, as their destination neared, they were engrossed in an amicable conversation about nothing of any consequence.

The day fell into its usual pattern. Sapphira had been assigned to assist a dedicated team who were excavating a set of *insulae*. So far it was a lot of digging with little reward; the trio of modest dwellings seemed determined not to relinquish their relics without a fight. What kept them going was that, given the results from other insula in the vicinity, there was a decent likelihood of finding *something*.

To their delight, several pieces of pottery were extracted during the morning. In between helping to sift through the piles of dirt, in case they had overlooked tiny fragments, Sapphira mapped their location and sketched the individual shards. Signore Valana, the gentleman in charge of the group was confident there was more awaiting their eagle eyes and careful fingers.

By noon, Sapphira was smeared with dust and other assorted detritus, from her face to her boots. Trudging along the ancient street to one of the water troughs scattered throughout the ruins, she removed the hated bonnet and rinsed her face, rubbing a wet hand around her neck to cool down. She glanced down at her clothes, and heard her mother's voice upbraiding her, relieved it was in her head not next to her.

Twirling her bonnet by its ribbons, she found Leofwin

waiting for her in their usual spot.

"Busy morning?" he asked, amused by her state of dishevelment.

"Somewhat, but…" Sapphira sat down in the shelter of the crumbling wall and described what they had achieved, gesticulating wildly in her enthusiasm.

Leofwin listened with half an ear, the rest of his attention fixed on her animated countenance. Hester's words teased his subconscious as the happiness in Sapphira's voice washed over him.

Her hair, no longer confined under the bonnet was unravelling from its severe bun, glossy ringlets coiling around her face. Under the dark crest of her eyebrows, green eyes, fringed by inky lashes — such a contrast with her blonde hair — glittered like gemstones.

Again, he experienced that peculiar jolt; it resembled recognition, although of what eluded him. Leaning back, he felt the rough stone of the wall through his shirt. A welcome solidity in the nebulous jumble of his mercurial emotions.

Lust. That was the only rational interpretation. His body craved release and Sapphira was the only eligible female within a thirty-mile radius who was unencumbered. Lust — pure and simple.

He nodded in satisfaction. Now he knew what it was he could expunge it.

His gaze on Sapphira, Leofwin refused to acknowledge the derisive jeers reverberating in the far reaches of his mind.

Oblivious to Leofwin's epiphany, of sorts, Sapphira prattled on about this and that.

"Goodness, forgive me, I have monopolised our conversation. How was your morning?" she apologised when Leofwin gathered up the remnants of their luncheon. "Are you going to throw away that last piece of bread? If so, might you allow me to dispose of it?"

His forehead wrinkled in puzzlement.

"The dogs," she elaborated, squaring her shoulders in anticipation of the customary reproof.

"Not as gratifying as yours..." bypassing this — he knew it would do no good to tell her not to feed scraps to the dogs — Leofwin handed her the crust and went back to her question, "...although we have exposed a decent area within the building in which we are working. No artefacts, but tomorrow, we can tackle the rooms where such things are likely to be buried."

"Do you find that there is a pattern to the areas where most artefacts are unearthed? Say for example a kitchen or a dining room — it is called a triclinium, yes?"

"Yes, and yes, it is, well remembered." He praised, genuinely impressed. "The parts of houses where, typically, people spent much of their time is where we are finding objects which create a picture of their lives. I imagine the inhabitants fled without worrying whether their bed was made, or the crockery neatly stacked, or children's toys tidied away. I also suspect most expected to return, not be killed or see their town vanish under a thick blanket of ash and lava, leaving them destitute."

Leofwin shrugged, not in dismissal of the horror wrought on Pompeii, but in regret. He sighed and got to his feet. "Let us not be mired in melancholy for what we cannot change. The afternoon awaits." A quick glance at the sky caused a frown. It was cloudless, but the blue was slightly dull. "Do not tarry at day's end. I think there might be a storm in the offing, and we do not want to get caught in it."

"Thank you for the warning. I shall meet you at the amphitheatre."

"Good girl," he stowed everything in his satchel and slung

it over one shoulder. With a casual wave he disappeared around the corner.

Smothering a snigger at being referred to as a girl, Sapphira retraced her steps to the insulae.

The heat became oppressive, making Sapphira — who had already removed her jacket and loosened her cravat — wish she could shed her riding habit and work in her chemise. Best she could do was leave her bonnet on a pile of rubble at the entrance to the insula and pin up errant locks of hair. The sheets of paper on which finds were documented and sketched, served as a basic fan to waft her hot face.

While Sapphira was not afraid of storms, she preferred not to be outside when one hit, and kept a leery eye on the sky.

The group worked hard, and, in what felt like the blink of an eye, the afternoon was over.

A chorus of goodbyes were being said, and Sapphira was pulling on her jacket when she spotted one of the strays, sniffing around her bonnet, nudging it with his nose to tip it over. She grinned at the dog's antics, remembering she had stashed the hunk of bread underneath her hat. She was within an arm's length of the makeshift hatstand when the dog snatched at the ribbon and scarpered, his new treasure swinging wildly from his jowls.

"Hey, you little rascal," Sapphira squawked, "that's not edible." She grabbed the bread thinking she could trade it for her bonnet, and took off after the creature, who led her a merry dance along a maze of streets and through what looked like narrow alleyways. Familiar with the twists and turns of the site, the dog stayed several feet in front of her, enjoying the game.

Eventually, he came to a halt, tail wagging, tongue lolling

out of his mouth, and with what could only be described as a huge grin on his furry face. Sapphira swore the dog was laughing at her.

"Bad dog," Sapphira panted. "Here, you have this and let go of my hat." The sadly maligned article was probably ruined, but she did not want the creature to swallow the ribbon. She broke a corner off the bread and tossed the crumbs between her and the dog.

For several minutes, the pair was involved in a standoff. Sapphira, perched on a convenient corner of wall, cajoled, cooed, and dropped more crumbs, but the stray refused to relinquish his booty. Eventually, desire for food won out. Spitting the hat onto the dirt, the dog gobbled up the crumbs, then sat on his haunches, head cocked, waiting for this weird human to part with the rest of the bread.

Picking up her bonnet, Sapphira — needing a moment or two to cool down — resumed her seat. The dog inched closer, checking to see whether there were any more treats. Finding none, he laid his head on her knee, his velvety brown eyes beseeching her.

"You are a scamp," she scolded good-humouredly. "Look at my hat."

The dog, totally unrepentant, scattered the dust with happy sweeps of his tail.

"Time to go, Scamp. The perfect name for you." Unable to resist his endearing face, she risked a quick pat on his scruffy head. "I'll see you soon. Hark at me talking to a dog," she smirked, as the newly dubbed Scamp trotted off, eminently satisfied with his afternoon's frolic.

Sapphira got to her feet and glanced around. *Where was she?* Concentrating on not tripping over random clumps of debris or uneven stones, as she chased the dog, Sapphira had lost all sense of direction.

She backtracked until she came to a street, but it was not

one she recognised. The sky was darkening, and the breeze had strengthened which, thankfully, moderated the heat.

With Lord Osmund's warning about the weather ringing in her ears, Sapphira took the path to her right thinking it would lead her to the Forum. It was a dead end, at least the remainder of the road had yet to be excavated.

Trying another, she was pleased to note its length was unhindered, and she spied a cross street at the opposite end. Humming under her breath, she was hurrying along when the murmur of nearby voices snagged her attention.

She peeked through two doorways... nothing. At the third, she saw two men crouched over a mosaic. There was only a small portion visible, which although uneven, and missing some pieces was still beautiful. A simple flower motif in black tesserae, repeated across a background of white.

Aware she had no time to dawdle — doubtless they would be afforded the chance to examine the piece soon enough — the thrill of witnessing so important a discovery, had Sapphira watching the men wipe the mosaic with a damp cloth. The pattern glistened, the miniature tiles barely dulled by age and burial.

A low rumble caused the two men to look upwards.

"It's now or never," one of them said, loud enough for Sapphira to hear. Expecting them to cover their find with a layer of dirt, as seemed to be the usual procedure, Sapphira was shocked to see the man who spoke lift a corner.

Speechless, she stared as the mosaic cracked into two sections, several tesserae falling off. Removing the fragment, he shoved it into a large sack which his partner-in-crime held open.

Without thinking about the consequences *at all*, Sapphira gave vent to an eldritch screech and barrelled towards the pair.

CHAPTER NINE

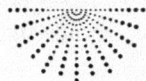

"*S*top! Thief! What are you *doing*? You cannot take that, 'tis a priceless artefact. You have no right..." Sapphira launched herself at the man closest to her, using her bonnet to beat him with one hand, while scrabbling to reach the sack with the other.

"Who the bloody hell are you?" The man goggled at the virago bearing down on him. Hair billowing around her like Medusa's snakes with a crazed look in her eyes, he considered the possibility she was an escapee from a local asylum, while ducking to avoid the demented flailing of her straw hat.

"A concerned citizen," she shrieked and continued to batter him. Her bonnet, already suffering irreparable damage at the jaws of Scamp, gave up and disintegrated.

"Gawd woman, leave it out. This is none of your business."

"If you are stealing, it *is* my business."

"Not stealing, merely appropriating a saleable commodity."

"One which is not yours."

"Not stealing if the item is not owned," he huffed, grabbing Sapphira's wrists. "You finished yet, Walt?" He threw this question over his shoulder at his accomplice who was stuffing a little pile of statuettes into the sack on top of the mosaic fragments.

"Ow, that hurts. Let me go, you scoundrel." Sapphira paused in her bid to twist free of his clutches, unable to credit she was having this argument.

It was all the man needed. "Here, you deal with her, I'll take the sack." He all but flung Sapphira at Walt who wrapped one arm around her waist and clapped a hand over her mouth.

"Quit yer yammering," he commanded menacingly, "Or it'll be the worse for yer."

All this served to do was make Sapphira struggle harder. His iron grip was as claustrophobic as an enclosed space, and she could feel panic begin to take hold.

She jerked her head backwards, momentarily slackening the hand clamped over her mouth. Sapphira bit down hard, her teeth sinking into the sensitive web of skin between Walt's thumb and forefinger.

"You little bitch," howling in pain, Walt retaliated with a brutal slap to her cheek.

Exploiting her advantage, Sapphira ignored the sharp sting of the blow, wriggled free, and ran pell-mell for the street. Not quickly enough.

"Nev, stop her," Walt bawled.

Nev dropped the sack and caught Sapphira by her skirts, his fingers snarling in the material. Hearing a loud rip, Sapphira spun around, only to find herself trapped once again. Her scream drowned by a crack of thunder.

A large hand fastened around her mouth and nose.

Sapphira couldn't breathe. Her panic escalated. Spots appeared before her eyes, and tears spilled down her cheeks.

She squirmed frantically, grappling at the hand with desperate fingers, to no avail. If anything, the man's grip tightened

A grey mist obscuring her vision, Sapphira had a brainwave.

She stopped fighting to take a breath and slumped.

Leofwin was pacing up and down the path by the amphitheatre. *Where the devil was she?* A few of the men with whom she had been working, dashed past, wishing him a cursory goodnight in their hurry to get home before the worst of the storm hit.

No sign of Miss Beresford.

Damn, but she was heedless.

Signore Valana was coming his way. "Valana, have you seen Miss Beresford?"

"She is not already here?" The supervisor was startled. "Miss Beresford left the insula, ohhh, more than half an hour ago. She did mention you wanted to leave promptly because of the weather. I assumed she was coming to meet you."

"I have not seen hide nor hair of her since luncheon."

Forks of jagged lightning split the mass of roiling clouds, followed seconds later by a long roll of thunder. The storm was almost overhead.

"I cannot imagine she will delay. No one wants to be abroad in a tempest," Signore Valana raised his voice over the whine of the wind.

"I hope you are correct. Go..." when Valana made as though to turn back into the ruins. "...no need for us both to get saturated. Get you home."

"Two can cover more ground."

"As you say, she will doubtless arrive momentarily."

Leofwin assured his friend. "I'll track her to where you were working."

Reluctantly, and only because his home was some distance away, Signore Valana did as Leofwin bade.

Making a quick detour to the old, and thankfully solid, shed, where his stallion, Vulcan, and Sapphira's mount, Minerva, were stabled, Leofwin retrieved his cloak from the bag strapped to Vulcan's saddle. Patting the horse on its rump he latched the door securely and set off.

"Witless wench," he ground out, as he trudged through the ruin. "Just once, could she listen to instructions. I do not deliver them for the good of my health." He groused his way to the insulae, his irritation mounting when there was no sign of Sapphira.

"Now where am I supposed to look?" He peered into a few of the surrounding buildings and streets but it was as though Sapphira had vanished into thin air. Odd, given the excavated sections of the site were relatively minimal.

That said, he was cognisant of how easily a person unfamiliar with the criss-cross layout of Pompeii could get lost, Leofwin made a concerted effort to control his anger which was now laced with an ample dose of concern. The sunlight had been snuffed out, and he could smell rain on the wind.

Where the devil was she?

"You cork brained ass. You've gone an' killed her." Walt's dismayed gaze was fixed on the woman lying in a crumpled heap. Streaks of lightning flickered in the gloom giving her ashen features a spectral aspect. An ear-splitting crash resounded among the insulae. The storm was upon them.

"Better dead than tattling on us," Nev retorted. "Come on,

we need to get outta here before someone decides to look for her. Stupid, stupid fool. Couldn't leave well alone. Now she's paid."

Walt, binding an old handkerchief around his sore hand, agreed and levied a spiteful kick at the prone woman. "Bitch," he repeated with a sneer.

Shoving the last of the purloined artefacts into the sack with more haste than care, and with the rain beginning to pelt the ground in earnest, the pair legged it.

It took everything Sapphira had not to recoil or scream when Walt's boot connected with her thigh, thankful it was a glancing blow and that the noise of the storm eclipsed her agonised groan. She remained motionless, praying they would not return and, ignoring the teeming rain, counted to one hundred, slowly.

Tentatively squinting through half-closed eyelids, Sapphira sucked in a huff of relief. She was alone. Not particularly comforting, but less distressing than the alternative. She levered herself onto one elbow and took stock.

She was lost, filthy, and soaked. Her dress was torn, her right hip ached like the dickens and her face throbbed. Worse, she was dreadfully late. What a mess.

Dragging herself to her feet, Sapphira bit her lip so as not to cry out from the sickening pain lancing through her hip and down her leg. She checked the damage to her skirt, heartened to note the tear was not too obvious, hidden by the soft folds of the material.

Above her, clouds scudded across an angry sky; this storm was far from over. Hugging the wall, she limped along the street as quickly as she was able, her feet slithering on cobbles slick with water. The wind whipped at her hair and plastered her wet dress to her skin.

Shivering uncontrollably from cold and shock, Sapphira

plodded on doggedly, hoping against hope she would come to a street she recognised.

Leofwin's alarm intensified. Their occasional spats aside, Miss Beresford had never given him the impression she was wilfully irresponsible. This could only mean her failure to meet him was unintentional. It was why that concerned him.

A methodical man, he had checked the excavation plots which might have distracted her, finding them all empty. The two night watchmen he spoke to during his search had not seen her but agreed to keep an eye out.

Glad of his cloak in the downpour, Leofwin was debating whether he ought to wait at the amphitheatre, when a bedraggled figure appeared around a corner some distance ahead of him. He saw her glance up and down the street and then sag.

It was Sapphira.

The relief coursing through him was almost overwhelming. He took one stride towards her, when something deep inside him clicked. Shocking in its intensity. How had he not realised? Then it dawned on him that he had but, since this was an emotion neither looked for nor coveted, he had quashed it.

Happiness warred with exasperation, as he made haste towards her, shouting her name.

Sapphira heard a voice over the tumult. Uncertain whether it was her imagination, she hesitated. It came again.

"Miss Beresford."

Stiff with cold, she pivoted awkwardly in the direction of the sound.

Lord Osmund! Oh, thank goodness, she was no longer

lost. Sapphira tried to reply but her mouth refused to heed her brain, and her teeth were chattering.

Then he was next to her, wrapping her in his cloak, chivvying her along the street. "Keep moving. You need to keep moving."

"Sorry, so cold," she gasped, forcing one foot in front of the other, her saturated garments and aching thigh making every movement twice as difficult.

"What happened? No, never mind, that can wait. We shall have to stay here until the storm passes. The stable will be dry."

Exhausted, Sapphira who struggled to match his pace at the best of times began to lag.

"Stop dallying, we must get to shelter." Leofwin urged, without looking at her.

"Just leave me." Sapphira implored. "I cannot..."

"Do not be foolish. You will catch your death," he interrupted.

His brusque tone had the desired effect, and Sapphira mustered up the last of her strength. Moments later she was being hustled into the stable. Minerva and Vulcan nickered softly, tossing their majestic heads.

Removing his cloak from her shoulders, Leofwin shook off the water, droplets flying everywhere, and hung it on a thoughtfully placed rusty hook. Rummaging around in one of his saddle bags, he retrieved the picnic blanket and bundled Sapphira into it, before settling her onto the warm straw.

"Sit there. Can you do that without getting lost?" he appealed, not very kindly.

Tired, frightened, bruised, and drenched, Sapphira's frayed nerves snapped.

"Go to hell, and while you're there, do the world a favour and forget the way back."

Leofwin's jaw dropped. "*What* did you just say?"

"You heard."

"Your ingratitude knows no bounds. The reason I adjured you to be here in a timely manner was in order for us to get home before the storm. I waited, asked everyone whether they had seen you. None had, but all assured me, you would never, especially in light of the deteriorating weather, be so thoughtless as to ignore my request. I scoured the site for you, gave you my cloak when, finally, I found you, and this is the thanks I get? *Go to hell?*"

He was working himself into a fine rage.

"If you would permit me to explain…" Sapphira began.

"What is there to explain? Thoughtless chit."

"Thoughtless?" Sapphira smacked her forehead with her palm. "Oh, my lord, you are the most boorish oaf I have ever had the misfortune to meet."

She met his outraged glare with matching one of her own. "I am wearied of treading on eggshells around you. You might be my host and I am sorry if my unexpected presence has upset some invisible balance, but *you* are not easy to live with. One moment you are friendly and polite even helpful, the next, taking great delight in finding fault with everything I do or say.

"Have you *any* idea what it feels like to be an unwanted guest? How arduous it is, predicting your mood, preparing myself for your jibes and superior remarks?

"Yes, I made mistakes. I will continue to make mistakes. Italy is not like England, a country I had never left prior to this visit, by the way. The language, the people, the country-side, even the air, everything is foreign, and it takes time to adjust. Neither am I an antiquarian or art historian. Every day I am faced with a miscellany of new experiences, challenges, and information to assimilate, and am doing my best.

"Hester assured me you were a considerate gentleman who would be sympathetic to my reasons for accompanying her. Had I realised my being here was going to be so onerous a burden, I would not have subjected you to it." Sapphira was shouting now, terror from her ordeal of the afternoon morphing into a temper the like of which she had not surrendered to for an age.

That it was the culmination of everything she had repressed since that awful day in April, did not register. What *did* register was that she was not prepared to deal with Lord Osmund's unfeeling attitude. *I'll wager he would be upset had he been imperilled*, she fumed inwardly.

Uncaring that the storm had yet to abate, Sapphira flung off the blanket and staggered towards the door.

"Miss Beresford…" Stunned at her fury, Leofwin put out an arm to halt her flight.

"Leave me alone," she roared, and hobbled into the darkness.

CHAPTER TEN

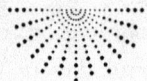

*L*eofwin was so flabbergasted that Sapphira's ungainly gait went unnoticed. Never in his life had *anyone* shouted at him and here was a slip of a woman lambasting him with no respect for his status. Sapphira's words battered him in much the same way as had the rain.

Abruptly, his own temper, which had reached boiling point, fizzled out. He grabbed his wet cloak and hurried through the stable door to see Sapphira splashing over the muddy ground, gesticulating erratically. Her tirade not requiring an audience.

His lips twitched. She was magnificent.

"Miss Beresford," he called. She did not stop. "Please, Sapphira."

His use of her given name pierced Sapphira's outrage. She paused, then turned, which gave him time to cover the gap between them.

"What now?" Even in the gloom her baleful expression was unmistakeable.

"Miss Beresford, I grant my behaviour has been less than affable, and I had no mind to make you feel unwelcome. Hester is correct, I am normally quite the genial fellow."

"So, what is it about me that turns you into a dunderhead?" Unknowingly, Sapphira parroted Hester's remonstrance.

"I cannot..." he started, then shook his head. "No, that is not quite true. It is not you, per se, more your sex." He opened his palms in a vaguely contrite motion.

"My *sex*?" Sapphira was not sure *where* this discussion was going but it was not taking the direction she expected.

"Women, ladies, those of the female persuasion."

"Pray, do enlighten me." Sapphira would have tapped her foot, but her hip ached too much. Desperate to sit down, to rest her bruised body, to sleep, she was equally determined not to exhibit any such weakness.

"Would you agree to a bargain? If you come back to the stable, I shall enlighten you. A dunderhead I might be, but I am not wholly insensitive, and you need to be out of the cold."

Sapphira studied him, unaware her face, smeared with mud, was pinched and drawn or that her blonde hair hung in sodden ringlets around her face.

Leofwin quelled the impulse to haul her into his arms, purely to banish the chill... of course.

Neither noticed the rain had stopped. The thunder continued to rumble but it was faint now, the storm moving away to the east, drawing the angry clouds with it.

The swirling mass dispersed, and the sky cleared. As though unveiled by an invisible hand, the moon, protected by her heavenly guardians, glowed in ethereal radiance.

Around them, all fell still; even the breeze had dropped.

"Miss Beresford." Leofwin crooked his elbow. The longer Sapphira stayed outside the greater the likelihood she would be beset by sickness.

Acknowledging it was unwise to loiter in the chill night, Sapphira was about to accept the proffered arm when an odd glimmer to her right caught her attention.

Unsure whether it was anything more than a distant flash of lightening, she peered down the street she had traversed with such frequency.

In front of her, a phenomenon, unknown until this moment was revealed.

Soft moonbeams fell on an array of white stones, placed strategically among the slate-grey cobbles, illuminating the ancient road.

Sapphira was awestruck.

"Oh, they are like stars in the mist... how ingenious," she breathed. "Such a simple technique, yet the effect is incredible, granting the inhabitants of Pompeii the ability to see their way at night."

"I agree, 'tis almost unearthly." Then as Sapphira gave a violent shudder. "Miss Beresford, please, accompany me back to the stable. Harangue me there if you so choose, I probably deserve it, but you *must* get out of this damp air."

Fatigue was the deciding factor. All Sapphira wanted to do was climb into her lovely warm bed — a futile desire and, at this point, a mattress of straw and a horse's girth for a pillow was as inviting a prospect.

She hooked her arm through his and, with one last glimpse at the display of Roman innovation, they returned to the stable.

Inside the wooden shack it was pitch black. Leofwin left the door open, allowing a glimmer of light to creep through.

"Here is the picnic blanket." He plucked it off the floor and handed it to Sapphira. "Do you require assistance, with your... errr... garments?" he asked awkwardly.

"Thank you, I can manage." Sapphira assured him, thankful she was wearing her riding habit, not a day gown.

"Let me know when you are ready." He walked out and vanished around the corner of the stable.

Thwarted by cold fingers, Sapphira fumbled with her wet clothes, frustrated she had to tolerate so many layers. Eventually, she undid the buttons on the jacket and divested herself of it, followed by the skirt, cravat, and habit shirt. She hung them on the hook Leofwin had used earlier for his cloak, removed her boots and stockings, then vacillated.

Her chemise, gossamer fine and shorter than normal, fell to the top of her thighs — her modified riding habit with its split skirt did not allow for the standard length. Damp or not, she had no intention of removing this last garment, even though it only afforded her the minimum of modesty.

Huddling into the meagre warmth of the blanket, she called softly, "I am changed."

There was a long silence, but just as a scream clawed at her throat, she heard the pad of boots on the wet ground.

Leofwin poked about behind the horses and found five extra bales of straw stacked in a corner. Using three, he formed a makeshift bed. "There you go, it will be prickly, but you will be off the floor."

"What about you?" Sapphira spoke through clenched teeth.

"I shall persuade Vulcan to become my pillow." His reply echoed her own thoughts. "Are you comfortable if I close the door? I do not want you to end up in a draught. You have my word I shall not breach your trust."

Sapphira was so tired, she was scarcely able to form an

answer. With a huge yawn, she said, "I have no qualms in that regard, but I should like to hear the rationale behind your capricious behaviour. To snap at me without questioning the reasons for my delay was unnecessary, especially given you have no idea of the hair-raising experience I endured. You sir, have no patien—" mid-word, slumber overtook her.

The mirth playing about Leofwin's mouth at the suddenness by which Sapphira fell asleep, faded when her remark came back to him. *Hair-raising experience? What the deuce?* He opened his mouth to ask, then thought better of it. Sleep was more important than explanations. They could wait until morning.

Covering Sapphira with his cloak, he closed the door, inched his way to where Vulcan stood, and coaxed the gentle giant down onto the straw strewn floor. Curling up between the stallion's legs, head resting on the creature's warm body, Leofwin brooded over what she meant by hair-raising. Nothing came to mind. His thoughts became muddled and, shuffling until he was comfortable, dozed off.

At some point during the night, Sapphira stirred, becoming aware of a prickling sensation against her skin. Memory flooded back. She shot upright, the improvised bedding slithering off her shoulders, and peered into the obscurity, getting her bearings. The sounds of the horses breathing and the smell of their warm bodies, strangely soothing.

Pinpricks of moonlight filtered through the wooden slats, enough for her eyes to adjust to the darkness. On the floor no more than three feet in front of her, she spied a large and oddly shaped hump. Wrapping the cloak around her, she tiptoed closer, to see Lord Osmund sprawled against Vulcan.

She took a moment to study him. Even in the gloom, she perceived a weariness etched on his angular features, and the inclination to stroke her hand along his jaw was almost irresistible.

Appalled by her train of thought, she coerced her wayward brain back to the mundane and brushed gentle fingertips along his arm. He felt cold to her touch, not surprising, especially since she was using his cloak. Despite the bulk of the two horses, the interior of the stable was cool.

There was a sensible solution, but Sapphira hesitated. Knowing was one thing, implementation was a whole other issue. An icy draught skittered through the walls, making her shiver, and she threw prudence to the winds.

Leofwin jolted awake. He blinked, momentarily disoriented by his surroundings and whatever had disturbed him. Slivers of light crept through the numerous cracks in the walls. *Had the dawn roused him?* He recognised the stable, recalling the storm and subsequent hunt for Sapphira.

One puzzle solved.

He was no longer cold; a material of some weight had been tucked over his shoulders. He realised it was his cloak, which could only have been placed there by Sapphira. *When had she done so and why?* He was musing over this mystery when a slap, accompanied by a flurry of indecipherable babble created a third conundrum.

Leofwin jerked backwards. Something moved with him.

He glanced down and his jaw dropped.

Sapphira?

It was obvious she had been lying in the crook of his arm.

How in the world had she ended up there? He racked his brain but could not remember agreeing to so indiscreet a sleeping arrangement.

Sapphira lolled against him. The picnic blanket was askew leaving little to Leofwin's imagination.

Unable to help it, his gaze travelled the length of her lissom figure, coming to an appalled halt at the sight of an ugly welt on her thigh. The surrounding bruise, blossoming in shades of yellow, brown, and purple, disappeared under the negligible undergarment, which somehow managed to guard her dignity.

A more detailed inspection revealed another blemish — hard to distinguish under grubby smudges — discoloured the side of her face. *What the hell...?*

Before he had the chance to process this, her flailing hands struck him again and, unwilling to suffer a battering, he grasped them, while trying to decipher her garbled muttering.

Sapphira's eyes flew open. Even though he could see terror lurking in their emerald depths, there was no recognition. Her vision was turned inward.

"Sapphira, 'tis me, Leofwin." He spoke in measured tones seeking to calm her, but it was plain his voice did not penetrate her nightmare.

She fought him like a wild cat, her incomprehensible ravings unnerving the horses. Vulcan shifted restlessly but settled at a word from Leofwin. It was imperative he arrested Sapphira's internal torment.

He instilled a firm note into his voice. "Sapphira Beresford, what is all this nonsense? You will wake the dead with that clamour."

No reaction. Her face had contorted into a mask of fear, and gibberish spilled over her lips.

What... or who... the dickens had she encountered?

With no time to waste contemplating this, he tried again. "Miss Beresford," he barked.

Sapphira stilled. Her blank gaze faded, and her focus

returned.

She stared at Leofwin for what felt like an age, then drew a shuddering breath, and gripped his forearms. "I am safe?" she husked.

"You are safe," he affirmed, fighting the temptation to hug her.

"Oh, praise the good Lord and everything that's holy." Sapphira's head dropped to his chest as she strove for composure. "Forgive me, my lord... I..."

He patted her on the shoulder in what he hoped was a comforting manner. "Hush, there is naught to forgive. You suffered a nightmare is all."

Sapphira straightened up, a red stain colouring her pale cheeks when she noticed her state of undress. "I... err... but... because..."

"Again, do not fret. Neither of us has behaved inappropriately." He spoke gravely, conveniently disregarding his earlier perusal of her scarcely clad form. "Thank you for sharing the cloak, its warmth was a boon."

"You were cold, it was the least I could do."

"No, the least you could do was to ignore my discomfort."

"Yes, well..."

There was a brief silence.

"I ought to dress." Sapphira said, making no attempt to move, distracted by the nightmare and Leofwin's solid presence. He was so close, she could feel the heat from his body, and wrestled with an inexplicable yearning to fling herself into his arms, driven by an overwhelming need to be held.

A faintly exotic fragrance teased her nostrils; she detected myrrh and honey and possibly calendula, but it dissipated before she could be certain.

Suppressing a similar desire, Leofwin rose to his feet. "I suspect your attire is not quite dry. We will hasten for home as soon as you are ready." Hand on the door, he turned. "Perhaps we might revisit our bargain on the way."

Sapphira stared at his retreating figure. *What bargain?* She ransacked her brain for an answer, but the previous night was naught but a blur. *Oh my, what on earth have I agreed to?*

Setting that aside for now, she lifted her habit shirt from the hook, and held it up. Although a tad crumpled, it had survived remarkably well. The material had stiffened overnight and seemed determined to impede her. Grumbling under her breath, she finally she got it fastened.

Inspecting her skirt, Sapphira was relieved to note the rip was not as bad as it had sounded, although she was unsure whether the garment was salvageable. Her aching leg hampering her every movement, she shimmied into the begrimed article, and hooked the broad straps over her shoulders.

Leaving the cravat for the moment, she did battle with her jacket. By the time the buttons were done up, the chill of the early morning air was dispelled.

Sitting on the bales of straw she had used as a bed, Sapphira pulled on her stockings and boots, the damp leather making her grimace in distaste. Her hair felt like a bird's nest, but without a mirror, she made do with running her fingers through it, then tying it back with the cravat.

Satisfied she was presentable as possible, Sapphira went to find Leofwin, who was standing several feet from the stable, hands on hips, staring at the imposing grandeur of the amphitheatre.

He spun around at her approach.

"Thank you." She offered a shy smile, acknowledging his tact.

He bowed. "Give me a moment to saddle the horses."

"Let me help."

With a mind to the bruising he had observed, Leofwin shook his head. "Enjoy the fresh air, I'll not be a moment."

He was as good as his word. Before long, the pair were astride their respective mounts and trotting out of Pompeii.

CHAPTER ELEVEN

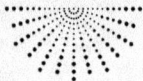

The sun had yet to make an appearance, but its rays pushed back the last of the night through a cloudless sky. As they rode, the pink of dawn yielded to turquoise, and warmth began to permeate the air, paving the way for a perfect summer's day.

"What happened?" Leofwin's question broke the companionable silence which had descended as they left the ruin.

"I saw two men in the process of stealing a mosaic and decided to stop them." Sapphira's tone was bland.

"I'm sorry, what did you just say?" His eyebrows shot under his hairline.

"One of the stray dogs stole my bonnet. I chased him, retrieved my hat and... errr... was making my way to meet you when I came across two robbers who were removing the mosaic, which was not the only artefact they had stolen. There were other things as well, small carvings." That she had been hopelessly lost at the time was a detail Sapphira deemed unworthy of mention.

"And your injuries? How did you come by them?"

"What injuries? I am fine," Sapphira hedged.

Leofwin quirked a sceptical brow. "Do not prevaricate, Miss Beresford. Your face is taking on all the shades of the rainbow and, not only are you favouring your right leg but also, I noticed you wincing when you mounted Minerva."

She stared straight ahead, wondering how to paint the picture without sounding witless. To plunge headlong into so fraught a situation without due consideration was reckless and she knew it. Anyone with half a brain would have gone for help. The result could have been far worse.

"Miss Beresford," her host pressed.

With a resigned huff, Sapphira capitulated, and provided a succinct account of her ordeal.

Leofwin listened aghast. Sapphira had shown remarkable courage in her gambit to foil a robbery brazen in its execution. The market for ancient artefacts was a lucrative business and those intent on stealing were merciless in their persistence. He knew of people who had confronted treasure hunters alone only to suffer grievous beatings for their troubles.

Then there were the thieves themselves. Since the authorities had appointed a crew of watchmen at Pompeii, looting the site under cover of darkness was risky enough. To chance it in broad daylight — especially given the number of people roaming the ruins in their respective capacities — was nothing short of lunacy.

Perhaps that was precisely why. Strangers could remain inconspicuous if they endeavoured to blend in with the regular teams.

When Sapphira expounded on how she received her bruises, the wrath which suffused Leofwin, while understandable, far exceeded the justifiable outrage he would feel had anyone, let alone a woman been treated thus, and shook him to his core.

Summoning up the discipline which had become ingrained during the war, he set aside his inner turmoil and quizzed her on what she could recall of the vagabonds.

"Both were reasonably tall, although not as tall as you," she began. "Their clothing was similar to what everyone else on the site wears, which is why I did not think anything of their actions."

She cast her mind back, concentrating.

"They are very definitely English, roughly spoken, with coarse accents. The man who kicked me is called Walt. He is stocky, and dark haired. Nev was the one who almost suffocated me. He is more wiry and older than Walt, at least ten years older I would gauge, with fair hair and a beard. Will that be helpful?" she concluded with a hint of pride, pleased she had remembered something.

"Extremely," Leofwin replied. "Given the circumstances, I am impressed at your powers of recollection."

"Perhaps because I watched them work for a few moments before I realised what they were up to," she mused. "I was so furious, I did not consider the consequences. How dare they think it is acceptable to remove such antiquities."

"You could have been killed," he countered. "Hester will not let you out of her sight for the duration."

"But I was not killed. Yes, it was terrifying and, despite looking as though I was in a brawl, the marks are superficial. I refuse to allow those blackguards to spoil my time here."

"You are an unusual woman, Miss Beresford," Leofwin's tone was contemplative.

"Why thank you, kind sir." Sapphira effected a curtsy. "We are back to Miss Beresford? Yet you called me Sapphira last night, several times." She arched a pointed brow.

"I... errr..." Leofwin felt himself blushing... actually blushing.

Sapphira manoeuvred Minerva alongside Vulcan and reached across to press a hand on his knee. "If you are amenable, might we start again? The informality you share with Archer and Hester is enviable and, while I am not a close friend, perhaps I might be included for the remainder of my time here. We are thousands of miles from Society and its constraints. Who does it hurt if we forgo convention?"

She held his gaze, not easy when you are riding a horse.

Her touch, light though it was felt like a brand, and Leofwin could not have denied her, any more than he could fly to the moon. In truth, the rules were a tedious business.

Here among his fellow enthusiasts, he was Osmund, or Leofwin. All those he worked with knew he was a marquis, but he never stood on ceremony and had begged to be treated as an equal. Initially, his new colleagues were deferential but, once witness to his dedication, they soon forgot he was nobility. It was liberating.

"I concur," he smiled, and patted her slender hand still on his knee. "If you agree to return the favour, I should be honoured to call you Sapphira."

She smiled, her lovely green eyes twinkling. "Sapphi," she corrected. "Only granted to a select few. Now, I believe you mentioned a bargain. To be fair, I am hazy about what I agreed to, but you brought it up, so..." she removed her hand from his leg and opened her palm.

Ignoring the curious sense of loss so simple a gesture elicited, Leofwin elaborated. "I offered to explain my behaviour in exchange for you returning to the stable with me."

"Ahhh, now this I *am* interested to hear." She shuffled awkwardly in her saddle. "I shall be relieved when I can change out of these clothes," she grumbled. "Everything is sticking to me."

The image of her lying in his arms, popped into Leofwin's head, lingering despite his determination to dismiss it. He swallowed to clear his throat which was suddenly clogged. *How could a woman, one he did not particularly like... conveniently forgetting his recent revelations... reduce him to incoherence?*

He glanced at Sapphira who seemed oblivious to his confusion. He swallowed again. "As you might expect, my life was mapped out for me from birth. I was primed to assume the dukedom. Everything I did or said, conditioned me. Even my thoughts were not my own.

"Since I knew no different, that in itself was not the issue. What I baulked at was being pursued by ambitious mothers, who seized every opportunity to parade their daughters in front of me. Somehow, they had discovered there was no arrangement in place, meaning I was fair game.

"I know my duty, but the pressure became untenable. I could not attend a ball or a picnic, without being pestered. Exasperated, I informed my parents I would wed when I was ready and not before, and if that meant never, so be it. I was almost grateful for the wars. They provided a legitimate excuse to disappear. It is a terrible thing when being embroiled in a battle to the death is less abhorrent than repelling prospective brides."

Sapphira chuckled softly.

"I am glad you find my woes entertaining," Leofwin said dryly.

"The picture in my head is humorous. It resembles a Gillray satire. Lord Osmund, resplendent in his military uniform, fending off a regiment of simpering ladies armed with fans and parasols." She bent over and slapped her saddle, laughing unrestrainedly.

Her merriment was infectious and, in spite of himself, Leofwin joined in.

"Oh, oh, I'm sorry, but..." Sapphira spluttered as another gale of laughter overtook her. Sucking in a long breath, she became serious. "I do empathise, possibly more than you realise. The obstacles life throws at us can be taxing and the only way to consider them dispassionately is from a distance. Mind, going to war is a tad extreme," she opined with an exaggerated eye roll.

Leofwin shrugged. "Oh, I don't know, if the endless mud, hail of canon fire, rain of bullets and rapidly accumulating dead bodies doesn't put things into perspective... what will?" he jested.

Sapphira stared. This was a completely different aspect of her host. His wry, tongue-in-cheek wit matched hers. "Lord Osmund, you are proving to be quite the comedian."

"I thought we had consented to a less formal arrangement. My name is Leo, and only granted to a select few." He winked.

She inclined her head in acquiescence. "Pray continue. You found war more congenial than Society. In my head they are one and the same, but that is another story. Then the war ended..." she left that one for him to pick up his explanation.

"Ah yes, my behaviour. I hoped when I was discharged from the army, things might have changed. Lamentably, even the threat of invasion by a foreign power was not enough to sway those redoubtable Mamas. The first ball I attended after my return was my last. Apparently, my injury, from which I was still recovering, was merely an added attraction. I became a focus of their pity, and they vied to be seen tending to the poor wounded solider. It was nauseating.

"Then, reprieve. Aunt Maud bequeathed me the villa. Her marriage to an Italian nobleman was against her parents' express wishes, and she never set foot in England again. I was a child when she left and have no idea why she named me beneficiary, but it was a timely blessing.

"I booked the next available passage to Naples, threw a few belongings in a trunk, and farewelled my family. That was six years ago, and it was a decision I have never regretted."

"Have you been back? Do you miss them... your parents and siblings? Do you have siblings?" Sapphira prodded.

"I have made the journey once. It was a joy to see my family and I stayed at Witringham Abbey, avoiding London completely. Yes, I miss them, and thankfully my mother is an incurable letter-writer, so I receive regular updates on their lives."

"Do you get lonely?"

He considered this. "Occasionally, especially at certain times of the year when we gathered to celebrate a birthday or Christmas. For the most part I prefer my own company. I always have, and circumstances have made a solitary existence easier."

"Am I right in positing that your dyspeptic veneer is a shield to keep people at arm's length? A way of preventing a repeat performance?"

Leofwin was about to refute her charge — he enjoyed an amicable relationship with his colleagues — then paused. Sapphira was not incorrect. He fought shy of extending any friendship beyond working hours. Outside his staff, the only other people to visit his home were the Dynhams, and now Sapphira. His private life was just that, private.

"I have never given it serious thought, but you might be right. I am a confirmed bachelor, entrenched in my ways. I have no desire or will to change."

"I understand your rationale. I too have a fancy for a life unencumbered by emotion."

The words in Hester's letter came back to him, and Leofwin swivelled in his saddle to pin Sapphira with a hard stare.

"*Now* what have I said," she exclaimed.

He did not reply, and they rode on for a while without speaking.

They were approaching the villa when Leofwin asked, "Sapphi, why did you come to Italy?"

"Hester invited me."

"She told me you required a spell out of England."

"She was being kind."

"Have we not reached an accord?"

"What if we have? My woes are of no significance."

"Hah, you have woes. A trouble shared is a troubled halved." His expression, one of gentle encouragement.

"You are persistent, I give you that."

"Only when I believe it necessary. Come now, what makes your smile dwindle and your cheeks pale for no apparent reason? You retreat into your shell when you think no one will notice. Some of the blame lies at my feet, but not every instance."

Mimicking her earlier gesture, he stretched out and patted her knee. A faint tingle snaked along his arm, gone almost before he registered it. "Please."

Sapphira glanced ahead. The driveway leading to the villa was in sight. "Might we postpone this until later? We are nearly home, doubtless Hester and Archer will need placating, and I am desperate to be rid of these clothes."

With sleight of hand, Leofwin caught Minerva's reins, bringing both horses to a halt. He studied Sapphira's face. She returned his stare unflinchingly.

"As long as you do not renege."

"You have my word."

They shared a smile and something else, tantalisingly elusive, began to flourish.

Fate viewed their interaction with smug satisfaction. *So far, so good*!

CHAPTER TWELVE

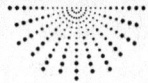

*I*t was early evening before Sapphira saw Leofwin again.

Whether there was someone on lookout or the sound of the horses' hooves acted as an alert, neither of the two weary riders knew but, as they reached the villa, doors flew open, and people descended on them from every direction.

Sapphira, trying to ignore the throbbing muscles in her bruised thigh, had barely dismounted, when the womenfolk, Hester included, swooped. Whisked to her bedchamber, Sapphira could have cried when she saw the hot bath being prepared.

She was assisted out of her unyielding clothes by a tutting Amalia, whose cheerful scolding escalated when she spotted the livid marks on Sapphira's cheek and leg.

Bombarded with questions, no one paused long enough for Sapphira to answer a single one. The din began to resemble a marketplace, with the stall holders vying to be heard. If she hadn't ached so much it would have been hilarious. As it was her lips twitched when she begged them to take a breath.

"Please, I cannot distinguish a single word. One at a time, or I swear my head will explode, and then where will you be? Covered in foul matter and no answers forthcoming."

Her rather gruesome statement worked, and everyone shut up.

Sapphira grinned. "First things first. Amalia, my apologies for the deplorable state of my clothes. There was an... incident, about which I will be happy to apprise everyone, but might it wait until I have had a bath, and perhaps a short nap?" Despite doing her best to sound jaunty, her voice lacked animation.

The dark circles under her friend's eyes which were beginning to rival the deepening purple of Sapphira's cheek, prompted Hester to take control. Anxious to know what had kept the two of them out all night, she reined in her curiosity. Time enough later. After dispatching one of the maids to fetch a plate of food and a hot beverage, Hester ushered out everyone else save Luisa.

"Come up to the salon when you are rested," she said as she closed the door.

Removing the last of her garments, Sapphira stepped through the arch into her dressing room. The lightly scented water was steaming. Never had a bath looked so inviting.

"Thank you, Luisa," Sapphira sank into the warmth, careful not to slop the water over the sides of the tub. "You have no idea how I have longed for this moment."

"Take your time, Miss. I shall return shortly." Bustling about the room, Luisa gathered up the remainder of Sapphira's sadly maligned clothes and left quietly.

Sapphira wallowed... there was no other word to describe it... in the luxury of her bath. The heat seeped into her bones, reviving her tired body. Propping her head on the rim, she almost floated, allowing the water to ripple over her skin. *Bliss.*

Soaping herself, she ensured every last smear of mud was erased. Lusia organised for the water to be changed, then took charge of washing Sapphira's hair, gently combing out the knots.

Reluctantly, and before the water cooled to the point of discomfort, Sapphira climbed out of the tub to be wrapped in a large drying towel. She walked over to the closest window and leant on the frame to gaze out over the bay. The sunlight sparkled on the azure water, and the balmy morning air drifted past her, carrying a sweet floral fragrance.

Sapphira breathed deeply. "'Tis so beautiful," she murmured.

"We are fortunate, *sì*." Luisa came to stand beside her. "My family, we have lived here for generations. Papa says why leave when perfection is already on the... hmmm... we say *soglia di porta...*?"

"I think maybe, threshold, maybe doorstep..." Sapphira translated, "...and I agree wholeheartedly."

"You will be sad to go?"

"More than I believed possible," Sapphira's reply held a pensive note and Luisa nodded sagely.

"Ahh, you are falling in love with Campania. Your heart, he knows." Luisa tapped her chest then her head.

"Certainly, it will be an extraordinary memory."

"Memory? Is that all? You do not wish to stay?"

Sapphira turned to face Luisa. "A tempting notion but my life is in England."

"Pah, you are here, England is there. Does she miss you? Do you miss her?" She tapped her head again. "We shall see." Luisa did not enlarge on her comment. "Come now, you are ready for *la dormita*. These bruises will require ointment. I will fetch him when I wake you."

As though Sapphira was a child, Luisa ushered her to the bed and tucked her under the covers.

Before she reached the door, Sapphira was asleep.

Leofwin, who had fared rather better than Sapphira, made do with a thorough wash and change of clothes before joining Archer and Hester in the salon where he inhaled several cups of strong coffee.

"Are you going to tell us what happened?" Archer quizzed his friend, after a silence during which they sipped their drinks and Leofwin munched through a plate of eggs and ham.

"I think I ought to wait until Sapphira joins us, this is really her tale. I was merely a bystander."

"'Tis Sapphira now?" Hester teased with a sly smirk.

"We have reached a rapport," Leofwin's bland reply gave nothing away.

"Because…" Hester stretched out the word, her brows forming a testy line.

His mouth twitched at her expression. "Patience, Lady Hester. You will hear in good time. I *can* say it is a story worthy of a London broadsheet." Before Hester could protest, he changed the subject and refused to be drawn any further regardless of how often she badgered him throughout the day.

Sapphira slept the sleep of the just, not waking until the afternoon sun filled her suite with golden light. Appreciating the comfort of an actual bed, she lay for several minutes, mulling over the events of the previous day.

Leofwin loomed large in every scene, even those he had not been involved in. Ignoring his cantankerous attitude, she conceded he was exactly the right person to have next to you in a crisis. He had shown himself to be solicitous and, with the benefit of hindsight, Sapphira supposed — if she was feeling magnanimous — she could understand his indignation at her tardiness.

Not that she was about to let him off easily. Yes, they had set aside their differences, but the proof of the pudding, as the adage went, was in the eating.

A puckish grin hovered in reminiscence of their most recent altercation. In other circumstances she might enjoy pitting her wits against Lord Osmund. He would be a worthy opponent.

All this introspection was delaying the inevitable.

Throwing back the covers, Sapphira sat up, and gingerly swung her feet out of bed. She inspected her leg; the bruise looked angry and was painful to her touch. Shaking her head, she padded across to the armoire and rifled through her clothes.

Possessed by the need to arm herself, metaphorically speaking, she chose a deceptively simple gown of rich turquoise silk. It was one of her favourites, and knew it complemented her eyes and hair.

She was lifting it down, when there was a quiet knock and, at Sapphira's invitation, Luisa entered.

"Ahhh… you are awake. The sleep, she was good, sí? You feel refreshed?" the young maid asked.

"Thank you, yes. I confess my slumber last night was… sporadic." Sapphira chuckled.

"I have the ointment. Permit me…" Luisa jiggled a pot under Sapphira's nose and indicated she should recline on the bed.

"I can manage," Sapphira felt moved to point out.

"Tomorrow yes, today, let me give you the care." Luisa persuaded gently.

Sapphira acquiesced and, after draping the dress over one of the chairs, settled on the bed. Pressing her lips together so as not to grimace when Luisa massaged in the balm, she caught a familiar scent, recognising it from the previous night.

"Might I be so bold as to ask whether Lord Osmund requires the succour of this salve?" Sapphira pried.

"*Sì*, for his scars." Luisa didn't go into further detail, concentrating on ensuring she had covered the still expanding bruise. "Miss Beresford, how did he happen?" nodding at the discoloured skin.

"I met with foul play."

"*Scusa?*" Luisa's eyes grew round.

"I witnessed a robbery and thought to stop the thieves, who were unhappy with my interference. Please keep this to yourself. I have yet to apprise Lord and Lady Dynham of my misfortune."

"Of course, Miss. You are brave, *sì*?"

Sapphira gave a rueful smile, "No, Luisa, I think reckless is a better description. I was lost and scared, a situation exacerbated by the storm. If not for Lord Osmund…" she did not finish, acutely conscious of what might have happened.

"I am glad he was there to rescue you," Luisa patted Sapphira's hand. "He has… hmmm… the valour."

"Indeed, he does," Sapphira's reply was soft, wistful.

Wiping her hands on a damp cloth, Luisa smiled, and withheld her opinion. One shared by the rest of the staff. Time would tell.

Donning her gown, Sapphira stood while Luisa fastened the buttons then tied the filmy ribbons in a neat bow. A sheer cream wrap, and satin house slippers completed the ensemble.

She studied herself in the pier glass with a critical eye. The livid mark on her cheek could not be hidden by even the most artfully arranged hairstyle. She stroked it tentatively and winced. *If I ever see either of those two rogues again, I shall exact my revenge,* she thought fiercely, then laughed at her bravado.

"You look *molto bellissima.*"

"You are too kind." Sapphira blushed. "Are they in the salon, or on the terrace?"

"The terrace, Miss. The one below."

Sapphira took Lusia's hand and squeezed. "Thank you," her quiet gratitude obvious.

Sapphira made her way down to the lower level, the numerous steps not helping her sore leg one jot, obliging her to pause once or twice to catch her breath and ease the throbbing.

The angle of the sun told her it was late afternoon... *goodness I have slept the day away.* Voices floated to her on the breeze and when she reached the terrace, Leofwin and Archer leapt to their feet, the marquis pulling out a chair for her.

Acknowledging his courtesy with a smile, she sat down, feeling two pairs of eyes boring into her. She shot a questioning look at her host.

"Despite Lady Hester's persistence, I did not crumble." Leofwin read her thoughts.

Sapphira heaved a sigh. "Is there any chance you might be prevailed upon to pretend this never happened?" She eyed Hester and Archer, optimistically

They shook their heads. "Absolutely not," the couple replied in unison.

"Sapphira Beresford, if you knew how worried we were, you would not ask so ridiculous a question. No sign of either of you, and a storm raging. We sat up long after midnight, all manner of scenarios playing in our heads… none of which ended happily. You arrive home in a state of dishevelment, have been hurt, and spent the night with a man who is not your husband. I *knew* agreeing to you going to the site without a chaperone was a mistake," Hester fretted, wringing her hands.

"Hester…" Leofwin began.

"No, Sapphira came at my behest, I am responsible for her well-being, not to mention her reputation. What were you thinking, Leofwin?" Hester reproached.

"Hester, pray calm yourself. None of this was Leo's fault." Sapphira used the diminutive without thinking, not noticing the look Hester shot her husband, or the gleam in Leofwin's eyes. "Lord Osmund was the consummate gentleman. If not for him, I should likely still be wandering the ruins seeking a way out. 'Tis worse than a maze." Her attempt at levity fell on deaf ears.

"Sapphira…"

"Hester…" Sapphira mimicked. Then took pity on her friend who was genuinely upset. "This whole debacle started because Scamp stole my bonnet."

"Scamp?" Archer queried, baffled.

"One of the strays," Sapphira elaborated.

"I warned you not to feed them," Hester upbraided.

"I know, but the poor darlings are hungry and, before we get into an argument over whether I ought to stop feeding them, I warn you right now, it would be a waste of breath. Back to my story.

"After chasing the little terror for several minutes, I managed to catch up with him. You never saw a dog so pleased with himself." Her face crinkled, comically. "I offered him a hunk of bread left from luncheon, which was probably the reason he nabbed my hat in the first place. It took some coaxing for him to drop the bonnet and take the crumbs, but food won out. He is such a poppet," she mused, remembering his sweet face when he laid his head on her knee.

"What does a dog have to do with you ending up bruised and limping?" Archer asked, acquainted with Sapphira's tendency to go off on a tangent.

"When he ran off, presumably on a quest for something else to steal, I realised I had no idea where I was, and could not remember the route I had taken. To someone who has worked on the site for a considerable time, I presume the differences in the streets and paths are obvious, but they all looked the same to me, and several are blocked at one end. As did the buildings, all partially excavated, with nothing to distinguish one from another. I ended up walking in circles.

"Then I heard voices and oh, the relief, thinking I was about to meet up with one of the teams who could direct me to the Via dell'Abbondanza. Unfortunately, they were not legitimate employees, they were thieves."

"*Sapphira…*" Hester's hand fluttered to her throat, mindful of where this might be leading.

Sapphira was notoriously impetuous. Once upon a time, she had subjected a group of youths to a furious tongue-lashing for mistreating a donkey, uncaring that she was a woman on her own, she was outnumbered, and they had sticks.

To be fair, the boys had fled in the face of Sapphira's vitriol, and she rescued the donkey, but it was not the first time she had ignored her own safety. Laudable her actions may be, but she had not yet learnt that avoiding danger was usually smarter than confronting it head-on.

Sapphira placated, "I know, I acted foolishly but remember, I was lost and had no idea where any of the others were. I did yell, but no one heard. Moreover, I was incensed at their brazen behaviour. Robbing artefacts in broad daylight. The nerve.

"So, I did what any self-respecting man would have done, and ordered them to stop." She shrugged. "Of course, they took no notice, leaving me no alternative but to... err... step into the breach, as it were."

CHAPTER THIRTEEN

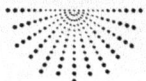

"*H*ow did you receive your injuries," Archer interposed.

Sapphira sent a speaking glance to Leofwin, who smiled his encouragement. "They are not really injuries, just bruising. Fine…" when it looked as though Hester was going to argue, "…but you must promise not to berate me."

There was a lengthy silence. Hester frowned at her friend, whose expression did not waver. Archer grasped his wife's hand and murmured something for her ears only.

Several more seconds ticked by.

"You have my word." Hester's tone was nothing short of grudging.

While they were talking, Amalia had served drinks and placed a large shallow dish laden with cheese, dried fruit, olives, and flatbread in the middle of the table.

Suddenly hungry, Sapphira filled her plate with a selection. She eyed her friends. "Permit me a moment or two. I am famished."

A low growl attested to her remark, which raised a

chuckle and eased the tension. The others followed her lead, and peace descended while they partook of the spread.

Sapphira popped the last corner of bread into her mouth, sipped her wine, and grinned at Hester.

"Back to my tale. There were two men, Nev and Walt. I tried to stop them taking the mosaic, a scuffle ensued, resulting in Walt, errr... detaining me. Not prepared to be held captive, I bit him, here..." Sapphira recounted the episode in detail.

"The storm probably saved my life. They had to get away and didn't stop to check whether I was alive or dead, although I heard Walt telling Nev he'd killed me. Then, Walt kicked me, in retaliation, I suppose... he *did* curse a lot when I bit him. His boot hurt like the dickens but, thankfully, a crack of thunder was louder than my groan.

"I counted to a hundred and when I opened my eyes, they were gone, but now I was lost, sodden, and coated in mud. I forced myself upright, praying I would find the way to the amphitheatre before it got dark. Lord Osmund would be wondering where I was, doubtless annoyed because I had delayed our departure. Given our frequent clashes, it was conceivable he had decided to teach me a lesson and abandon me for the night."

Leofwin spluttered, "I would never..."

She smiled across at him. "Of that, I have no doubt but, I was exhausted, in pain and becoming increasingly pessimistic. What to do for the best? Keep walking or hide somewhere? I cannot tell you how long I trudged but, eventually, I turned a corner and, to my abject relief, Lord Osmund saw me. He escorted me back to the stable, checked I was not badly hurt, and was kind enough to build me a bed out of straw bales. We went to sleep, and then came home."

She deliberately omitted their quarrel and what had

happened during the night. There were some things even your best friend did not need to know.

Hester and Archer were staring at her as though she had grown two heads. Sapphira swallowed on an unladylike snort of mirth.

"You might have been killed," Hester croaked.

"But I was not. I am here hale and hearty."

"Humph," Hester grumbled. "I might contest that."

"Was it an experience I wish to repeat? No. Perhaps it was not the most judicious course of action, but I was there. If I had gone for help it would have been too late."

"It very nearly *was* too late. Sapphira, please pause and count to ten before you risk life and limb. You are not a child, and I should like you to be around a while longer," Hester reproached, tartly.

Sapphira hobbled around to where Hester was sitting and gave her a hug. "Forgive me, Hester. I had no mind to cause you, any of you distress, and you have my word, I will do my best to think before I act."

"Of course, I forgive you, only…"

"I know." Sapphira, after another quick hug, returned to her seat.

Archer, determined to divert their conversation before it became emotional, asked Sapphira whether she could describe the robbers, which she could and did.

"Their faces are imprinted in my head. I do not imagine this was their first, nor will it be their last foray into thievery. Leo mentioned how lucrative the trade is in stolen artefacts, and the mosaic they were removing was a stunning example. At least it was until they broke it into pieces…"

Sapphira stopped, her sorrow at such wanton destruction for coin, intense. Collecting herself, she continued, "Then there were the other items. Several small carvings, and who knows what else they had in the sack, which was full."

She took another sip of her drink. "Do you think they will be found?"

"The men or the relics?" Leofwin asked.

"Both."

"Unlikely to improbable. They will already have a buyer lined up."

"Oh, how aggravating," Sapphira hissed. "All that time buried, only to be snatched by the unscrupulous. I could weep."

Seated alongside, Leofwin patted her arm. "You never know, they might make a mistake. Now, to change the subject, I think dinner is about to be served, then as I recall, we had a deal."

"A deal? What is going on?" Hester asked, Leofwin's conduct not going unnoticed.

"Nothing important." Sapphira blushed.

One look at Hester's face told Sapphira this was not going to be answer enough.

"I agreed to tell Lord Osmund why I accompanied you to Italy," she said in a rush. "Happy now?" She narrowed her eyes at Leofwin.

"Eminently." He rejoined, wholly unrepentant.

"And how is this a deal?"

"He explained why he is such a curmudgeon," Sapphira replied pertly.

Archer guffawed. "Perhaps we ought to have warned you, Leo, Sapphira does not suffer fools gladly."

"I agree, Dynham," Leofwin shot Archer a mock fierce glare. "A decent friend and fellow officer to boot would have acquainted me with this trait, well in advance. Forewarned is forearmed."

"And miss the fun? Not a chance. The entertainment

value alone you pair have provided was worth the three-week voyage."

"The very fact you deem a caution necessary, merely proves my point," Sapphira asserted. "Did I hear you mention dinner?" She looked towards the archway, hopefully.

Leofwin shook his head in genial resignation. "You win... temporarily, but no amount of prevarication will deflect me from my goal. Miss Beresford, you gave me your word. Do not disillusion an old grouch." He waggled his eyebrows theatrically.

Somewhat mellow after a glass or two of wine on an empty stomach, Sapphira chortled, "You are not old. Stop with the dramatics."

Hester and Archer stared at each other, the same thought running through their heads. *What the dickens happened last night?*

Hester jabbed her finger at Sapphira then Leofwin. "Enough now. I think I preferred it when you two were at odds."

"I'm sorry, Hester. I forgot myself." A trifle shocked at her giddiness, Sapphira sipped her drink, then all but dropped the glass on the table. The wine had loosened her tongue and seemingly lowered her inhibitions. She drew a sobering breath.

"Hester invited me on this trip because, less than a month prior to our departure, my betrothed left me at the altar, and I mean at the altar." Her bald statement effectively dousing any lingering levity.

"Beg pardon?" Leofwin was suitably dumbfounded.

"I was to be married to a man I have known since child-hood. It was arranged, but I thought he lov... bore an affection for me. A sentiment I reciprocated. There was no indication he felt otherwise, but on the day we were supposed to be married, he vanished."

Facing the bay, Sapphira did not see the moonlight glittering on the water, instead her vision was filled with the scene at the church. The whispers of the guests, her father's anger, her unsuspecting mother, her own humiliation.

"Sapphi." Uncaring how inappropriate it was, Leofwin reached for her hand and interlaced their fingers. Lost in memory, Sapphira did not realise.

"He ran away with my sister."

It was only the second time she had said those words. They still possessed the power to unravel her. She felt a sob rising in her throat, and swallowed, convulsively. No, no, no, no, no, she would *not* cry over this. Neither Jeremy nor Gisela deserved her tears.

She felt a gentle squeeze and glanced down. Leofwin was holding her hand. He was holding her hand!

Bewildered, she raised her eyes to meet his. His gaze was warm with sympathy.

"I am appalled you were treated so callously and understand why you hanker for a life unencumbered by emotion, but I hope your soul heals. Your erstwhile betrothed's loss is another man's gain. A man who will give you the world and expect nothing in return. Who will treasure the love you bestow on him, not toss it aside."

Sapphira gaped. "My, my, Lord Osmund, you are quite the poet." She broke the subdued hush which had fallen when he finished speaking.

"If the occasion demands." He smiled and released her fingers.

She felt bereft without his touch, adding to her confusion.

"On the bright side, had he not behaved so callously, you would not be here. In my humble opinion, a travesty."

Sapphira blushed. "Thank you," she whispered.

Hester and Archer held their peace.

Fortuitously, Amalia appeared to announce dinner and, quite naturally, the conversation turned to less weighty matters.

"How are you feeling, Hester?" Sapphira asked while they enjoyed a popular Neapolitan meal made up of vermicelli pasta, herbs, and lightly roasted vegetables.

Initially sceptical of the cuisine, Sapphira had fast become a convert, and this particular dish was one of her favourites. It seemed anything could be eaten with the peculiar looking food called pasta.

The locals used it rather like the English did potatoes and could be a simple repast or a feast. In fact, the diet was less rich all around. An abundance of vegetables, fish, and fruits, with smaller portions of meat and fewer courses.

The best part — pasta was fun to eat, twirling it around a fork, not chopping it up... although, if not careful, any sauce ended up splattering the diner.

"I confess to being a trifle indisposed. It comes and goes. Doubtless something I ate, or perhaps too much sun," Hester replied.

"Ought you to consult a doctor?" Sapphira studied her friend who still looked peaky.

"I am certain to be fine. Another day or two's rest and I shall be fit as a fiddle."

"We are a pair," Sapphira pulled a grotesque face, making the others chuckle. "The ache in my leg has yet to dissipate, and the mere thought of mounting a horse ties my stomach in knots."

"Then we shall enjoy some relaxation here at the villa," Leofwin interposed. "I am blessed with a private stretch of beach. The water is warm at this time of year, and a swim can prove quite the curative."

"How risqué," Sapphira quipped. "That said, I do believe I

could be tempted. I have heard tell of the healing properties of sea water. What say you, Hester?"

"I have been persuaded to dip my toe into the bay. 'Tis invigorating," Hester revealed. "Leo and Archer enjoy a swim when we visit in the summer months. Can be a tedious exercise for ladies. My bathing attire is entirely proper, but the amount of material in the suit leaves me more likely to drown than swim."

"We are far from home and Lord Osmund says the beach is private. Might you trim the garment to make it lighter? I did not bring a bathing suit. In truth, I do not own one, but perhaps I have something which can be adjusted." Sapphira said.

"Why are we back to Lord Osmund?" Leofwin complained. "I thought we had agreed on Leo?"

"I... errr... was not certain... only... now..." Sapphira stammered.

"Please, you are no longer Miss Beresford to me. I think of you only as Sapphira, you must return the favour."

"Oh, I am more than happy to think of you as Sapphira." That young lady winked as the rest of the table burst out laughing.

Sapphira felt the press of a foot over hers and looked across the table at Hester who inclined her head towards Leofwin. Sapphira shook her head unobtrusively, which made Hester purse her lips and bob a vehement nod.

With a resigned huff, Sapphira began, "There is one more thing..." then hesitated. Although the pretence seemed absurd after the revelations of the evening, it was liberating being plain Miss Beresford.

The foot pressed harder.

"You *are* a criminal?" Leofwin crowed and slapped his good leg. "I knew it."

"Leo," Archer chided, managing to keep a straight face. "You think we consort, nay travel the world with villains?"

"Indubitably," Leo retaliated.

"Very droll," Hester said. "Let the girl finish."

"Thank you," Sapphira grinned at her friend. "As I was about to say before I was so rudely interrupted... criminal indeed, tsk... in the interests of full disclosure and, given we appear to have reached a rapprochement, there is one more thing I ought to tell you. My father is the Earl of Templeton."

CHAPTER FOURTEEN

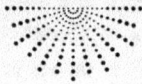

*I*f Sapphira had wanted to take the wind from
Leofwin's sails, she could not have found a better
tactic. The marquis gawked at her in stupefaction.

"*You* are the lady, Brunswick jilted?" he blurted out, then
palmed his forehead. "Dash it all, Sapphi, that was unconscionable. I spoke without due consideration for your sensi-
bilities." He hastened to apologise for his lack of tact.

Heat flooding her cheeks, Sapphira brushed aside his
apology. "It is of no matter, I am more surprised you heard
about it, this far from England."

"You forget my mother and sister are inveterate scribes.
They deem it imperative I am kept abreast of even the
smallest snippet of news about home, be that extracted from
an accredited broadsheet or overhead rumours. They did not
mention the name of the woman in question, and I have been
away too long to recall, or care about, who is betrothed to
whom. I can only reiterate my sincere regret that you
suffered thus."

A lengthy and rather awkward silence descended.

"Now you know why I needed a refuge. Had I been plain

Miss Beresford... nonentity, the... errr... incident would not have registered. Regrettably, being the daughter of an earl, my humiliation and that my sister was involved, provided enough fodder to satisfy the most cynical of gossips. Two, maybe even three if you count Jeremy, for the price of one."

Her mouth twisted cynically. "It is what it is and only to be expected. We all know that for some the downfall of others is akin to daily nourishment, they cannot live without it."

"Your parents must have been devastated," Leofwin said.

"Papa was furious and wanted to call out Jeremy. 'Tis a good thing they were far away from The Towers. Papa is a fine shot." She gave a wry smile. "As for Mama, I cannot fathom what she was thinking. She blamed me for not being attentive enough," Sapphira shook her head in recollection of her mother's perspective on the situation.

"*Attentive* enough? Had anyone else suggested I was less than solicitous to my betrothed, I would likely have slapped them. Mama was more concerned about Gisela than my embarrassment. Then again, until that moment, Gisela could do no wrong in her eyes. Poor Mama, confronted by the notion her perfect little darling turned out to be as fallible as the rest of us, she had no idea how to handle the knowledge."

Sapphira could not prevent a hint of bitterness creeping into her voice. Mentally she forced it aside and smiled brightly. "But 'tis over and in the past. If they are genuinely in love, I hope they are very happy together."

"You are a better woman than I." Hester tapped her lips contemplatively. "If Archer had run off with my sister, the misery I would have rained down on them would make Hell sound like a picnic in the park."

"Hester Chatham." Archer was floored by his, normally gentle, wife's remark.

"Don't say I didn't warn you." She wagged a finger, which

Archer grasped, and kissed the tip. The look they shared was a meeting of minds, of a love no one could threaten — its strength palpable.

Sapphira turned to Leofwin in faint appeal.

Understanding, he launched into a discussion about nothing of great significance and the remainder of the evening passed in light-hearted banter.

Her long sleep during the day leaving her wide awake, Sapphira stayed on the terrace when the others said their goodnights.

"Do not stay up too late, Sapphi," Hester exhorted when she kissed her friend's cheek. "You need your bed."

"Just a few more minutes. I believe a little star gazing is in order," Sapphira replied.

Voices fading as the three ascended the steps to their respective bedchambers, left Sapphira in blessed silence. She walked to the edge of the terrace and propped herself against one of the pillars, breathing in the delicate scent of some night-flowering blossom.

The moon's pale luminescence, reflecting on the restless obsidian sea, reminded Sapphira of the legend of the moon spinners.

In Greek myth, nymphs spin the light of the waning moon down to earth, until there is a moonless night when all creatures are protected by the darkness. On that night, the nymphs wash their spindles releasing the light ready to be spun again for the new moon.

Tonight, entranced by the ethereal scene, Sapphira would not have been at all surprised to see the legend materialise in front of her.

In the distance, the dark humps of Capri and Ischia floated in the bay, like misshapen guardians, hardly discernible unless one squinted.

Cloaked in the velvety darkness, Sapphira pondered recent events. Who could have believed when she left England mere weeks ago, she would end up in a brawl with a couple of looters? Now *that* was a story to titillate the rumour mill.

Her initial fright, while hovering on the periphery of her mind, had been overtaken by outrage and no small amount of frustration. The scene played in her head with annoying repetition. If only she had been able to thwart them — acknowledging it was improbable she would have lived to tell the tale, had she persisted.

"Naught you can do," Sapphira admonished herself, sinking onto the low parapet which bounded the terrace. Swivelling around, she dangled her legs over the wall and hummed a tune.

Forgetting where she was, Sapphira removed the simple hair comb keeping her chignon in place and ran her fingers through the heavy tresses, unravelling the twist.

"Oh, the relief," she murmured to the empty air, absently turning the comb in her hands.

Hidden from view, Leofwin's breath caught when Sapphira's hair, gleaming silver in the moonlight cascaded over her shoulders. He could not explain why he had back-tracked to the terrace — he never could, not even when he reminisced on this moment years later; the night everything changed — and was busily inventing and discarding excuses for his reappearance.

When she joined them earlier, he had detected a vulnerability underneath her usual blithe insouciance. Not unexpected given her recent experiences here and in England. What *was* unexpected had been an almost chivalrous desire to protect her from further woes — to be the man she turned to, relied upon. A sentiment which took root in his subconscious.

Not to mention his body's response to the way that stunning gown flowed around her when she moved — clinging in all the right places, or how the flickering of the candles highlighted the gentle curve of her cheek, and the sparkle in her green eyes as she teased Hester.

He decided an offer to help her up the steps might sound reasonable, conversant with how awkward they could be for someone with an injured leg. He was sprightly now, but it had been a feat of endurance the first few months after they had been laid.

It was the best he had and, straightening his shoulders, left the seclusion of the shadows.

His, "Lady Sapphira," spoken in a modulated tone so as not to alarm her, had the opposite effect and in no way prepared him for what happened next.

His footfall going unheard, Sapphira gave a panicked squeak, twisted on the stone capping, and instantly vanished from sight.

"*Sapphira!*" He darted forward to peer over the wall. Beneath him, in what looked like a cocoon of turquoise silk, lay Sapphira. Her vexed expostulations about numbskull marquises sneaking up on their unsuspecting victims had him biting his lip to hold his laughter — a reaction he deemed imprudent — in check.

"I seem to be forever apologising to you, my lady," he said as he slid over the wall, careful not to jar his bad leg. "Perhaps one of these days, we might meet without any drama."

"It is my unending hope." Stuck in a bush, Sapphira's reply was tart. "Pray tell, how are we supposed to get back over the wall?"

"With difficulty. I suggest we go down to the shore, then

take the steps. 'Tis the easiest option. Let me..." he reached her side and hauled her out of the bush, which, thankfully was not riddled with thorns, and the silk of her dress slithered off the soft leaves virtually unscathed.

"The way I am going, I shall be in dire need of a new wardrobe," she grumbled, pulling her skirts around to inspect them for damage. "This is my favourite gown," her words a melancholy wail.

"Fret not. Save a random leaf, and perhaps an odd smear, the dress is intact," Leofwin assured, praying it was so. The lack of light below the terrace left him clueless as to whether he spoke the truth.

"Take my arm." He crooked his elbow and at Sapphira's hesitation added, "The ground is uneven and on a slope. The last thing you need after yesterday, is another tumble." He jogged his elbow invitingly.

Begrudgingly, Sapphira linked her arm through his, and they slithered their way down to the beach.

"What possessed you to sit on the wall?" Leofwin asked.

"What possessed *you* to creep up behind me?" Sapphira parried.

"I was not creeping, I never creep," Leofwin defended. "I assumed you would hear my approach. Next thing I know, you had disappeared. It is fortuitous the ground slopes away gradually at that point, better than the steep drop further around."

"Yes, that might have proved a mite disastrous." Irony laced her tones.

He bit back a chuckle. "Now, now, no need for sarcasm. No harm done."

"Except to my dignity," Sapphira reproached.

The ground levelled off and, in seconds, they were walking along the hard packed beach. Sapphira stopped to watch the white ruffles rushing up the sand. The constant movement unchanged for millennia, grinding innumerable tiny pebbles into beige dust — mesmerising.

She felt a gentle tug on her arm.

"My turn to apologise. I could watch the sea for hours. I spent most of the voyage doing much the same thing, there is something untamed yet soothing about the roll of the waves. The changing hues of the water depending on the weather, or the time of day. The crew thought me addled." She grinned.

Leofwin responded in kind and squeezed the fingers resting on his arm. "Your hand feels chilled, time enough to admire the sea when you are rested and healed."

"'Tis only bruising, Leo."

"Yes, but you were also cold and wet for a protracted period. While I do not believe you have suffered adversely, I am not prepared to tempt fate."

Sapphira knew he was correct, but she did not want the evening to end, although for why escaped her. "Fine," she acceded, tilting her head to study the flight of steps. "Advance, Lord Osmund."

Straight-faced, Leofwin struck out on the climb. Here in the open, the glimmer cast by the moon was just enough to light the way. It was slow going, and at one point Sapphira succumbed to a bout of hilarity.

"You find this funny?" Leofwin quizzed.

"I do. Imagine how ludicrous we must look, reeling our way up the steps as though in our cups. I am mightily relieved there are no witnesses. Not only is it amusing, but also it takes my mind off the twinge in my leg. No doubt you are fighting a similar discomfort."

"I am pleased to say, my daily walks and years of climbing these steps has inured me to the once painful pangs, but your description does summon up a picture of a comical duo."

They reached the lower terrace. Someone had snuffed out the candles and tidied the table.

"One more flight and you're there," Leofwin encouraged.

"A moment," Sapphira said and limped across the darkened stones to the wall, in search of her wrap. It had gone. "My wrap."

"It cannot have blown away. Amalia probably recognised it and took it to your suite," Leofwin consoled.

"I hope so." She let her gaze rove the area below the wall where she had fallen. No sign of her wrap, or her comb for that matter. Tomorrow.

The compulsion had increased to irresistible and, before his head could talk him out of it, Leofwin had closed the gap between them, making Sapphira jump when he materialised out the gloom.

"Stealth does not become you," she castigated on a strangled yelp.

"Then this will seem positively indecent," he murmured and, before she could blink, swept her into his arms and stifled her protests, such as they were, in a kiss which all but undid her.

Sapphira's immediate impulse was to batter him into oblivion.

Her hands curled into fists, only to slacken when *the* most delicious sensation, its beauty akin to rose petals unfurling after the rain, began a slow glissade. From her nape to her toes, infinitesimal frissons spiralled out along every vein, the wonder — ineffable.

His lips moved against hers with such intoxicating sweetness, tears pricked her eyes. It was her first kiss... ever, and, as first kisses went, it was heavenly. Involuntarily, her arms stole around him. Her fingers clutched the fine brocade of his waistcoat as he drew her closer, moulding her to him.

Sapphira lost all awareness. Her thoughts were flying off in every direction, her body refused to do her bidding, and her heart was beating so loudly, he was sure to hear it. Brazen did not *begin* to describe her response.

Leofwin's behaviour might contravene every single rule, but never had anything felt so right.

Trembling with the force of his emotions, Leofwin broke their kiss and lifted his head.

They stared at each other, expressions impossible to read in the darkness.

"My lady, I cannot excuse what came over me. I must have been taken by a madness induced by the moonlight," Leofwin rasped.

Sapphira, her head swimming, tried to untangle his words. "You think it mad to kiss me?" she muttered.

"No, I think it sublime, but I gave you no chance to object. Not particularly honourable."

She gave a deep-throated chuckle, the sound thrumming through Leofwin.

"Ahhh. The *galant* hero. Yes, I suppose I ought to be offended by such audacity, but it might interest you to know, I have absolutely no objection." Her impudent tone, at odds with her shy smile.

"In that case..." He recaptured her mouth. This time it was not so sweet.

CHAPTER FIFTEEN

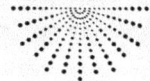

Sunlight danced over Sapphira's eyelids. Sleepily, she pushed herself up on her elbows, wondering why it was so bright, then remembered. She had gone to bed in such a haze she had forgotten to close the shutters. Throwing back the covers, she padded across to the window and, resting her shoulder against the frame, stared out at the view.

The memory of Leofwin's touch sent tingles tumbling down her spine, and a pink stain flaring up her cheeks. His second kiss was at the same time tender and fervent. A possession, a brand. Pressing cool fingers to her hot cheeks, she pondered the day ahead.

*How am I going to face him? Never mind facing **him**, what about Hester and Archer?* Hester could read her like a book, however hard Sapphira strove to disguise her feelings.

"Bloody, bugger, and dammit." Her favourite — if forbidden — expletives spilled over tight lips.

Leofwin had escorted her to her suite, dropped a light kiss on her forehead, and wished her pleasant dreams. *Pleasant dreams. Good gracious, if only he knew,* the pink darkening to scarlet. *Maybe kissing me was of little import. Maybe he kissed lots of women? No... he claimed women were to be avoided at all costs. So, why did he kiss me? He* had *said it was heavenly.* A smile curved her lips. *It truly was.*

Her mind went off on a tangent. *What if he had a mistress? A woman whom he visited for the sole purpose of satiating the carnal appetites, her maid had insisted beset men with uncomfortable regularity.* The notion spawned another ache, naught to do with her bruised thigh. *It seemed improbable, in light of his sentiments in that regard, but what do I really know about him?*

She frowned, recalling a conversation with Alice about a month prior to her wedding day. Alice, knowing the nobility rarely discussed the intimate details pertaining to marriage, had felt it her duty to apprise the unworldly Sapphira of what would happen on her wedding night.

Alice's somewhat lurid description, which reduced Sapphira to a fit of giggles, also gave her food for thought, and she had dared broach the topic with her mother, hoping for clarification.

Lady Templeton, flustered at so personal a question, shooed away her daughter. "Young ladies do not talk about such things, Sapphira. A good husband will teach his new wife how to... errr... take care of his needs."

Sapphira sought out Alice, demanding to know more. The maid, who was unwed, provided Sapphira with a litany of expectations. Ribald and, undoubtedly, garnered from a dubious source, the recital *did* serve to enlighten the uninitiated. Sapphira, weeding the wheat from the chaff so to speak, was perturbed by the mention of mistresses. Innocent she might be, but she was not an idiot, neither was she deaf.

Men and their mistresses were a titillating topic of gossip among the *ton*. Sapphira had a vague understanding that whether a husband either kept or took a mistress was directly related to a lack of affection within their marriage. Wives were expected to be above reproof, although there was an occasional whisper. It seemed rather one-sided but, given women had little autonomy, not without merit.

She could hear Alice now.

"Men have urges and if their wives refuse to oblige them, husbands will seek satisfaction elsewhere."

"What if the wives are not satisfied?" Sapphira had asked.

"My lady, a gentlewoman does not have *urges*." Alice, the expert, had reproved with faint distaste.

"I beg to differ, Alice," Sapphira murmured, her body pulsing at the mere thought of Leofwin's kiss.

All this introspection was getting her nowhere. Dragging her gaze from the sunny vista, she headed for the dressing-room, pausing at the armoire as she did so, her fingers stroking the turquoise gown. She ran her eyes over it, spotting a few grubby marks — testament to her altercation with the bush.

Hopefully, Amalia would know how to remove them. Not only was it her favourite dress, but now it held sentimental value. She might dream of being romanced, but Sapphira was realistic enough to acknowledge any dalliance with Lord Osmund would be fleeting. Their lives were bound to different countries, at least currently. The future? That was another matter entirely.

Washed, dressed and, aside from her sore cheek and hip, feeling none the worse for her recent drenching, Sapphira found herself strangely hesitant to return to the terrace. In truth, nothing had changed, yet everything was different.

Come on my girl, you are an adult. You have been stranded at the altar and sailed halfway round the world. You have braved the underworld and battled thieves. Breakfast with the man who kissed you into a dizzy spiral last night pales in comparison.

Taking a moment, she concocted a perfectly delightful statement in readiness for Leofwin's justification of his actions. She would dismiss them with regal disinterest as though men were in the habit of losing their wits and kissing her in the moonlight.

A snigger slipped over her lips at her nonsense, but it had served to quell her anxiety.

Composing herself, she opened the door…

…and came face to face with Leofwin.

Had he been there all night? Don't be fatuous, Sapphira.

Staring at him agape, her nicely rehearsed speech abandoning her, Sapphira was perplexed by his presence. His rooms were on the upper level.

"Hester?" she said the first thing that came into her head.

"Is at breakfast," Leofwin replied.

"Then… err… why…?"

"I was passing and heard your door click. 'T'would be impolite not to wait."

Nodding abstractedly, she scrabbled for a clever riposte. With none presenting themselves, she made do with a smile. "Thank you."

"'Tis a fine day for a swim," he mused as they descended to the lower terrace.

"To be sure," she agreed, looking straight ahead, missing Leofwin's quickly smothered mirth.

Sapphira, cursing her stiff leg, made haste down the last few steps and blew onto the terrace like a miniature gale. "Good morning," she greeted them over-brightly. "Such glorious weather. Lord Osmund declares it a splendid day for a swim. What say you, my Lord Dynham? Hester, do you feel up to testing the waters?" She beamed at the pair who were taken aback by their friend's exuberance.

"Are you ill?" Hester's brow furrowed in concern.

"Not I," Sapphira exclaimed. "Merely glad to be alive and determined not to miss a moment."

Sinking onto her usual chair, she applied herself to the array of food with gusto, chattering non-stop, asking artless questions but leaving no time for replies.

Hester and Archer were thoroughly nonplussed, while Leofwin remained coolly unperturbed, managing to maintain his habitual reserve.

"Well, that was delicious, thank you. Time to consult with Amalia and Luisa regarding swimming attire. They may have some suggestions that will serve our purpose." Sapphira trilled and was gone.

"Good gracious me, what was that about?" Archer enquired. He checked his pocket watch. "I am exhausted, and it is not yet ten."

"I could not possibly imagine," Leofwin answered, but his expression told a different story.

"Leofwin Colleville, what have you been up to?" Hester wagged her finger at the marquis. "I know that look. Archer gets a similar one when he has forgotten something important. Like the anniversary of the day we wed, or my birthday." She gave her husband an arch grin, who returned it sheepishly.

"I do not tell tales," Leofwin refuted, unfazed by Hester's withering glance.

"So, there is a tale?" Hester leapt on his words.

"Maybe, maybe not." Leofwin teased. Standing when Hester shot to her feet, he opened his palms in a conciliatory manner. "Least said, soonest mended. If Sapphira wishes to share, she will. Now," he changed the subject, "I need to speak with Nuncio regarding the beach." He bowed and departed.

"What was the why of that?" Hester grilled her husband as Leofwin disappeared along the passageway linking the terrace to the domestic sphere.

"You know as much as I, dear." Archer patted her hand. "How are you faring now you have eaten?"

"I am wearied of this ailment. Mayhap Leo is correct and a dip in the sea might..." Hester gulped and went a queer shade, dashing off before finishing her sentence.

Archer followed more slowly, ruminating over his wife's malady. In all the years he had known her, she had never been unwell, and this marked the third day, with no sign it was easing. In fact, it seemed to be getting worse.

When he pried further, Hester had admitted to feeling occasionally bilious since they disembarked from the ship, but had given it little thought, ascribing it to the upheaval of travel and a change in diet — something she had concealed from everyone, not least her husband.

Archer's anxiety was deepening, but Hester had demanded his oath not to tell anyone.

"It comes and goes," she had assured him. "It will doubt-less blow over, and I have no mind to spoil our visit over something as trivial as a queasy stomach."

He made a decision. A breach of vow would be worth her wrath.

He found her in their suite, head over the chamber pot, tears streaming down her cheeks.

"My love, this cannot go on. You must allow me to

summon a doctor." Archer rarely put his foot down but in this he was adamant. He set aside the porcelain and, using a damp cloth, wiped his wife's hot face. He held her close and kissed the top of her head, the fear she was seriously ill besieging him. "Come, back to bed for you. I shall speak with Amalia."

Gently removing Hester's dress, he tucked her into bed. Before he had closed the shutters dimming the room, she was asleep.

Deep in thought, he wound his way to the kitchens where he found Amalia discussing the day's meals with Bruna, Leofwin's cook.

"Might I have a word?" he asked, quietly.

Amalia said something to Bruna in Italian and ushered Archer out. "The kitchens are no place for a lord," she tsked mildly.

Archer laughed in spite of his concerns. "You know we do not rest on our titles here, Amalia. I should like to ask your advice."

"Of course, anything."

They walked as they talked and, by the time Archer had outlined Hester's symptoms, they were in the formal garden which circled the upper level of the villa.

Amalia listened attentively, then asked a few pertinent questions, some of which Archer was at a loss to answer.

"I appreciate the sickness only manifested three days ago, but you must understand, Hester is never ill." Archer concluded.

Amalia guided him to one of the wooden benches strategically placed under the trees. "Sit," she instructed. "While I think you will not be happy until you have spoken to the *dottore*, I believe illness is not what besets your lovely wife, not in the normal sense."

Elbows on his knees Archer had been gazing out over the

garden. Now, he twisted to study Amalia, his bewilderment apparent. "Normal sense?"

Amalia, with typical Italian effervescence, grasped the hand closest to her and shook it rigorously. "The *Signora* Hester, I suspect she is with child. Her malaise is merely the babe making the havoc in here." She pointed to her abdomen.

"Hester is with child?" Archer repeated stupidly, the words bouncing around his head. You could have knocked him flat with a feather. He knew Hester wanted children, as did he but, thus far, they had not been blessed and both assumed it was not to be. They had talked it through, buried their sorrow deep, deep down, accepted the improbability, and planned their lives accordingly.

Now in a heartbeat it seemed their greatest wish might be a reality.

"Yes, oh Signore Archer, is this not the most joyous news?"

"Joyous news? Yes," Archer was reduced to parroting Amalia, the ability to function, quite thoughtlessly, deserting him.

"Come, you must set at ease *la Signora's* mind," Amalia chivvied.

"She sleeps," he croaked, his brain awhirl.

"Then I think you should have the caffè. He will help the head. Very strong today, very strong." Amalia all but dragged Archer to the salon, where she pushed him unceremoniously into a comfortable chair and commanded him to stay put.

Archer registered that she was giving him orders instead of the other way around but, in truth, he was glad. At this precise moment, he was unsure whether he could put one foot in front of the other, never mind countermand the voluble housekeeper.

Time passed but Archer did not notice. Suddenly, there

was a flurry of movement and the salon seemed full of people.

"Dynham, what's this I hear? Congratulations are in order. What a day. I have sent for Guarino. He is a grand fellow, trained in London you know. Clever but not pompous. Trust him with my life. I daresay he'll be over shortly." Leofwin clapped his friend on the back.

"Hester…" Archer began.

"Yes, yes she ought to be told, this does concern her." Leofwin winked, drawing a half smile from Archer, "for now let her sleep. Poor girl has been looking fatigued."

"This is marvellous news." Sapphira knelt on the floor next to Archer who had yet to regain his wits. "I am so happy for you. Even more so knowing Hester's indisposition is a cause for jubilation not anxiety." Secretly grateful for the shift in attention.

Amalia reappeared bearing a tray laden with steaming hot coffees and a selection of pastries dripping with nuts and honey.

"We've just eaten breakfast," Archer said faintly.

"Who cares?" Sapphira interjected, paying little heed to civility. "A little of something decadent can be good for the spirit." She was wholly unable to prevent the bloom of crimson from washing up her cheeks, and studiously avoided looking in Leofwin's direction.

She heard his low chuckle and felt the subtle brush of his fingers across her shoulders as he reached for a cup. Her heart thudded. *How did he do it?* With effort, she maintained her poise and handed Archer a pastry, "Try one, and you'll see I'm correct," she cajoled.

The beach was forgotten — for the time being at least.

CHAPTER SIXTEEN

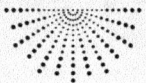

*D*octor Guarino duly arrived and, with a protective Amalia at his side, examined Hester.

His gentle interrogation, framed to extract a wealth of crucial information, left him inclined to accept Amalia's assertion but, he judged it too early for a definitive diagnosis. He could not rule out a simple stomach ailment.

While Amalia rearranged Hester's clothes and helped her under the covers, Doctor Guarino carried a chair to the bedside. Settling onto the cushioned seat, he pondered his words.

"Doctor?" Hester appealed, her features wan. Normally unflappable, she was terrified. Inexplicable lethargy, acute sickness, constant discomfort — all manner of possibilities had taken root in her head, none of which ended happily.

"Lady Dynham, although I have my suspicions regarding your condition, it would be presumptuous of me to make an official prognosis."

"P-prognosis," Hester stammered, her fears crowding in. That word did not sound positive.

"If I offer you my opinion, and ask you to be patient until

the symptoms manifest, would that help?" He beamed benevolently, thinking he sounded reassuring. All this did was send Hester into a panic.

"*Manifest?*" she squeaked. "How? What else are you waiting for? Is it not enough that I am casting up my accounts with indecent regularity?" She closed her eyes, and blurted out, "Am I dying?" to be disconcerted by the doctor's roar of laughter.

"My dear, dear lady." He patted her right hand lying on the top of the covers. "You are far from dying, but what I surmise afflicts you, takes time to become obvious."

"I am glad my state of health amuses you," she grumbled, frowning, his oblique reference adding to her puzzlement.

Tutting in exasperation at the medico's prevarication when, to her, it was plain as the bulbous nose on his face, Amalia went around to the other side of the bed. "Signora Hester, *il dottore* is trying, badly I agree..." ignoring Doctor Guarino's humph, "...to tell you, he believes you to be carrying a child. Something I too believe."

Hester's jaw dropped. She shook her head as though attempting to clear the picture, but the scene did not change. Her stunned gaze seesawed between the doctor — whose bushy brows had arched encouragingly — and Amalia who was smiling in delight.

Shuffling up on her pillows, she tried to speak, but nothing came out.

"Let me summon your signore," Amalia said and walked to the door. Opening it to peer around the jamb, she swallowed a grin at the sight of Archer pacing up and down the corridor. "Signore," she hailed him.

Archer was in the room and holding Hester's hand almost before Amalia had finished speaking. "My darling." He scrutinised her face, reading the gamut of emotions lurking there, the overriding one being incredulity.

"He says... she thinks... I don't... oh, Archer." Overwhelmed and not convinced she wasn't dreaming, Hester, uncharacteristically, burst into tears.

Archer gathered his wife against him and rocked her, his own eyes suspiciously damp. "Thank you," he murmured to the two watching whose faces were wreathed in smiles.

"I shall come often." Doctor Guarino stood to take his leave. "The good lady needs rest, but fresh air and gentle exercise are as revitalising. In this, Signore Osmund has the perfect abode. Amalia..." He indicated the housekeeper should follow him. Bowing politely, he walked from the room, Amalia on his heels.

"A babe. Archer, I cannot believe this." Hester hiccupped, sniffling. "Are you sure I am not in some sickness riddled delusion?"

Archer kissed her soundly. "Does that feel like a delusion?"

She burrowed closer, revelling in his embrace. "No, that feels blissful. What of the others? Does everyone else know?"

"I am afraid they do. It would have been nice to tell them together. My fault entirely."

"How so?" Hester did not really care, she just wanted to listen to her husband talk while she coaxed her brain into some semblance of cohesion.

"I asked Amalia for her advice. When she delivered her hypothesis, shock rendered me temporarily incapable, and she took control of the situation. I presume she informed Leo, because the next thing I know, he and Sapphi were congratulating me, and the doctor had been called." He huffed a regretful sigh.

"For us to be the first to know and announce our news together would have been my preference. I am sorry I ruined that chance," he bemoaned.

Hester nestled her head under his chin and draped one arm over his waist. "Oddly, I am not disappointed. They are our greatest friends; I do not begrudge them knowing before I did. Mind, if the doctor expects me to curb my daily routine for the next several months, he is sorely mistaken. No…" when Archer began to interrupt, "…I am aware of the dangers associated with childbearing. As far as I can tell, it makes no difference whether the mother stays in bed for the duration or scales mountains and, while I give you my word I shall take every care, I cannot sit idle."

Archer swallowed his half-formed argument. "That's all I ask"

"Do we stay here, or risk the voyage home," Hester mumbled, sleepily.

"Plenty of time to make plans, love."

Yawning, she snuggled against him, "I love you." Her voice was fading.

"I love you too."

Archer heard her breathing even out. Lifting his legs onto the covers, he dropped a tender kiss on her hair, and fell to contemplating the momentous changes they were about to face, unable to suppress a smile of unvarnished joy.

At Leofwin's insistence, Doctor Guarino checked Sapphira's bruises, reassuring that young lady all was healing nicely. After a brief chat with Leofwin, he arranged to return a week hence, unless required prior.

As the doctor's carriage trundled down the drive and out of sight, Sapphira who had eavesdropped on their conversation, shamelessly, remarked, "'Tis true then? Hester *is* with child?"

"He refuses to commit, although his instinct affirms that is the case," Leofwin's tones were formal.

"Why?"

"Why what?"

"Why will he not commit?"

"While the likelihood is that Hester is increasing, it is early days and thus other explanations for her sickness cannot be excluded. It might be that she is suffering from naught but a common stomach upset."

"But his medical experience tells him it is not the latter?"

"It does."

"Amalia is also confident. She says Hester's complexion is the giveaway, although I am unsure what she means," Sapphira mused. "Goodness, what a morning, and there was I thinking a swim would be the highlight of the day."

"There is nothing preventing you from fulfilling that highlight." Leofwin contested.

"Mayhap this afternoon, when the day is still warm, but the sun is not quite so intense. If I venture into the water now, 'tis certain my skin will burn despite my best efforts to remain covered."

"Nuncio has rigged up a sizeable canopy of sorts to provide shade. I regret we cannot stretch to a bathing machine, but I'll wager we can contrive a way to enjoy the water without scorning convention."

"*I'll* wager you are far too late." Sapphira sallied.

Leofwin's expression started to crinkle in bafflement, then his sharp mind guessed her inference, and he shot her an unrepentant grin. "I have never been one for the rules. "

"You don't say," she shot back drily.

"My lady Sapphira, would you do me the honour of joining me for another caffè?" Motioning towards the pot perched on the low table between the two sofas.

It was still steaming and Sapphira could not deny the aroma was irresistible.

"Thank you, I should be glad to." She pushed her cup across the marble surface of the table. "Hopefully, Hester will feel up to joining us later. A quick plunge in the sea as the day cools might be just the thing."

Their conversation followed a different topic. The excitement did not wane but, until Hester put in an appearance any more celebrations were on hold. A comfortable peace descended on the villa.

Putting their heads together, Sapphira and Luisa had manufactured what the former deemed to be acceptable swimming attire from a pair of pantaloons and a chemise. It *did* expose a tad too much shoulder, and it was *impossible* to cover Sapphira's slender ankles, but was, otherwise, entirely suitable.

"If I wear a wrap until I enter the water, I do believe it will suffice. Moreover, I imagine it will be much easier to launder than the suit which poor Hester will have to wear," Sapphira said, holding their handiwork at arm's length to study it, a trifle giddy at the prospect of paddling in the bay. One more activity to add to her growing list of exploits.

"It is a seemly garment, my lady." Lusia nodded her approval.

How those in the domestic sphere had become acquainted with her status, Sapphira had no idea — she blamed Leofwin — she had apprised him less than a day ago, yet the staff were already using her title. *This* was why she had wanted to keep it secret.

"Luisa, please, my name is Sapphira. If you insist on addressing me as my lady or Lady Sapphira, I shall pretend I cannot hear you. I have been here for more than a month and I thought we shared a cordiality, an affection even."

"Sì, my lady, but…"

"No buts and no my lady. Sapphira or nothing. Yes, I know it is not customary but, please indulge me in this one thing. My time here, in your beautiful country, is like a dream and in dreams anything is possible." She reached out to clasp Luisa's hand. "Please."

Luisa recognised that arguing would get her nowhere and, after a brief internal battle, acquiesced. "I should be honoured to, my lad… Sapphira." She blushed.

"There now, that wasn't too hard, was it?" Sapphira smiled and released Luisa's fingers. "Time to trial our design."

With Luisa's help, Sapphira changed clothes, checking and double checking in the mirror to ensure she was not revealing any more than she ought.

Satisfied, she rummaged through her drawers for her favourite, well-worn but relatively presentable shawl. Made from fine wool, she had worn it multiple times when on board ship because its generous proportions enveloped her from head to toe, much like a cloak.

"Perfect." She shook it out, then slung it around her shoulders. "Behold… the epitome of modesty. Now, would you consider me too bold if I go barefoot? I really do not want to wear my boots or get sand in my slippers."

Solemnly, but with a mischievous twinkle in her eye, Luisa assured Sapphira no one would notice.

Cheering gleefully, Sapphira chose a broad-brimmed straw bonnet. Ramming it over her hair with little regard for the neat style Luisa had wrangled it into that morning, she tied the ribbons under her chin. "Ready."

Sapphira couldn't believe what Nuncio and his small

team of men had achieved in a couple of hours. A large expanse of what resembled a ship's sail had been stretched between several sturdy wooden poles. A similar sized sheet formed a protective wall around two sides, leaving the other two open to catch the slightest draught.

The result was a sort of tent; its interior spacious enough to house a table, four chairs, and a gaily patterned rug scattered with huge cushions in richly coloured silks. To Sapphira, the bookworm, the setting evoked descriptions of the Bedouin encampments in far off lands, she had read about in one of Papa's geography tomes.

Dusting the hot sand off her toes, Sapphira stepped inside, instantly feeling cooler. The first one down, she removed her bonnet and hung it off the back of her chosen chair, which she turned to face the water. It was so peaceful. Even the birds and insects were stilled under the blazing sun.

Making herself comfortable, she contemplated the endless ocean.

Midnight blue at the horizon, softening to turquoise near the shore, the sea was like liquid glass, barely a ripple disturbed its surface.

The islands in the bay, hazy in the afternoon light, reminded her of the previous night. The heat which flooded up her cheeks had nothing to do with the warmth of the sun and triggered an impulse to fling herself into the blue depths to cool off.

With Sapphira to think was to act. She was halfway across the sand, when her name was hailed, arresting her steps.

"Sapphira."

Leofwin.

For a split-second, she debated whether to wait or continue to the water. She had shed her shawl and her hat still dangled from the chair. It was easy to justify her attire in the sanctuary of her bedchamber, but the fact remained, she was scantily clad.

Give him his due, Leofwin's eyes never left her face. To Sapphira's confusion, this both reassured and rankled. *Is not my figure attractive? Sapphira... really?* she upbraided inwardly, as the heat which had receded, flared up with added brilliance.

CHAPTER SEVENTEEN

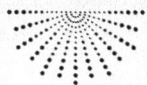

"My lord," she curtsied when he reached her side.

"Back to titles?" Leofwin sighed. "This is becoming tedious but, if you must... Lady Sapphira, permit me to escort you to the breakers. While the bay is generally calm, it can change without warning. Never go in alone, for if the current strengthens you could be dragged out to sea."

His genial expression had morphed into a bland mask, and Sapphira found herself wanting to rub her chest to ease a curious twinge. His words stuck a chord, however, and she fidgeted uncomfortably. By maintaining the formality, she was deliberately erecting an invisible barrier. Her behaviour was perverse, and it did not become her.

"My turn to apologise," she smiled tentatively. "I am at sixes and sevens after last evening, and at a loss as to the best way to move forward."

"Ahhh... your... errr... ebullience at breakfast did not go unnoticed." He gave a wicked chuckle.

"You might laugh, but we are at a crossroads. In the past two days our relationship has altered beyond recognition.

We cannot revert to our previous cordiality, although I value that part of our... err... friendship. Our mutual aversion to courtship and all it entails leaves me in limbo, and before you say something you will regret, I respect your decision. I do not expect you to do anything so drastic as to fall in l... develop an abiding affection for me and sweep me off my feet, but I..." she faltered, not exactly sure where she was going with this. "... I will be leaving soon," she finished lamely.

"Mayhap we do not overthink things and see where the days take us," Leofwin suggested, ignoring a peculiar jolt in the region of his heart at the knowledge Sapphira would be gone before the days had much of a chance to take them anywhere.

There was a short silence.

"I like that idea," Sapphira paused then added ingenuously, "I said to Luisa that being here is akin to a dream and in dreams anything is possible. Perhaps..." Diffidently, she angled her head, her green eyes holding his, hoping he understood what she dared not articulate.

It took every ounce of self-control for Leofwin not to drag her into his arms and kiss her senseless. He took refuge in clasping her fingers. Bowing over them, he grazed his lips against her knuckles. "Perhaps."

They stared at each other, the sultry air simmered with an, as yet, incomprehensible emotion, one neither was prepared to acknowledge.

"I have a favour to ask." Sapphira's question broke the hush.

"One I am happy to grant, should it be within my power." If Leofwin was thrown by the abrupt switch in conversation, he hid it well.

"Please will you teach me how to sea bathe? Not paddle

or splash about in the shallows, actually swim."

"My lad... Sapphira, I... errr... that is..." Leofwin floundered. To teach anyone to swim involved a reasonable amount of touching. More than might be considered decent between a man and a woman... and a lady no less. "Would not Hester be a more sensible choice?" he deflected.

"Under normal circumstances, yes, but it will be all Hester can do to coax Archer into allowing her to get her toes wet, never mind going deep enough to swim. Oh, he is in for a bumpy ride."

Sapphira giggled, the carefree sound extinguishing the residual tension. "Thus, I shall not make her life more difficult by asking her to be my tutor. That leaves you and Archer. We know Archer will not take his eyes off his wife so, whether you like it or not, the responsibility lies with you." She waited, expectantly.

Aware her argument was flimsy, she tossed in for good measure... "This is a dream, remember."

Tickled by her impudence, Leofwin relented. "On your head be it. Give me two minutes. Go, dabble your feet."

The sand at the breakers was hard-packed, making it easier to walk. Sapphira relished the feeling of the water sweeping over her toes and lapping up her ankles... *utterly divine*. Unable to help herself her gaze slid to the tent where Leofwin was stripping out of his clothes.

She came to a standstill when he emerged into the sunlight. Her eyes grew round, and her pretty mouth hung open. *This* was what men looked like when disrobed. *Praise the good Lord and all his saints*.

Not unfamiliar with the male anatomy — she had visited the British Museum and wandered a sufficiency of art galleries — Sapphira's only other reference was her younger brother who, along with one or two of the stable boys, often cavorted in the lake at The Towers... usually in the nude. At fifteen, Glanville's juvenile physique bore little resemblance to the figure striding towards her.

Leofwin was wearing what looked like cut down pants, so short they scarcely covered his thighs. He might as well have forgone them completely so snug was the fit.

As he splashed through the shallows, she stared unabashed at the scarring on his right leg, and the defined musculature of his broad chest. Her heart rate tripled, and her breathing caught. *Leofwin was... was...*

"Is something amiss, Sapphira? The heat? You look a trifle distraite."

She came down to earth with a bump. *The **heat**... distraite... if only he knew...* "No, no, I am quite all right." Fists balled at her sides to calm her fluttering insides, and resolutely keeping her eyes above his chin, she chirped, "Lesson One."

Initially reserved and determined not to gawk, Sapphira quickly forgot she was in the company of a practically naked gentleman and concentrated on following his instructions.

Hilarity ensued. No matter how assiduously Sapphira tried, she could not coordinate her arms and legs to produce the streamline technique Leofwin demonstrated as he carved his way effortlessly through the water.

She studied the movement of his arms and legs and attempted to replicate it, with little success. She *did* succeed in going under and swallowing mouthfuls of salt water.

Their merriment echoed around the bay, attracting the attention of Sapphira's fellow guests who were making their way down the steps, looking forward to a constitutional along the sand.

Hester, spying their two friends in the water, no chaperone in sight, quickened her pace.

Archer looped a hand around her elbow. "My love, they spent the night together, alone, in the middle of an empty ruin. If anything untoward was going to happen, that is where it would have occurred. They are not so witless as to abandon their sanity in full view of the neighbourhood."

Hester turned to him, her eyes troubled. "I am concerned, Archer. Never mind that the pair of them are virtually naked... together... in the sea... there are undercurrents here that I fear might wash them away if they do not pay heed."

"Would that be so bad?" He raised a brow.

"Archer, of course it would. You know as well as I do that should their relationship exceed the bounds of... amity, Sapphi will be ruined, along with any chance of a good marriage. How could they?"

"I should leave well alone, my dear. They are old enough to know what they are doing. Do you honestly think Leo would blight a young lady's reputation for a few hours of fun? Give him... them... some credit."

"But."

"No, Hester. Trust me in this." Archer's expression told Hester he was not to be swayed.

In general, an easy-going man, this inexorable side of Archer was new, and Hester rather liked it. Not that she was about to tell him that. "Fine," she acquiesced grudgingly, "but one wrong move and I expect you to interfere. Sapphi is under our protection. I take that responsibility seriously."

"As do I, but she has reached her majority, and is entitled to make her own decisions. Moreover, Sapphi is an canny personage. Let her be." Archer squeezed his wife's elbow.

They meandered towards the tent, observing Sapphira striving to conquer the — to Leofwin and Archer — inordinately simple sidestroke. She sank beneath the surface to reappear, gasping yet determined.

"What about backstroke?" Archer hailed Leofwin.

"Good thinking." Hester nudged her husband.

"I have my moments." He grinned.

Leofwin slapped his forehead, in what the couple on the shore guessed to be a 'why didn't I think of that?' gesture. They watched him speak to Sapphira who nodded eagerly and launched herself into the water.

There was *a lot* of splashing and Sapphira's legs seemed to have a mind of their own but, after a few minutes, it was as though something clicked in her brain, and she swam several feet.

Her crow of delight was lost because, in her elation, she forgot the stroke and disappeared.

Laughing, Hester and Archer took a seat and availed themselves of the refreshments someone had thoughtfully provided.

Sapphira emerged from the sea coughing and spluttering but her face was a picture of joy. "I did it, I actually managed the stroke. Did you see?" She clapped wet hands in glee.

"You were superb," Leofwin assured, dazzled by her euphoric smile.

"Again." She glanced over her shoulder and was about to fling herself backwards when Leofwin caught her hand.

"The afternoon is waning and there is a brisk edge to the air. This might be a good time to stop for today. It feels easy when you are in the water, but your muscles will be sore tomorrow. The sea is not going anywhere and, while the weather holds, we can come down every day."

Sapphira's expression which had dropped, brightened. "Truly? You would take the time to help me?"

"Of course. You need plenty of practice. Mayhap, once you feel competent with this stroke, we can try the side stroke again."

She pushed her streaming hair out of her eyes uncaring

that it had unravelled and was forming a sodden tangle down her back. "We can but hope." She made a cheeky face. "I fear your efforts may be in vain. That said, I cannot recall when last, I had so much fun. What a memorable dream."

Slowly, Sapphira waded out of the surf, heedless to the fact her wet clothes were plastered to her svelte figure, leaving little to the imagination. A red-blooded male, Leofwin deemed it prudent to remain in the sea until his reaction to the sight was not so... obvious.

"I shall follow shortly," he called after her, and struck out briskly, swimming parallel to the shore. It was not until he had reached the rocky outcrop delineating the border of his property that he had his body under control.

As she reached the soft sand, Sapphira was met by Hester carrying a large drying sheet.

"Oh, thank you, I was just thinking how impolite it would be to drip water all the way to my bedchamber." She beamed, as Hester wrapped the sheet around her.

"You looked to be enjoying yourself." Hester avoided pointing out that her presence at the water's edge was necessitated by how transparent Sapphira's outfit had become now it was wet.

Ushering her friend into the tent, she picked up another sheet from the neat pile which one of the staff had placed on a stool, and started to rub Sapphira's hair.

"Thank you, Hester. Yes, it was amazing, although 'tis a good thing Leofwin is patient. His instructions were simple, but my brain did not seem able to translate them into actions," she replied breezily.

Archer — who, ever the polite gentleman, had averted his gaze when Sapphira came out of the sea — quipped, "Leofwin. Patient? There are two words I never thought to hear in the same sentence."

"I am the veritable model of patience," a deep voice, laced with humour proclaimed from beyond the makeshift shelter. Leofwin appeared. "Brrrr, how quickly one cools." He towelled himself rigorously, glad to feel the warmth creeping back into his chilled limbs.

"Not so's you'd notice," Archer contradicted.

Archer's sly dig earned him a cuff to his shoulder, as Leofwin reached over to pick up a glass of lemonade, which he drained in one go. They shared a brotherly grin.

"How are you feeling, Hester?" Sapphira asked. "I am so happy for you both."

"I have yet to come to terms with the notion," Hester admitted with a wry smile. "Mayhap, by the time this confounded nausea subsides, I shall be convinced. It seems too much like a dream at the moment."

Sapphira met Leofwin's gaze, and her mouth curved in a sweet smile. "Of late, I have discovered that dreams come true when least expected."

There followed a brief hiatus during which Sapphira and Leofwin retired to their respective rooms to divest themselves of their wet clothes, rinse off any residual salt and sand, and get dressed. Rejoining their friends, what remained of the afternoon vanished in convivial and occasionally nonsensical conversation about all things baby related.

Amid this, Amalia deposited a platter of bite-sized cakes and biscuits on the table, along with a carafe of locally brewed white wine with which to toast the expectant parents.

When the sun began its slow descent to the far horizon, muting the vibrant colours of the day to softer hues, the four made their reluctant way to the terrace for an early dinner.

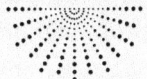

CHAPTER EIGHTEEN

"*H*ow is your leg, Sapphi?" Hester asked, while the crockery was being cleared away in readiness for dessert.

"Much better, thank you. Interestingly, my execrable attempts to swim seem to have eased the ache, although Leofwin tells me I shall be sore everywhere on the morrow."

"It does take a little while for one's body to become used to this form of exercise," Archer interposed. "Remember how you were, my love?"

"I waddled like a duck for two whole days," Hester chortled at the memory. "I did not think I would stand upright again... ever and refused point blank to go back into the sea for nigh on a fortnight, despite everyone assuring me it was the only way to lessen the ache."

"Oh no, I hope not to be affected likewise," Sapphira groaned. "I wish to get back to the site forthwith, not be hampered by additional aches and pains."

"At least you have been warned." Hester smiled across the table.

"I propose we make the most of this lovely weather and

spend the next few days here or hereabouts. There is no need to rush our return to the ruins, they will not vanish…" leaning back in his chair, Leofwin spotted Sapphira's face, and added wryly, "…thieves and vagabonds aside."

"Do we not need to apprise the site supervisor about the theft?" Sapphira asked.

"I have sent a missive to Valana detailing the incident. He will deal with the appropriate authorities, who will doubtless organise an investigation. As the relic hunters cared not for injuring a woman in pursuit of their goal, I have expressed my opinion that they must be considered dangerous and approached with extreme caution.

"I included your description of both men, an unexpected fortuity, which Valana will circulate among the teams. Hopefully, they will be tracked down and a suitable punishment meted out." Leofwin replied.

"It is all we can do." He shrugged. "Regrettably, all over the world, sites like Pompeii are targeted by the unscrupulous. It is impossible to have a guard on every corner. Moreover, no one would be prepared to offer up the coin required to secure their loyalty."

"I would like ten minutes with the person behind that theft," Sapphira growled.

"Because confrontation worked so well for you the first time," Hester contended dryly. "Please leave well alone, my dear. I do not want to tell your parents you were kidnapped, or worse, murdered, by bandits."

"Pooh," was Sapphira's considered response. "Lightning never strikes the same place twice."

"One can only hope," Archer's tone was wry.

Hester excused herself early claiming weariness, Archer at her elbow. At the edge of the terrace, she paused. Their absence meant Leofwin and Sapphira would be alone together, unchaperoned... again.

About to retrace her steps, she heard Sapphira say, "Wait for me, I too feel an urgency to be abed. Ooof," she groaned when she rose to her feet, "I stand, or rather hunch, corrected. I can already feel my arms stiffening." She gave an experimental wriggle, to the amusement of the other three.

"It will soon pass," Leofwin consoled. "But might take another swim or two."

"Humph," Sapphira grumbled and caught up with her friends. "Good night, Lord Osmund," she threw over her shoulder sedately, his quiet laughter following her into the darkness.

Her nighttime ablutions complete, Sapphira stood by her open window and stared into the night. Tired she might be, but she was also restless. Her mind would not settle, too many questions without answers, muddling her thoughts, not least that her host had taken up lodging at the forefront of her mind.

She could not deny their burgeoning attraction, but was it genuine or a fantasy engendered by recent circumstances? Was it even mutual, or was he just being kind? *That kiss was anything but kind.* What did it matter anyway? Her departure loomed, she would return to England, their paths unlikely to cross again.

Captivated by the moon on the water, she was plagued by a vague melancholy. Luisa was right, Campania *had* stolen her heart. *Only Campania?* Her mind taunted.

Despite a day of excitements in one form or another, sleep hovered maddeningly out of reach. After tossing for what felt like hours, Sapphira yielded to the inevitable and got up. Pulling on her dressing gown, an aged and well-loved voluminous garment which turned her into shapeless mass, she crept barefoot from her room.

Closing the door with a quiet click, she paused... which way to go? The atrium on the upper floor was always accessible. Being less familiar with the layout of that room, there was a reasonable chance she might bang into, or... and more probably... trip over, a piece of furniture, disturbing those of the household who slept on that level.

The terrace. That was the obvious option, yet she dithered. *What if* he *was there? Will he suspect my appearance to be in expectation of reprising that kiss? Woman, stop over-thinking this. Why should he be there at this hour?*

Stealthily, she descended the steps, wincing when her tight muscles baulked at so rude an awakening. The terrace looked to be deserted. Heaving a sigh of relief, she relaxed and made her way carefully across the cool tiles, hands out in case she walked into a stray chair or table corner in the darkness.

Her fingers finding and gripping the back of one of the chairs, she moved it closer to the perimeter wall, then spun it around to overlook the bay. She shuffled down on the seat until she was almost reclining, then lifted her feet to balance her heels on the stone capping. Hands clasped over her stomach, she inhaled a long slow breath.

The scene before her was timeless. *How many others had sat on this hillside and admired the same view? How many lost their lives in the catastrophic eruption of AD 79?*

Shrouded in the velvet of the night, the silence was almost complete.

Leofwin had not left the terrace. It was long past midnight, but he felt strangely unwilling to end the day. Although he had dismissed Amalia for the evening, the faithful housekeeper — familiar with his lordship's periodic insomnia — had brought him a last cup of tea with a brandy snifter before seeking her own bed.

Since then, he had become one with the darkness, sitting in a corner of the terrace, while the fun of the afternoon played on repeat in his head. Sapphira's antics and uninhibited abandon tugging a smile from a sombre mouth.

There was something brewing. While impossible to deny, he was not disposed to embrace it. Regardless, to suppose they could share more than a brief romance was futile. He lived here, she, thousands of miles away.

Their kiss had awoken something he did not believe he possessed.

Desire.

Well, he admonished inwardly, *extinguish it*. In less than a month, she'll be naught but a dream. That reminded him of Sapphira's earlier comment. *In dreams anything is possible.*

The muted ding of the grandfather clock up in the salon struck two. He needed to find his bed. About to stand, his movement was stayed by the scrape of metal on tile. Unaware he had company; the sound froze him in place.

He watched Sapphira pick up one of the chairs and carry it over to the low wall, off which she had fallen the previous night. *What the devil was she wearing?* The sack-like garment was terribly unflattering.

Swallowing a grin while grumbling under his breath, for there was little chance he could avoid detection, Leofwin coughed quietly.

Sapphira bounced out of her chair and, pivoting on her bare feet, assumed a pugilistic pose, increasing Leofwin's mirth.

"Who goes there?" she demanded her tone fierce rather than frightened. "Show yourself."

Laughter rumbled through Leofwin's chest. She

169

continued to surprise him. This woman possessed the heart of a warrior.

"'Tis only I." He schooled his features and stepped forward, the moon's pearly glow accentuating his angular countenance.

"You!" she hissed. "How is it, every time I seek a moment's quietude you interrupt?"

"I was here first. You interrupted me," he contested.

"Oh… well… oh," she faltered, her righteous indignation deflating. She chose a different tack. "Could you not sleep either?"

"I have not yet been to bed. Slumber and I have an unpredictable relationship. Sometimes we are in harmony, sometimes not. 'Tis an impediment I have borne since the war and have grown accustomed to fitful sleep."

"Normally, I fall asleep the instant my head touches the pillow. I cannot think what has me wakeful."

"Mayhap it is nothing more sinister than an eventful day or two," Leofwin suggested. "To be expected in the circumstances."

"Mayhap," she agreed.

"Would a brief constitutional help?"

Sapphira gaped at him. *A walk? At this time of night? Was he addled?* "Where?" she asked bluntly.

"Along the beach."

Alone… with a man… in the darkness. How deliciously illicit. Sinful it might be but, enthralled by the notion, she was sorely tempted. *Who would know?*

"Perhaps a short stroll will facilitate repose," she said before her head could talk her out of it.

"Oh," Sapphira exclaimed when they stepped on to the beach. "'Tis like the streets of Pompeii."

A softly glistening path stretched out in front of them, the moon winking off the crystallised dust.

"I often come down here at night. I appreciate the solitude, the knowledge I am completely alone save the moon and the sea." Leofwin said as they picked their way to the hard-packed sand.

"Yet, besides your staff, you live alone... when not hounded by guests," Sapphira contested.

"It is not the same. I am always alert to their presence, even in my private quarters. Voices, footsteps, doors banging. Here, there is no one and nothing, especially after dusk."

"I think I understand. I have a penchant for midnight promenades around the grounds at home. It is my way of rebelling, and being fortunate to observe the activities of a variety of nocturnal animals adds to the attraction. My family remains ignorant. They believe me to be staid; the eldest child who abides by the rules and always does as instructed... makes me sound utterly dreary. When I look back, I can see why Jeremy ran off with Gisela. She is a far more attractive prospect."

"You *do* understand that rebellion is only effective when witnessed," Leofwin remarked, his amusement apparent.

"Of course, I do." She gave a merry chuckle, then shrugged. "It was the best I could manage, and why my decision to sail around Europe left them dumbfounded. I think that caused them more heart palpitations than my being jilted. Let us talk of other things. Of escapades and excavations. Now I have discovered Pompeii, I have a mind to continue across the Mediterranean to explore the East. I have heard wondrous tales of the Pyramids and Petra."

"A grand plan," Leofwin encouraged. "Do not stop at Petra, follow the ancient Silk Road to China."

"Oh, the sights I would see," Sapphira loosed her arm and twirled a jig, which brought Leofwin's attention to her bare feet.

"Sapphi, your feet must be freezing," he chided.

"Not a bit, and now I can do this…" she hoisted her dressing gown and danced into the sea, splashing through the breakers. "Come on in, the water's fine."

Entertained by her hoydenish tendencies, Leofwin reached out to grasp her hand while keeping his booted feet out of the water.

"Take them off," she urged.

"Whatever for?"

"Because it is fun, and a little fun is good for the soul." She came out of the water and pirouetted along the sand. "I recall Hester once commenting that you were stuffy. Personally, I do not believe a word of it, but…" she drew out the last word, her expression mischievous.

"Stuffy. *Stuffy?*" he expostulated and hurried after Sapphira. Catching up, he snagged one of her hands and hauled her against him, capturing her mouth in a searing kiss.

Sapphira pushed him away, tapping a trembling finger to her lips. "Stuffy," she croaked.

Anchoring her to him, Leofwin bent his head.

"Did that feel stuffy to you?" His heart thudding, he broke their kiss to search her face.

"I do not believe that example provided adequate evidence to make a reasonable judgement," Sapphira replied demurely, leaning backwards. "Might it be possible to repeat the experiment?" She cocked her head, a wicked smile playing around her mouth.

Her sauce rendered him speechless. "Miss Beresford… m-my Lady," he stuttered, robbed of coherence. That he had dared flout convention was bad enough, but this…? Still, he could not deny her audacity entranced him.

"Oh, back to titles, are we? This is becoming tedious, but

if we must…" Sapphira echoed his words of earlier, accompanied by a dramatic sigh. Dipping a curtsy, she feigned affront. "My dear, Lord Osmund, my analysis was stymied by a woeful lack of information. An honourable gentleman would ensure a lady was in possession of all the pertinent facts before demanding an informed decision," she paused. "Do you by chance know of one?" She batted her lashes winsomely.

"Why, you imp…" Leofwin needed no second bidding.

Their escalating passion was only tempered when a wave crashed over their feet, the shock of the cold water making Sapphira squeal and dash up the beach.

"Botheration," she grumbled. "Of late, it seems my lot in life is to get wet." She gathered up the hem of her dressing gown to squeeze it out. "Ugh."

"We ought to return to the villa," Leofwin's petition was half-hearted at best.

"Must we? I am enjoying our repartee, and 'tis such a shame that wave interrupted your argument. Your… errr… eloquence was most persuasive."

"Your dressing gown…" Being a gentleman, he made a token protest.

"Can be carried, like this," she demonstrated. "Please Leo," she wheedled. "I am wide awake and once back in my suite, reality eclipses fantasy."

"It would be discourteous indeed if I was to crush your dream."

Dressing gown clutched in one hand, Sapphira slid her other through his arm, and they meandered along the beach, falling back into light-hearted conversation.

It was a pattern they were to repeat every night.

CHAPTER NINETEEN

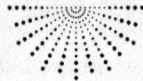

For the remainder of that week, the company did not stray far from the villa.

Letters were written and stacked neatly on the salver ready for dispatch.

Journals, for those who completed them, were updated.

Constitutionals taken, and the neighbourhood explored.

It was a relaxing interlude and proclaimed to be the perfect tonic after the hubbub of the preceding days.

Sapphira's bruising diminished; the discolouration on her cheek fading more quickly than that on her hip. While the features of the thieves were imprinted on her mind, as plainly as the toe of Walt's boot was imprinted on her thigh, she sketched the duo.

A passable artist — her skills evidenced in her journal and in the site records at Pompeii — she managed to pen a reasonable resemblance. Close enough that anyone seeing them, would have no problem recognising either man in a hurry.

"Please remember to take these with you when next we

head to Pompeii," Leofwin implored. "Valana will be most impressed. Much easier to recall a drawing than a verbal description."

"You truly think these will help?" Sapphira asked.

"Categorically. The detail is remarkable."

Sapphira blushed, inordinately pleased by the compliment. "Let us hope it helps," was all she said, however.

While Hester and Sapphira were otherwise occupied, Archer and Leofwin lazed on the terrace, puffing on their pipes and discussing business or politics.

The sole upside to the clouds of smoke was that the odious aroma of the burning tobacco repelled the biting bugs who, it seemed, had developed a taste for the blood of the recently arrived English visitors. They swarmed at dusk, millions of them, but so tiny they were almost invisible to the human eye. Worse, their hapless victims did not discover they had been made a meal of until it was too late.

"Is this normal, or have they come out in their multitudes because we are fresh meat so to speak?" Sapphira wailed, one particularly tiresome evening. "I will never complain about England again."

"Hah, 'tis no different. Midges are as bad as these little horrors, but because we eat outside infrequently, we get attacked less." Archer countered.

"It is the time of year. Naught we can do. Unless we eat our meals in the salon, we must grin and bear it. Amalia has some ointment that reduces the itchiness of the bites." Leofwin mollified.

"Humph, I would prefer not to be their main course at all," Sapphira groused, scratching her head. "The one thing keeping them at bay are your smelly pipes." She motioned to the men. "Mayhap we ought to put some tobacco into little bowls, light it and place the bowls around the terrace." She looked at the marquis hopefully.

"You would elect to breathe in that noxious aroma over fresh sea air?" Hester pulled a face. "No, thank you very much. I prefer to take my chances with the gnats. They are at their most voracious when the sun is setting, or when the breeze drops. The solution is to adjust the time we eat, so 'tis only we four with appetites which require slaking." She gave a decisive nod.

The leisurely days had worked wonders for Hester, whose zest for life was resurfacing. With helpful suggestions from all the women on Leofwin's staff — regardless of whether they were mothers — she had begun to manage the debilitating nausea.

A few drops of lemon in tepid water or crushing a mint leaf snipped from the plants in the herb garden and inhaling the fragrance were the two easiest remedies.

The most efficacious was a tisane concocted from ginger, lemon, and honey. The former, renowned for its health-giving properties, although a precious commodity and used sparingly was lauded by Amalia and Bruna.

A small knob of ginger root was sliced into a pot of simmering water and left to steep for about an hour. A popular restorative, especially in the winter months when minor ailments were rife, Bruna had the timing down to a fine art. After draining the liquid, she added a squeeze of lemon juice, a spoonful of honey, stirred gently and served immediately.

The ginger slices were dried carefully and wrapped in muslin, ready for re-use.

Despite Dr Guarino's assurances that the sickness was

worse in and usually confined to the early stages of pregnancy, the ginger tea was a godsend for Hester, mitigating the nausea to a tolerable severity.

Determined to become a proficient swimmer, Sapphira cajoled the others into taking to the water, most afternoons. She received little resistance. Following the storm, the weather had become hot and sunny and to cool off in the sea was a relief. Even little Mariella joined them; her childish shrieks of joy echoing around the bay.

In between teaching Sapphira the finer points of swimming strokes, Hester was happy to float on her back, enjoying the buoyancy of the surf, while the two men raced up and down the private bay.

After their evening meal — later, as Hester had suggested, to avoid being eaten alive — the four developed a partiality for lingering over coffee and a digestif. Conversation flowed effortlessly and they were never at a loss of topics of discussion.

Fresh air, full stomachs, and a glass or two of wine tended to have a soporific effect and, without fail, before the clock in the salon struck eleven, the household — to all intents and purposes — was fast asleep.

Had anyone thought to peek out of their bedroom, they might have been startled to observe furtive figures slipping between the shadows. A sharp ear might have overheard muffled voices.

By unspoken agreement, Sapphira and Leofwin continued their nightly trysts. How one knew the other waited was a mystery neither questioned, accrediting it to tacit approval by a higher authority.

Arm in arm, they sauntered along the beach, doing little more than enjoying the tranquillity and being able to talk without restraint.

Their brief acquaintance had already revealed a shared appreciation of books... no matter the topic... and history in all its forms. A partiality for quiet places and the countryside as opposed to large social gatherings and busy cities.

Now, they discovered this extended to art and music — although Leofwin professed to be tone deaf. Where better to debate their admiration than here on the Italian Peninsula — home to some of the most gifted composers of both.

Of course, *any* lull in their chitchat was filled by heated kisses but, interestingly, although the illicit intimacy was heartfelt and craved, it was their conversation which cemented this fledgling bond.

"I am looking forward to returning to Pompeii," Sapphira said, shortly after midnight on Monday morning, when they turned at the end of the cove to head back to the villa.

"I also. Save my sojourn in England, this is the longest I have gone between visits."

"Really? Goodness, you are dedicated indeed."

He shrugged. "No, 'tis more an obsession, an addiction almost. Being on the site sustains me as much as food. I cannot explain it, it just is."

"No need to justify your avowal, I do believe I understand. While perhaps not *quite* as immersed as you, Pompeii haunts me. She captured my soul when first I set foot on her ancient soil, and I have not yet had sufficient time among her ruins."

"Hah, finally, I have persuaded you into assigning femininity to inanimate objects," he teased.

"Fine." She threw up her hands. "I accept the premise and bow to your superior intellect."

"As you should," came his smug riposte.

"Be careful, or you might trip over your ego... again," she taunted.

They bantered back and forth, trying to outwit each other, their voices camouflaged by the crash of the surf. Reaching the steps, as had become his habit, Leofwin gathered Sapphira close, his lips seeking hers.

As had become *her* habit... Sapphira's rational side commanded her to stop this lunacy, while her romantic nature basked in the delectable sensations wrought by his kiss.

'Tis just a dream, she insisted, determined not to probe any more deeply into the chaos running riot in her mind.

Banishing reason, she embraced the illusion.

The next day saw all four at Pompeii, with Hester steadfastly refusing to stay at the villa.

"Do not even think it," she had forestalled Archer's reservations, knowing he wanted to wrap her in layers of soft blankets. "I cannot put my life on hold for the next few months. I will take every care, but a horse ride and a little excavating is unlikely to result in any problems. If it soothes your anxiety, I will ride side-saddle and should I feel tired, I shall rest. Trust me, my love."

Looping her arms around his waist, she canted her head to hold his gaze. "Do you think me addled enough to risk our baby?"

Glad they were in the privacy of their bedchamber, Archer kissed her with ardent fervency. "Of course not, I simply..."

Hester placed a gentle finger on his lips, stemming what she guessed would be one of his well-reasoned and possibly long-winded arguments. "Hush, I know. Let us take one day at a time. I am not infirm, and women have continued with their daily lives while expecting, since time immemorial."

"But none of them were my wife." Archer huffed.

Hester chuckled. "What a relief, think how exhausted you would be."

"Lady Dynham, the things you say."

"*Moi?*" The picture of innocence, Hester reached up for another kiss before patting her husband's nicely toned behind. "Much as I would like to spend the next hour or so… debating this issue," her fingers tiptoed up his spine provocatively, "we must not tarry. Pompeii awaits."

"Hey, not fair," he groaned.

"I daresay you will exact a forfeit later." With a flirtatious flounce, she turned to complete her preparations, laughing at Archer's, "Assuredly, I shall," which floated after her into the dressing room.

The higgledy-piggledy profile of Pompeii shimmered under the summer sunshine, creating the impression the whole site was a mirage.

"How marvellous to be back," Sapphira pushed her bonnet off her forehead to view the amphitheatre with delight, as the horses clip-clopped through the gap in the pines towards the stable. "I have missed seeing this leviathan every day."

The others agreed and, once the horses were settled with hay and water, they strolled past the imposing grey structure and onto the Via dell'Abbondanza.

"Did you know the Romans effected a most ingenious

method of lighting the road at night?" Sapphira addressed this remark to Hester and Archer.

"What do you mean?" Hester was mystified.

Sapphira told them about the tiny white stones. "See." She pointed them out. "You do not even notice them in daylight, but it is magical to see them under the glow of the moon. As though stars have fallen from the sky to illuminate your way. Ingenious, those Romans, very ingenious."

A thought struck her. "Mind, how did they find their way when it was raining? I'll wager there was a lot of tripping up and a lot of cursing." Her irreverent tone prompting the others to laugh.

"I confess I was clueless," Archer said, "but am not surprised. Their resourcefulness is legendary."

They chatted about sundry Roman innovations while they made their way along the ancient street, and soon the melody of voices belonging to the groups scattered among the ruins reached their ears.

"Would you consider me insensitive if I asked whether you might attempt to retrace your steps to the place where you witnessed the theft?" Leofwin asked — delicately for him.

Anticipating this question, Sapphira had already ruminated over her response. The idea was daunting, but to decline the request left the investigation incomplete.

If they knew precisely where the theft had occurred, they would have a better chance of figuring out the probable access point, or points, used by the treasure hunters. Patrols could be increased if the area appeared to be particularly vulnerable.

"I am happy to do anything I can to assist," she replied, mentally bracing herself. "Although, I warn you, it might take some locating."

"If we are patient and check methodically, I have no

doubt we shall find it." Leofwin's calm confidence was persuasive and Sapphira found herself believing him.

The four split up. Hester and Archer heading for the section they had been assigned to previously, while Leofwin and Sapphira turned towards the insulae from where the sorry episode had begun.

Sapphira was greeted with enthusiasm by the group, their concern for her welfare, touching, if rather embarrassing.

"It was my own silly fault." She blushed. "Anyone with an ounce of sense would have sought help from the guards or one of the teams. I did not stop to think and suffered the consequences."

This was met with a chorused denial, turning her pink cheeks to scarlet.

"You showed remarkable courage, lass," a gruff man who hailed from the north of England, asserted. "Most of us are well into our prime, leaving few sprightly enough to confront robbers, never mind chase after the buggers... oh, beggin' your pardon, Miss."

Sapphira chuckled. "Nothing to apologise for, Mr Fernsby. I am not easily offended. Lord Osmund is of the opinion we can ascertain where it happened, despite my misgivings as to the likelihood. I got hopelessly lost," she clarified, at the circle of bemused faces. "The problem is, I was concentrating on not losing sight of the dog rather than which direction I was taking."

"I recommend using a piece of chalk to notch the walls at the end of each section once you've checked it. That way you know where you have been." Signore Valana suggested. "Here." He retrieved a chunk from a small sack at the entrance to the insula.

"Good plan, Valana," Leofwin accepted the chalk. "Come on, Sapphi, we ought not dawdle." He spoke without forethought, oblivious to the knowing glances shared among the group. "We shall return shortly… I hope." With a nod, he was off, striding along the street.

Hurriedly thanking her kindly colleagues, Sapphira followed in his wake. "Wait for me, Leo," she called. "I cannot match your stride."

Leofwin slowed his pace, waiting until she reached his side. "Sorry, in my eagerness, I forgot your temporary impediment." He grasped her hand and looped it around his arm. "Time to find the scene of the crime."

CHAPTER TWENTY

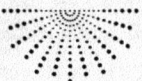

"*L*et me get my bearings." Sapphira said when they reached a cross street. One thing in her favour was that Pompeii, consistent with most Roman towns, was arranged in a grid pattern.

She studied the buildings and the road, then closed her eyes, sifting through her memory for the route. "I think we went that way, not straight across. It felt as though we were going downhill." The half-excavated street was on a slight slope.

Leofwin dashed a line of chalk at shoulder height on the wall nearest to him and they set off. It was slow going, and several times they doubled back, because Sapphira questioned every step.

Frustratingly, daylight proved a hindrance rather than a help. During the storm, buildings and streets morphed into a shadowy mass, and she had been more concerned with getting back to the amphitheatre and safety, than registering her route.

Under the bright sunlight, they transformed into individual dwellings and lanes with accompanying differences, and did not match the picture in her mind's eye. Everything was both more and less familiar.

"You might think the scatterbrained creature who led me on so merry a dance would do the honourable thing and offer a hint," she griped. "No gratitude."

"You are presuming he thinks like a human," Leofwin smirked.

"He is smarter than most," she rejoined.

Prepared to accept defeat, Sapphira spied something which did not fit. Lodged between two stones, fluttering in the breeze, a white ribbon.

"My hat," she crowed.

Leofwin stared at her, nonplussed.

She pumped his arm up and down, then pointed at the raggedy strip of silk. "That, it is my ribbon, one of the ribbons from my hat. Maybe Scamp *did* direct us here."

"Scamp?" Leofwin was stumped.

"The dog."

"Of course. A dog we cannot see, brought us here. Why did I not think of that?" He palmed his forehead.

Sapphira unhooked the ribbon, stuffed it her pocket and peered in through the closest doorway. Frowning, she scanned the ground. Grass and rubble covered the interior. If there was a mosaic under there, it was still buried. There was no sign anything had been disturbed since the initial excavations.

"We must be close." Leofwin said by her ear.

She spun to face him momentarily transfixed by the smoky grey of his eyes. He was so close.

Exploiting her distraction, Leofwin stole a kiss.

"My lord," she swatted his chest. "Catching a lady unawares, unconscionable." Her smile belied her admonishment.

"I was compelled."

"By whom?"

"Scamp."

Sapphira spluttered, "*Scamp?*"

"If he can lead us here without us seeing hide nor hair of him, he can compel me to kiss you…" Leofwin leered unattractively.

"Fiddlesticks," she rebutted through her mirth. "Come on we have work to do."

They continued on to the next building.

Sapphira stepped over the threshold first and froze. There, not three feet from where she stood, the fragments of her bonnet, only recognisable by the matching white ribbon squashed into the mud. Beyond, the denuded patch where once a mosaic had lain.

This was it. *Finally!*

"It was there, just there," she managed not to stammer. Relief accompanied by a twinge of fear coursed through her. A series of images chased through her head, and she sank blindly onto what remained of a flight of stairs.

Giving her a moment, Leofwin scrutinised his surrounds. Crouching in the exposed square at the far side of what was once the atrium, his fingers probed the dust, encountering tiny objects. Picking one up, he rolled it in his hand. Tessera. He twisted in place, his gaze landing on a few shards of pottery.

He glanced at Sapphira. When entering this house, she had paled and her lips were pressed together, but her normal colour was returning. She possessed a good deal of pluck for a gentlewoman.

He straightened. "Thank you, Sapphira. I imagine this is extremely unpleasant, but now we have a starting point." He chalked the doorway. "I think I know a less convoluted route back to Valana."

Without waiting for a reply, he took Sapphira's hand and pulled her upright. Linking arms, he was true to his word, and they reached the block of insulae in less than ten minutes.

"How on earth...?" Sapphira marvelled.

"You forget, I know this site like the back of my hand. I walk some portion of it every day, so the pathways are fixed in my mind. It was simply a matter of location. Once that was established the rest slotted into the map in my head."

"Goodness," was all she could come up with in reply.

He grinned and went on to give Signore Valana a succinct description of their discovery, before showing him Sapphira's drawings which had been tucked in his satchel.

"These are excellent, and will prove extremely useful. Thank you for taking the time." Signore Valana's praise was effusive.

"It was the least I could do," she demurred.

"No, the least you could do was absolutely nothing. You are quite something, Miss Beresford. I must speak with Fiorani." He bowed and hurried off towards the Forum, where he and his fellow supervisors had co-opted one of the more intact buildings adjacent to the Temple of Jupiter, for their daily meetings.

"He will be your devoted slave for life," Leofwin posited. "Now, I do believe 'tis time for a well-deserved luncheon. I wonder how the Dynhams fared this morning."

Replete, the four separated, heading to their respective corners of the site. Sapphira wound her way to the insulae and was soon immersed in her task, while good-naturedly fending off a veritable barrage of questions about her brush with the two vagabonds.

After kneeling or squatting for the better part of three hours, Sapphira's bruised thigh was protesting — something she was determined to keep to herself. What they didn't know, could not be used against her.

Which was all well and good in theory, but her laboured stride left little to the imagination.

"You have overdone it," Hester reproved gently, seeing how awkwardly Sapphira mounted Minerva.

"I am a mite tired, is all," Sapphira hedged. "A good night's sleep, and I will be restored."

Hester tutted but did not pursue it. Her friend was prone to be intractable if she felt cornered or challenged — a trait they shared. Instead, she changed the subject asking about the investigation, which kept them occupied the entire ride home.

The busy day saw them all retiring earlier than usual. Hester could not stop yawning, quickly setting the others off, until Archer declared it a night.

"It seems futile sitting here for the sake of it. An early night is naught to be ashamed of. In fact, I think it a boon." He all but dragged his wife with him.

Hester, who had been dozing in her chair, gave him a token show of resistance, but was too exhausted to argue.

Leofwin and Sapphira were amused to hear the couple bickering their way up the steps.

"She's asleep on her feet, I fail to see why she's squabbling with him." Sapphira chortled.

"I'll hazard, 'tis because she worries about leaving us alone," Leofwin said.

"If only they knew," she replied with wide-eyed innocence.

Leofwin smothered a bark of laughter. "Would my lady be interested in a short promenade?"

"She most certainly would, kind sir."

Suddenly it was July.

The month from the middle of which all excavations at Pompeii were suspended until the weather cooled. Despite the use of temporary shelters, erected to protect the workers, the summer heat made even an hour's work intolerable.

It was also the month when the three from England would set sail for home... or would they?

Hester and Archer had yet to decide whether they preferred to extend their time in Campania for at least a year, until the baby was born, or chance the voyage. Both options came with risk, but the main reason for Hester's vacillation was Sapphira. If they remained, Sapphira would have no chaperone for the return journey.

It was an ongoing discussion. Sapphira had assured her friends she would be perfectly safe with Captain Richards in charge, quickly dismissing their suggestion she too prolong her departure until the following year.

"And overstay my welcome?" she cried one evening at dinner. "No, no. I shall return as agreed. If you choose to stay and move to different permanent lodgings, the last thing you need is a third person under your roof, which means poor Leofwin would have to suffer me as a guest for the duration. Equally inconsiderate."

"Oh, I believe my suffering would be worth it," Leofwin who was leaning back in his chair with his eyes closed, drawled, without pausing to consider the impact of his words.

Sapphira flushed bright pink, while Hester and Archer pretended they hadn't heard.

Leofwin, realising what he had said, jerked upright and apologised profusely.

On the surface, it was naught but a throwaway comment and the other three, after some cheerful ribbing, made no further mention of it.

Sapphira stored it away to be brought out and dissected later when she was on her own. In her opinion, Leofwin Colleville rarely said anything he didn't mean. She had to be careful. They had vowed this… whatever it was they were doing… was only fleeting, a fantasy which could not be permitted to spill into their real lives.

Leofwin's remark had caught her off guard. The notion he wanted her to stay sent a delicious warmth rippling through her.

No, that way heartache lies.

She wrenched her contrary brain back to the conversation, to hear Hester gush with delight.

"I am a genius."

Spluttered laughter accompanied Archer's, "Yet, so modest."

"How rude." Hester elbowed her husband. "I think I have the answer. How about this? Sapphi, if we decide to stay, you could take Sarah as chaperone." Her personal maid had accompanied the Dynhams as part of their minimal contingent of staff. "She has family close to Dynham Manor and, since her father died, she worries about her Mama. A year is a long time for her to be away. I guarantee, if I offered her the chance to return with you, she would jump at it."

"What about you?" Sapphira countered.

"I'll wager I can persuade Leo to loan me Luisa, and I daresay Amalia knows plenty of local women who might be glad of some extra coin." Hester swiped her hands together. "There, I think that is a splendid idea."

"To avoid confusing me, make your plans and remember

to let me know when you have finished reassigning my staff," Leofwin's long-suffering tone raised a chuckle.

"Did you mean what you said?" Sapphira dared broach while Leofwin and she were taking their usual stroll.

"I have said many things, Sapphira, which one in particular?" he teased.

She stopped, unhooked her arm, and faced him. "That suffering me for a year would be worth it," she mumbled, diffidently. Unable to hold his penetrating grey gaze, her eyes fell away to fixate on the sand.

A gentle finger slid under her chin to tilt her head. "I rarely say anything I do not mean," his words echoed her own thoughts.

"But..." Sapphira heard the silent 'but' as loudly as if he had bellowed it. She shuffled awkwardly; this was becoming more complicated than she had anticipated.

"Your decision should be made here." He tapped her forehead. "Not here." He tapped her chest. "Reason not emotion."

At this oblique reference to their unspoken agreement, Sapphira felt as though he had doused her in a bucket of icy water. The nebulous notion that what they shared was *not* ephemeral, that what had been tenuous was becoming tangible, evaporated.

She forced a bright smile. "Quite, reason it is."

She changed the subject and somehow managed to keep up a flow of cheerful chatter for the remainder of their walk.

In the privacy of her bedchamber, Sapphira took a long hard look at herself.

"Your dream is becoming a nightmare," she railed at her reflection. "You knew what you were getting into when you started this. It was never anything more than a moment of magic. 'Tis your own silly fault. While he might be prepared to *suffer* my presence, it is on his terms. Don't do anything as rash as introduce emotions into the equation, Sapphi." She wagged her finger at the pier glass, then turned her back, unwilling to see the expression in her too perceptive eyes.

She sat on the bed and twiddled with the cover while she ruminated. Leofwin's remark was at odds with his behaviour. He knew the ramifications of an amorous entanglement with an unwed woman, whatever spin he wanted to put on it and however far they were from London.

He was not making decisions with his head — had he been, their nightly walks would never have happened. In that case, were his feelings deeper than he dared admit?

Following that train of thought, Sapphira mused over whether this might account for his odd remark. Had this developed into more than a dalliance, doomed before ever it started?

She forced herself to look beyond the enchantment of their clandestine trysts.

The answer had been there all along.

CHAPTER TWENTY-ONE

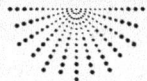

*H*ad Sapphira but known it, Leofwin was suffering a similar crisis of conscience. It seemed his mouth and his brain disconnected all too frequently when it came to Lady Sapphira Beresford.

He could picture her now, evaluating his words, words he ought to have had the perspicacity *not* to articulate.

He paced around his bedchamber, his mind in turmoil. While his head commanded him to hold fast, not to succumb to the heady emotions Sapphira elicited, his heart ridiculed his naiveté.

What was he to do?

You know exactly what to do, the voice inside his mind contested.

Which was all well and good but, as ever, when the heart is involved, it takes very little to throw good intentions into disarray.

Two weeks prior to Sapphira's departure, a mountain of mail arrived for the visitors. Most was for the Dynhams, but there were two letters for Sapphira. The first she had received since departing England.

Eager for news, she rushed to her bedchamber to read them at once.

One, from Lady Templeton, bewailed her daughter's absence. She was missing the Season. How did she expect to find a husband in the uncivilised wilds of the Italian Peninsula?

"If only you could see it, Mama. *Uncivilised...*" Sapphira pressed her lips together to suppress a rueful smile; her mother's distaste for anything... un-English, well-known.

She continued to peruse the epistle. It was doubtful Sapphira would recognise her poor dear mother upon her return, she had aged ten years with worry. On and on it went. A litany of woes, all of which related to her mother. There was no mention of her father, or Gisela and Jeremy, and not a single enquiry about Sapphira and whether her sojourn abroad had assuaged her distress.

By the time she had finished, Sapphira felt worse than she had after her run-in with the thieves. She loved her mother, but goodness she could drain one's energy.

The second letter was from Jeremy.

Seeing his name on the reverse, gave Sapphira a peculiar jolt. He hadn't featured in her thoughts for weeks. A conclusive indication, her feelings for him were not love. It was barely even affection. In fact, the more she thought about it, the more she realised, she had not missed him at all.

She pondered this revelation. For once, her sister had done her a favour. Relief, she was not bound to Jeremy for life, coursed through Sapphira.

Several instances, disregarded at the time, when they had clashed, popped into her head and she forced herself to view each one dispassionately. Shocked, she acknowledged that what she had believed to be gentlemanly concern was, in fact, disapproval.

Jeremy had not been her ally at all. He had been measuring her against some draconian standard, and she had fallen short of expectations. *I thought I knew him. How did I miss that?*

Lord Osmund was not the one who was stuffy, it was Lord Brunswick.

Something clicked in her head, like a flash of sunlight in a dark room.

Her epiphany of the previous night aside, Sapphira made a decision.

If ever she married, it must be to someone who did not want to rule, own, or control her. Who respected her. Who encouraged her to voice her opinion on any subject, no matter the significance. Who loved her beyond reason and explanation. Who, instead of quashing her eccentricities, lauded them. While she might defer to her husband, she would not submit — they would need to be equals.

As aspirations went, this fell somewhere between improbable and impossible.

A life alone was preferable to a marriage where she lost herself to suit her husband.

Dragging her attention back to the letter, Sapphira turned it in her hand, flummoxed that Jeremy had felt the need to write to her in the first place. *Was it an apology?* She dismissed that as unlikely; he was not one to admit his faults.

She tapped it against her chin.

Do I want to read it? Would it not be better to toss it in the fire?

What justification could he present to ameliorate his guilt? Was that even his motivation?

Sapphira frowned, a chill rippling across her shoulders. Guardedly, she broke the seal.

My dear Sapphira,

Excuse me… she was most definitely *not* his dear.

Doubtless, this missive will come as a surprise, and I beg you to read it rather than throw it away, which I suspect will be your inclination.

A reluctant grin tugged at Sapphira's mouth… acuity was *not* a trait generally associated with Jeremy.

Oh, for the power to turn back the clock. What I believed to be love, was nothing more than exhilaration induced by breaking the rules. Your sister was forbidden fruit and, she is something of a temptress. I was blinded by her astonishing beauty and flattered by her attention. For the first time, I felt needed. You never seemed to need me.

Sapphira could hear his whiney tone. How had she not noticed it before? *Because you too were blinded*, her inner voice piped up. She was also irritated that he blamed Gisela for his transgressions. Her lip curled in distaste.

The notion of running away to get married was exciting and, initially, we were deliriously happy. Scant days after our return home, I deduced I had made the greatest mistake of my life. Of the two of you, Gisela is the refined sister, the one whose accomplishments befitted a lady, not to mention sophisticated and charming. You must admit, gentility is not one of your finest traits.

Sapphira felt she ought to be affronted by this statement but, in truth, he was correct. That said, he made her sound like a clod-hopping milkmaid.

It is one thing to possess such qualities, quite another to exemplify them. I cannot deny, I am the envy of many a bachelor but, behind closed doors, Gisela is demanding and petulant. She assumes I shall curtail evenings at my clubs, to spend them with her. She expects to be entertained, showered with attention, pandered to. Sapphira, she is exhausting.

A caustic chuckle erupted… talk about hoist with your own petard.

I know I have made my bed, and deuce it is uncomfortable to lie on, but I have a proposal. A tad radical perhaps, but I think it will serve us both well. I miss you, Sapphira. I miss your chatter and your irreverent humour and your uninhibited ways. My mistake was not recognising your worth.
Given Gisela and I are unhappy, she may consider a divorce. Yes, it is a protracted process, but if she is amenable, might we resume our courtship where we left off?
If you are agreeable, mayhap we do not have to wait until we are wed to cement our vows.

Was this a bizarre joke? The man was a narcissist. Seriously, did he expect her, not only to forget the humiliation their elopement caused, but also be his mistress until such time as her sister could be persuaded to divorce him?

The insolence.

Sapphira could not stomach any more of this drivel. Balling up the sheet, she was on the verge of hurling it out of the window when something stopped her.

She needed to talk to Hester.

She tracked her friend to her bedchamber. Knocking, she entered at Hester's quiet, "Come in."

Hester, who was standing in the middle of the room, smiled a greeting at Sapphira.

"Good afternoon, what brings you here?"

"Excuse me for barging in, but do you have a few moments to spare? I have received a letter…" she wafted Jeremy's correspondence under Hester's nose. "It is… I am at a loss to describe *what* it is, except perhaps insulting."

Intrigued, Hester ushered Sapphira over to the two chairs positioned by the window. "Tell me."

"Better you read it, then you will see what I mean." Sapphira handed her friend the sheet.

Hester read, then reread the letter, appalled at the contents. She looked at Sapphira. "This… this…" she began.

"What does he think?" Sapphira interrupted. "That all he has to do is dangle divorce in front of me and I will fall into his palm like a… like a…"

"Ripe plum?" Hester offered.

"Yes, exactly. Like a ripe plum, desperate for whatever crumbs of affection he might cast my way." Ignoring the fact, she was mixing her metaphors. "Honestly, men, philanders the lot of them. They think all it takes is for them to crook their little finger, whisper a few sweet nothings and we will prostrate ourselves at their feet in adoration, while they play fast and loose with our hearts. Well not this lady… ohhhh, the arrogance… to toy with my emotions in so heartless a manner. Grrrr…" she fumed. "The man is a crass imbecile."

Sapphira continued her rant as she followed Hester through into her dressing room, their voices fading.

At that precise moment, Leofwin happened to be walking past Hester's door, which was slightly ajar. Catching the last part of Sapphira's tirade, his jaw fell open in shock. He came to an abrupt halt and stared at the door aghast.

Anger began to smoulder, obliterating his common sense.

So, he was some callous rake who gave no heed to her feelings, was he? Playing fast and loose, was he? Just having a bit of fun? Blithely ignoring the fact that, while he was not playing fast and loose, per se, he *was* having his cake and eating it too.

Typical. Just when he believed he had found someone with whom he could share his life, to whom he could open his heart, she proved herself to be as superficial as all the rest. He was a fool. What a relief to find out before it was too late.

Raking his hand through his hair, he stomped up to his rooms and brooded until dinner time.

Fate heaved a weary sigh... all her hard work destroyed in an instant... *oh, dear, dear, dear...*

Dinner that night was subdued. Each seemed lost in their own thoughts. Leofwin especially was cool and refused to be drawn into the desultory conversation Hester tried to sustain. Eventually she gave up, and they separated much earlier than was their habit.

The letter from Jeremy, while irksome and the cause of a bitter taste in Sapphira's mouth had proved something of a catalyst. She decided it was time for a heart to heart with

Lord Osmund. They were dancing around something profound, something she believed was worth exploring, even if confronting him left her vulnerable.

What if he declines to discuss it or denies any attraction? her head warned. *Then the memory of his touch will have to suffice. I would rather know now, than be mired in this uncertainty.*

When Sapphira descended to the terrace, there was no sign of Leofwin. The hour was late, *where was he?* Perplexed, she waited until it was obvious, he was not coming.

Now, what have I done? She dredged her brain, but nothing jumped out. Her shoulders slumped; Leofwin's absence was more eloquent than any excuses or explanations.

Furious — with herself for daring to hope, Jeremy for his grubby proposition, and Leofwin for being... well... Leofwin — she spun on her heel and, muttering balefully, marched back to her bedchamber.

A figure peeled out of the darkness.

Leofwin walked over to the edge of the terrace and stared out over the obsidian ocean. His resentment at what he had overheard continued to bubble, provoking an ungentlemanly spite. Determined *not* to join Sapphira for their usual walk, he found himself here anyway. *What am I, one of her stray dogs?*

When she crossed the tiles, he forced himself to stay hidden, interested to observe her demeanour when he failed to appear. Amazed she lingered, he was sorely tempted to step forward and confront her, to challenge her over those derogatory remarks.

He watched her expression crumple, and her shoulders sag. Heard her vexed grumbling. Sapphira's melancholy ought to have afforded him some satisfaction.

All it did was make him feel like a boor.

Sapphira roused with the dawn and took a solitary walk along the beach, her only companions — the gulls. The bay was tranquil, in stark contrast with the tumult inside her mind. She had lain awake most of the night, troubled by Leofwin's behaviour. It seemed out of character.

Mayhap he was indisposed; he had been very quiet at dinner. Thus far, they had met by happenstance, not arrangement and, given the consequences if exposed, it was conceivable either one of them might chose not to chance a rendezvous. Perhaps he was simply tired and preferred sleep to a constitutional, or his injury had caused him discomfort, or to continue their trysts was too great a risk.

There were any number of reasons.

None of which assuaged her growing apprehension he was withdrawing.

The increasingly annoying, rational voice in her head chided... *what did you expect? You are leaving in a fortnight. What benefit is there from extending your liaison, of dragging it out until the last gasp? This whole thing was a blissful illusion, time to say goodbye and move on.*

Heartsore, Sapphira retraced her steps, determined no one would know the depths of her sorrow. Maybe her lot in life was to be jilted, officially or otherwise. A wry smile hovered. Of one thing she *was* resolute... spinsterhood with all its negative connotations looked more appealing by the hour, which offered little solace.

CHAPTER TWENTY-TWO

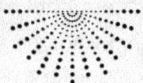

*S*apphira never knew how she managed to get through that day. From breakfast until they returned from Pompeii, she pinned a smile on her face and there it stayed. Not once did it slip… at least not in front of Leofwin.

She participated in the cheerful conversation as they rode to and from the site and maintained an unflustered demeanour at luncheon.

Only when she was among her own team did she allow it to wilt.

"Something amiss, lass?" Mr Fernsby probed when he had asked her to pass a trowel four times and she had not responded.

"Oh, I am so sorry, Mr Fernsby, here." Sheepishly, she handed him the trowel. "No, naught is amiss, I was merely woolgathering."

"All's I can say is, you must have made several bales." He studied her speculatively. "You're not worried about them thieves are yer?"

She smiled, but he noticed it did not reach her eyes. Her usual vivacity was sorely lacking.

"The thieves? No, I haven't given them a thought." Not quite true but they been demoted to second place in her head. "'Tis nothing except a tinge of sadness that I will be departing for England soon and I am torn."

"This country gets under your skin." Mr Fernsby nodded sagely. "I travelled here nigh on thirty years ago. I only intended to stay a month. I never left."

"You have not returned to England in all that time?" Sapphira was taken aback.

"No, my life is here, I am bound to this place. Leaving is not on my agenda, not until they carry me out in a box, and even then, it'll only be to the cemetery." He chuckled.

"Do you miss England? What of your family…" she paused and added delicately, "…your wife, is she with you?"

"I was fortunate to marry a local girl, Elena. She puts up with my compulsion to work on this site and I adore her from head to toe." A tall man, he twinkled down at Sapphira who felt a genuine smile crease her face for the first time that day."

"'Tis good to know there are men like you in this world."

She did not elaborate, but Mr Fernsby was a canny fellow. He had witnessed the way this young lady and Lord Osmund behaved around each other. He was also cognisant of how leery the latter was when it came to women.

The presence of a handsome and eligible marquis had set every maiden in the district a quiver but, with polite detachment, Leofwin kept them all at arm's length. Sapphira seemed to have broken through his barriers. Her wistful expression implied he had slammed them closed again.

"Plenty of us about, often right in front of your nose." He grinned and went back to digging the square he was working on.

No more was said, but Sapphira felt less despondent.

Which lasted until the evening.

The bay was suffused in gilded light when Archer strolled onto the terrace, prior to dinner, to find Leofwin already there, a glass of red wine by his elbow.

"Drink?" the marquis asked.

"Thank you." Archer took a seat and accepted the proffered glass.

The two men lit their pipes and sipped their wine, content to sit without talking, watching the sun glide towards the distant horizon.

The alchemy that was the sunset began, painting the sky a myriad hues impossible to replicate. From the blaze of orange fire where the heavens kissed the ocean, to the dazzling golden orb and its perfect fan of iridescent rays cleaving the darkening blue. From the clouds streaked with mulberry, magenta, and saffron, to the molten bronze of the sea.

Its timeless beauty stirred the soul.

Archer studied it and, rather poetically for him, mused on how the transformation mirrored life itself. Gloriously, extraordinarily, miraculously, and predictably, unpredictable.

His eyes on the spectacle, he said quietly, "What are you doing, Leo?"

"About?"

"Sapphira."

There was a lengthy silence. Archer twisted his head to see Leofwin staring out over the bay, spinning the glass around and around by its fragile stem.

"Leo?"

"There is nothing to tell." Leofwin replied curtly.

"Do not take me for a fool. Last evening, after days, nay weeks during which the rapport between Sapphi and you, has evolved from distant to affectionate, you regressed to your initial reserve. For her part, Sapphira is much too chirpy, a sign she is disquieted. What happened yesterday to cause such a reversal?"

"Naught but I have seen reason."

Archer frowned uneasily. "Seen reason? In what regard? Leo, please do not tell me you have overstepped your boundaries."

Leofwin stood up from his seat, propped himself against one of the pillars, and fixed his gaze on the wine in his glass. "You have nothing to fret about, Archer. Perhaps we stretched the rules a trifle, but 'twas a momentary lapse in judgement is all. I think she inveigled me. Suffice it to say, I am *done* with Lady Sapphira Beresford. She cannot be gone from my home soon enough. I should have trusted my instincts; women are nothing but trouble."

"*Stretched* the rules. Leofwin Colleville, good God, m—"

Tersely, Leofwin interrupted, "Credit me with some brains, Dynham, I have not besmirched her damn reputation, but I can understand why Brunswick chose her sister."

Deciding not to let Leofwin's unaccountable behaviour rankle, Sapphira headed down to the lowest level. She paused on the steps to admire the sunset, whose vivid radiance had waned to a more muted palate but was no less striking.

She breathed in the delicate fragrances drifting on the evening air, while imprinting the scene in her mind. Something about the immutable majesty of the view made the pang of parting acute. Too soon, this would be a cherished memory.

Mentally straightening her spine, she descended the last few steps. If Leofwin was alone she would demand an explanation. *Do I not deserve that much?* A bright smile on her face and a cheerful greeting on the tip of her tongue, Sapphira's approach was arrested by Leofwin's ruthless denunciation.

Frozen in place, mid-stride, Sapphira could not believe her ears. His words battered her, and she recoiled, the heat of humiliation flooding her cheeks. *What about our moonlight walks, the hours of convivial conversation? What happened to kissing me was sublime?* In that split second her dream was shattered. She spun on her heel and fled, almost bowling Hester over in her rush.

"Sapph—"

"Headache," was all Sapphira could husk, as tears clawed at her throat.

Perplexed, Hester entered the terrace looking over her shoulder. "Did Sapphira mention a headache?"

"Sapphira? She has not yet appeared." Archer said, "Why?"

"She just dashed past me looking distraught." Hester's intuition went into overdrive. Hands on hips, she jabbed a finger at the two men. "What were you two talking about?"

"I was simply reassuring your husband that he has nothing to fear regarding your charge. My intentions towards her are limited to her well-being while in my home and that is all. I have no interest in furthering our acquaintance."

"And, of course, this… errr… *opinion* was enunciated with your usual tact," she said tartly.

Leofwin had the grace to blush. "Perhaps I was less than polite but I stand by my words. Lady Sapphira has been a nice guest, but that is where our accord ends."

"Nice! *Nice?*" Hester threw up her hands. "Oh, how I itch to slap some wisdom into you. For someone with your intelligence, you can be staggeringly obtuse. I beseech you, Leo, do not let your prejudices destroy your chance at happiness." With a glare, she swept out. "I must check on Sapphi."

Fuming inwardly at the idiocy of men, Hester made her way to Sapphira's suite and knocked gently. There was no sound from within. She rapped again. "Sapphi, please open the door."

"I am fine, Hester. Please join the others. I shall see you in the morning."

Even through the door, Hester could hear the weariness in Sapphira's reply.

"Sapphi—"

"Truly, Hester. I-I require some time alone."

There was an uncompromising note in her friend's voice and Hester knew better than to press the issue. "I'll have Luisa bring you a light repast," was all she said, hearing a muffled, "Thank you."

Aware appearances were not quite what they seemed, Hester was also astute enough not to interfere... yet. This was between Leofwin and Sapphira. They were adults — or so they liked to believe — time to see whether they knew how to act like adults.

She was not about to hold her breath.

After another sleepless night, Sapphira dragged herself to breakfast looking decidedly peaky. Uncaring how unsuitable it was, she decided to wear her favourite gown. It was akin to donning armour, protection against Leofwin's resentment... however flimsy.

Hester's eyebrows shot under her fringe at the sight of her friend's impractical attire, but kept her counsel, and before long the foursome was trotting down the long driveway *en route* to Pompeii.

"What a lovely day," Sapphira remarked as they emerged from the dappled shade of the lane into the sunlight. It was already warm, promising a hot day ahead. "I pray it holds until my departure. In fact, if it might remain settled until I disembark in London, I would be most grateful." She glanced upward as she spoke.

"That is a big ask. I am not sure how much sway the good Lord has over the weather." Archer twinkled. "Although in the past, our return journeys have not been too squally."

"It will be what it will be. Calm or inclement," Leofwin intoned — somewhat pompously it must be acknowledged.

Sapphira bristled, and shifted in her saddle to put her next question to Hester. "Have you two made a decision?"

Hester's gaze swung to her husband. "We have," she replied, almost shyly. "We think staying here would be the better option. Archer has been discussing the possibility of renting a villa close by, with Leo. Apparently, there are several available. We hope to visit one or two at the weekend."

"Goodness, how splendid. I hope you are able to find a suitable abode before I leave, then I can assure your families you are both the picture of health, and your new accommodation is delightful."

"You think these two are deemed incompetent by their families?" Leofwin narrowed his eyes, waving one hand at the Dynhams.

"Beg pardon?" Baffled, Sapphira faced her host.

"To suggest you believe it necessary to *assure* their parents, implies they consider Archer and Hester incapable of something as insignificant as picking a villa. Yet somehow they have survived the rigours of travelling the world for nigh on a decade."

"Leo—" Archer began.

"No, Archer," Sapphira interrupted. "Evidently, Lord Osmund has a case of the blue devils. We must permit him to wallow. Doubtless, he has realised, his life is about to revert to its sedate norm. A magical summer, full of fun and jocularity, gone — nothing more than a dream." She used the word deliberately in hopes of jolting him out of whatever was causing him to be so fractious, accompanied by an impish grin, expecting a facetious wisecrack.

Which would have been his normal riposte.

The need to lash out, to hurt Sapphira, had Leofwin retorting bitterly, *"Dream? Magical?* Pah. In truth, I cannot wait to embrace the solitude. Three guests was one too many."

Hester's horrified gasp brought him to his senses.

He opened his mouth to apologise.

Too late.

Casting Leofwin a look that would have slayed a lesser man, Sapphira wheeled Minerva, the pair flying back along the dusty road. An impressive feat, given her choice of gown had forced her to ride side saddle that morning. Her hat tipped backwards to bounce against her neck and her hair began to unravel.

She was done.

No more head in the clouds, clinging to the possibility of a maybe. From now on, her feet would stay firmly on the ground. She had been a fool. Daring to hope. Trusting he was the one in a million who might be the perfect match. Folly. No more illusion, no more fantasy. No more being seduced by the silver tongue of a handsome man. No more...

Her vision blurred and she dashed a hand across her eyes. She would *not* cry; no man was worth her tears. She urged Minerva on, and the mare responded, rising to a gallop.

Horse and rider slithered into the stable yard, surprising the grooms, who were cleaning the loose boxes.

Sapphira dismounted and had vanished around the corner in a flurry of rich turquoise silk almost before any of them could blink.

They stared at each other in consternation, her agitation was obvious, and the antithesis of the Sapphira they had come to know. Contrary to Sapphira's belief, the staff in their entirety were cognisant of her midnight promenades with their master.

Behind closed doors, their favourite topic of discussion was whether Lord Osmund, finally, had met someone with whom he could be happy. In all the years they had worked for him, none had seen him so… carefree. Sapphira was the cause, of that they were confident.

This did not bode well.

CHAPTER TWENTY-THREE

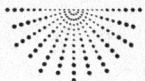

" *L*eo." Hester clutched her head, her appalled expression leaving neither man in any doubt of her dismay. "Never in my life did I... what... how could... *Leo*. Do please enlighten us as to the reason for that little display of petulance?" Her derision, withering.

His hands resting on his thighs, Leofwin bent his head. The desolation on Sapphira's face rocked him to his core, snatching his breath. He rubbed his chest in an effort to alleviate the stabbing pain in the region of his heart.

This was ludicrous. She had wounded him more savagely than the *crapaud* who had tried to kill him, and her aspersions festered, but the profound emotion she kindled in him had not diminished one iota.

It never would.

"Forgive me." He blew a resigned sigh. "I confess, Sapphira brings out the best and the worst in me. There is a contentious issue, one of which, I concede, considering her reaction, she is apparently ignorant, making my conduct incautious..." Hester's folded arms and steely gaze, had him amending that to, "…cruel, and I must right the wrong. She warrants the right to defend her actions."

"You talk in riddles, but please, do not expect me to argue." Hester, who would have tapped her foot had she not been astride a horse, swung her hand in the direction of the villa.

"What about the site?"

Hester's pursed lips informed him, in no uncertain terms, this was a woeful response.

He raised his palms in a conciliatory fashion. "'Tis a fair question."

"Given you know we are perfectly capable of finding our way there and back without escort, it is *not* a fair question, Leo," Archer tsked impatiently, as horrified as his wife. "Go, find Sapphira."

Without waiting for a reply, Archer turned his mount and clicked the reins. Hester and he continued along the road, neither gave Leofwin a backward glance.

Leofwin remained motionless for several minutes, rallying the thoughts churning through his head like a river in spate. His brutal condemnation was inexcusable.

Instead of letting emotions overrule logic, a *wise* man would have begged her to expound on her assertions, even if that meant admitting he had overheard a private conversation. Any man… any *gentleman* would collate the evidence *before* leaping to conclusions.

For a man who took pride in his objectivity, and his powers of discernment, who lauded integrity, tolerance, and dignity, Leofwin's conduct towards Sapphira demonstrated a paucity in every single attribute.

This was going to take more than a heartfelt apology.

He pointed Vulcan at the villa. The stallion — undisturbed by all this coming and going — trotted leisurely along

the dusty track, while his rider invented and discarded justification for his obnoxious remarks.

In the end, the truth was all that mattered.

Her ire dwindling, Sapphira's infuriated stride slowed, as her
internal debate spilled into a vocal flagellation. Trudging
aimlessly among the host of trees, currently blossoming in
riotous abandon to create a colourful canopy, she harangued
herself for being duped a second time.

The confusion lay in that she did not think Leofwin was a
man given to artifice. If he disliked her so much, why had he
not discontinued their walks? Why did his icy reserve melt?
To go from amity to enmity in less than an afternoon was
irrational and, while she acknowledged they had indulged in
their fair share of sparring, his harsh denigration was out of
character. Something was badly awry, but what remained
elusive. "Like his heart," she groused darkly.

Absently, she plucked a flower from a low hanging
branch, twirling it between her fingers, while marshalling
her rampant thoughts.

She slumped against the trunk of a tree. The truth of it
was inescapable. She loved Leofwin Colleville. She had been
in love with him for weeks, and neither his execrable
behaviour nor her imminent departure would alter it.

She had been living in a fool's paradise.

What a mess.

The crack of a twig underfoot snapped Sapphira's attention to the copse. Her encounter with the thieves reared up
in her mind and she could not quite suppress a shudder.
Although within screaming distance of the villa, by the time
anyone reached her...

"Lady Sapphira." A diffident voice intruded.

Leo. Her heart thudded. Even after everything he had said, he still possessed the power to undo her.

"What do you want?" She glowered.

"I am here to apologise, yet again. I spoke with—"

"Your words betray your heart, Lord Osmund," she strove to sound airy. "I was as much at fault as you. I was the one who *inveigled* you into a dalliance. I knew your aversion to the conniving females who stalked Society events, yet I dared to dream. I was naive enough to be lulled by your charm and the thrill of bending the rules."

Sapphira's tone hardened. "In truth, I should be grateful you enunciated your *lapse in judgement* before it was too late, although a gentleman would have had the decency to apprise the lady in question of his revulsion prior to announcing it to all and sundry." Flinging his own words back at him, she turned to walk away.

"*My* revulsion? What about your revulsion?"

She spun back and skewered him with furious green eyes. "What the *dickens* are you talking about? When have I *ever* given you the impression you revolted me?" Sapphira scoffed.

"Was it when I kissed you? Perhaps when I held your hand? Maybe it was when we embraced at the end of a walk, or when I risked everything to snatch an hour or two with you alone? Goodness, I had better be careful. It appears my mere presence is cause for abhorrence."

To prevent lurking sobs from spilling over, her mouth flattened into an implacable line.

"Sapphi,"

"Do *not* address me thus. You squandered that privilege when you deemed me extraneous to your bloody house party. How *could* you be so insensitive?" Sapphira raged.

"You did not stop to think of my sensitivities when you

called me a crass imbecile," Leofwin vented, his own temper fraying. "You think I am so shallow as to whisper sweet nothings in order to have you prostrate yourself at my feet?"

"Prostrate myself at yo—" About to refute his accusations, Sapphira stopped mid-sentence.

"Ahh, now the tables have tur—"
The sharp sting of her hand against his face shocked him into silence.

Stupefied, he stared at her, rubbing his cheek.
"You hit me. What the deuce?"

Sapphira's palm smarted from the blow. "You deserved it, you dunderhead. Did it cross your mind that I might have been talking about someone else? That the person I was referring to as a crass imbecile was *not* you? This... this whole fiasco is because you *eavesdropped*? Did you, for a single moment, think to *ask* me what precipitated my diatribe? What a radical notion. Nooooo... without any evidence to support your theory, you immediately assumed my remarks pertained to you.

"Well, Lord *the world revolves around me* Osmund, I shall afford you the courtesy you did not grant me and set you straight. I was talking to Hester, *in private*, about a letter I had received from *Jeremy*." Her voice rose several notches. "A letter, by the way, I would have shown you, gladly, had you given me the chance, but did you? No, instead of behaving like the intelligent nobleman you purport to be, you reverted to the grumpy marquis who thinks every woman is some kind of she-devil, out to trick him. Your outburst was reprehensible."

Her reproach bounced around Leofwin's head. Jeremy, she had been discussing *Jeremy*. Why had that not occurred to him? *Because you were afraid to trust that what Sapphira appeared to feel for you was genuine,* the voice of reason reminded. *Oh God, how the hell am I going to fix this?*

Head held high, Sapphira was weaving through the trees, her gown rippling around her in a silken cloud of turquoise.

He only had one chance. Chasing after her, he caught up as she stepped into the sunshine. Grasping one of her hands, he swivelled her around, reaching for the other to ensure she did not lose her balance and prevent her from fleeing.

"Lady Sapphira, I *am* a crass imbecile. I jumped, no… soared to conclusions without due consideration."

"Something which is becoming a habit, my lord," she mocked.

A ghost of a smile skittered across his face. "You are correct, I *should* have asked you what I had done to provoke such a tirade. That Brunswick might have been the cause never crossed my mind. In a split-second you went from my heart's desire to my heart's destroyer… and I lashed out. My behaviour has been unpardonable.

"I wish I could offer you a credible excuse, but I cannot. I have spent so long assuming the worst, it has become second nature."

He rubbed his forehead, desperately scouring his brain for the right words to rectify the biggest mistake of his life.

"I have been heedless and mean-spirited. My mother would be gravely disappointed. One among very few women whose opinion I respect. Hester is another, as are you," he added, almost as an afterthought.

"I'm honoured." Sapphira's curtsy, as sardonic as the curl of her lip.

Leofwin's brow furrowed. "I am floundering and do not know how to right this wrong, so, all I can be is forthright."

He looked her in the eye. As though carved from stone, she stared back at him, her face unreadable.

"I did not want you here." He had yet to relinquish his hold and felt her fingers flinch. He squeezed gently, gratified when she did not pull away. "A third guest, a stranger no less, upset my equilibrium. 'Tis easy hosting Hester and Archer, they are like family. They slot into my routine as though they never left, and I do not have to stand on ceremony. Moreover, there is no threat."

"*Threat?*" Sapphira blurted out, unable to stop herself.

"You know my views regarding those ladies of the *ton* on the hunt for a rich husband… any husband. A single woman — Hester's friend notwithstanding — coming to stay, troubled me. My defences were up before ever you set foot in my home. Then we met and, to my surprise, you appeared decidedly uninterested in me. It was as refreshing as it was disconcerting.

"Your candour, your repartee and dry humour, your unfeigned pleasure in your surrounds, your unqualified appreciation of Pompeii, and your staunch refusal to be cowed by my, yes, I admit it, irascibility, threw me. Hester took me to task several times, and, in truth, I could not have explained my rancour, had the good Lord himself demanded I do so," he paused.

"Until the day we visited Herculaneum."

Sapphira's brow furrowed. "What distinguished that day from the others?"

"Never mind you had the wit to fling my gibe back at me, you were terrified. Yet, instead of using it as a way to attract my attention, as would so many other women in the same distress, you pretended naught was amiss, to the extent of trivialising your panic. A trifle claustrophobic? You were rigid with fear. Your determination not to spoil the experience for the rest of us spoke volumes for your character, and I began to think I had misjudged you."

"Oh, how kind," Sapphira snorted and crossed her arms; secretly impressed he was baring his soul.

He gave a lopsided smile. "I was not wholly persuaded, but you systematically shattered every one of my defences in a manner a soldier of the realm, facing down his enemy, could not have bettered. You awoke in me emotions I presumed dead and, however hard I tried, I could not ignore them. Every day they increased, swirled, and flourished. If I believed in magic, I would allege you had bespelled me."

"*Bespelled* you? I brought it on myself, did I? 'Tis *my* fault you behaved like a numbskull?"

"No, no, please, that is not what I'm trying to say…" *this was going from the sublime to the ridiculous.*

"Then please, do make yourself clear, you lamentable man. Ohhhhh, Lamentable Leo, I like that." Sapphira chuckled suddenly. The tension in the air eased marginally.

This was getting him nowhere, but her flippancy was encouraging.

Blunt might be best.

"Sapphira, I was a blind fool. My attitude has been dubious at best, disgraceful at worst. My reasons are pathetic, and there are not enough hours in the day, in the week, to list them. My words were not a betrayal of what is in my heart, they were a shield. I do not expect you to forgive me, but I implore you to believe that my regret is sincere and from the heart. Is there any possibility we could start again?"

He held his breath.

While talking, he was positive Sapphira's outrage had begun to subside.

Sapphira's mind warred with her heart. In the rarefied world of the *ton*, men seldom admitted they were at fault in *anything* let alone matters regarded as private and personal. His apology sounded earnest and genuine. The very fact he kept tripping over his words, while making no attempt to justify his actions with platitudes or condescension was... to her chagrin... endearing.

It was the vulnerability in his gaze and the apprehension in his tone which had her heart beating her head into submission.

Ably assisted by the recollection of his sinfully seductive kisses.

He was still holding her hands. The tingle snaking along her arms was delectable.

Did she really want to retain the moral high ground to her own detriment?

No, she categorically did not.

Her departure loomed.

Could they recapture the dream?

CHAPTER TWENTY-FOUR

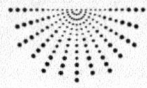

*T*hat was not to say she considered it appropriate neither did she intend to relent immediately…

"Your humble admission speaks to your valour. To reject so sincere an appeal would be ungracious…" the 'but' hovered unsaid.

While she had no mind to make him suffer for his folly… well not for too long… Sapphira gained a morsel of satisfaction when she saw him blanch.

"Sapph—"

"Hush, 'tis my turn."

He bowed.

"I was determined to scorn whatever excuse you contrived. Your disparagement of what I trusted to be a strengthening affection, inflicted an anguish more profound than Jeremy's rejection. This time, there was more at stake."

Sapphira perceived a dawning hope in the defeated grey of Leofwin's eyes and felt a corresponding elevation of her spirits.

Unbidden, she had the oddest notion there was something deeper at work here. Something elemental, as though an invisible hand was guiding them, immediately dismissing this as fanciful, ascribing it to her overwrought imagination.

"Regrettably..." she paused deliberately, suppressing a wicked snigger at the dismay he was fighting to conceal, then took pity on him, "...for my righteous indignation, your eloquence and obvious remorse made that rather more difficult than I anticipated." She nearly lost her poise at the slight relaxation of his stance but managed to school her features.

Not yet, Sapphira, not quite yet.

Before yielding her minuscule advantage, she continued loftily, "It appears we have reached an impasse. You want me to forgive your transgressions. I have yet to be convinced this is wise."

"Sapphira," Believing his hopes dashed, Leofwin with nothing left to lose, did the only other thing he could think of to persuade her. He released her hands and hauled her against him, anchoring her to his tall frame. Without giving her time to blink never mind remonstrate his temerity, he kissed her, hard.

Sapphira's thoughts careened off on multiple tangents.

You want this. Oh, how you want this, her traitorous heart encouraged.

No, he cannot erase his insults with a simple kiss, her mind refuted.

Simple... simple? her heart derided.

You are not ready to absolve him, her brain argued.

Are you sure? her heart countered.

Sapphira jerked back, and bunching her hands, battered his chest. "Leo, how dare you? I am not finished, you cannot..." her dissent muffled when he reclaimed her lips.

Her fists proving ineffectual, she considered kneeing him in his bad leg, as the now familiar euphoria ensorcelled her, banishing coherence. Briefly irritated at how easily she relented, the exquisite pleasure undulating down her spine was far preferable to bickering.

"Leo," she huffed when they came up for air. "Not fair…"

"Is it not said, the rules of fair play do not apply in love and war?" He twinkled.

"Yes but…"

"Sapphira, if you truly wish to argue," he kissed her nose, "I am happy to comply," he kissed her forehead, "but my aforementioned rule applies." He scattered featherlight kisses along her throat and across the exposed skin of her shoulder.

"Perhaps there is a third option," she husked.

He stopped his delectable journey long enough to look her in the eye. "Ahh, the lady has a solution to our dilemma. I am listening." He resumed his odyssey.

"Leo, stop, you are making my head swim." Her amusement was undeniable.

After sneaking one more body melting kiss and, with visible reluctance, he lifted his head and waited.

Sapphira tried to shepherd her thoughts, a futile exercise as they had no intention of being corralled, happily dancing a dizzying jig around her head. Not helped at all by Leofwin's heated gaze.

"I need to…" she disentangled herself, "…proximity to you, turns my brain to mush." She sent him a fierce glare, pacing to and fro in front of him.

"Perhaps there is a way to rekindle what has been lost," she began. "Yes, dreams can be ravaged by nightmares, and fantasy seems to be deceit, but the reverse is also true. Oftentimes, nightmares are eclipsed by dreams and what was deemed to be fantasy is revealed to be the truth."

Her rather erratic steps took her a short distance from Leofwin, who forced himself to remain where he was, leaning casually against a tree.

"My interlude here is drawing to a close. We entered into

this with our eyes open and our hearts impregnable. Neither of us was looking for a lifetime commitment. Courtship, marriage were not part of the bargain. So, I postulate we return to a point before this recent... errr... episode, and agree that this was, in fact, merely our illusion deviating from its predicated path. All we have to do is bring it back in line, and the dream continues until I depart. Moreover, Hester and Archer, never mind your staff and colleagues, should not have to bear the brunt of our discord."

Sapphira came to a standstill, a cascade of purple and white blossoms framing her svelte figure, her chin jutting out in challenge.

Leofwin pushed himself off the scratchy bark and stepped into the sunshine. "Your proposal has merit, but I have a question." His smile softened the formality of his response.

Sapphira arced a brow.

"Which point are we returning to? This one?" His face contorted into a grumpy grimace, incurring a smothered chuckle from Sapphira. "Or this one?" He stuck his nose in the air and swaggered, pompously, swivelling to drop a sly wink. Sapphira's laughter became a startled squeak when he gathered her to him. "Or this one?" He stole her breath in a tender kiss which quickly became fevered.

"This one..." she nodded on a croak.

Definitely this one... the ceasefire was sooooo much more fun than perpetuating hostilities.

Cool fingers collided with warm skin, searching and teasing, as lips tormented. Somehow Leofwin's jacket ended up on the dirt, quickly followed by his cravat, and the buttons on Sapphira's gown offered little resistance, delicate sleeves drifting down her arms.

The whinny of a horse penetrated impetuous senses and

the pair broke apart, trembling.

Blushing, Sapphira picked up the garments and shook off the dust. "People…" she mumbled, not very lucidly. "We ought to…"

"I could not agree more." With a dexterity that belied his injured leg, Leofwin caught Sapphira around her waist, swung her over his shoulder, and headed for the villa.

"Leo," Sapphira's shock at being manhandled thus, dissolved into giggles as she bounced like a sack of potatoes. "Are you kidnapping me?" Her words came in bursts like hiccups.

"In part," he admitted.

"*Really?*" she gasped. "Leo, put me down, I am not supposed to bend this way." Pummelling his back, to no discernible effect.

"All in good time."

"Please," she begged, "my breakfast does not appreciate such jostling."

The large flagstones marking the villa's curved frontage came into view, but Leofwin didn't slow down. Striding into the atrium, he turned right and crossed the salon, shoving through a door which opened onto a dim corridor.

Only then did he stand Sapphira on her own two feet. Giddy, she reeled, grabbing at Leofwin to prevent an ignominious fall.

"Goodness, I am all a dither," she sucked in a breath, convulsed with mirth. "Leofwin Colleville, I never did.

He steadied her. "Neither did I, but it seemed warranted."

She sobered at the glint in his eyes, and the air in the quiet hallway seemed to seethe.

"Where are we?" Sapphira had a reasonable idea but was playing for time. This was outside her experience, and she needed a clear head… *chance would be a fine thing*.

"These are my quarters. My personal domain. You are the

only person, other than Amalia and Nuncio, to be permitted beyond that door."

"Why have you brought me here?"

"I do not wish to be overheard, however inadvertently, and I want no more misunderstandings. What we share is too fragile, too precious. I might have been rather slow on the uptake, but I do not wish to waste the days we have left. That said, the dream is now yours to control."

Puzzled, Sapphira cocked her head. "I am not entirely sure I understand."

His gaze never wavered. "There are things I crave to do to you. I am besieged by an impulse to kiss you until your knees buckle, divest you of that glorious gown, uncover your body inch by delectable inch and worship you until you beg for mercy but..." he paused to brush his lips over her knuckles, "...my desires do not simply exceed the bounds of propriety; they obliterate them. Hence, the decision is in your hands."

Sapphira gulped and her colour heightened. "Errrm... I... errr..." the image his words evoked, was beguiling. *She* controlled the dream...

While unable to deny the irresistible yearning to venture beyond a kiss, this was unknown territory. She suspected their passion, once aroused, would not be slaked until... her thoughts spiralled out as heat uncoiled from her centre.

We have scarcely recovered our previous entente and here he was suggesting... her heart stuttered. *No, it is up to me. A few kisses, perhaps some slightly indecorous... exploration... hmmm... what was the harm? I am eminently sensible... I can call a halt at any moment... no problem,* studiously ignoring the unrestrained guffaws ringing in the back of her mind.

He was waiting, almost patiently.

Taking her time, she contemplated the angles and planes of his tanned face; noticing the crinkles at the corner of his eyes — laughter lines, and the errant lock of hair which fell across his forehead. Her gaze travelled down his throat to where his chest disappeared under the open neck of his well-worn cotton shirt.

Already privy to his masculinity — the vision of him walking into the sea, flickered behind her eyelids — she hungered to feel his flesh under her fingertips, to trace his muscles, to revel in the sensation of his skin against hers.

She sucked in a sharp breath.

This maelstrom of emotions, now awakened, would never abate. To surrender to her desires would give her a gift; a blessing to warm her during long, cold, lonely nights — the empty afterward.

To bargain with Leofwin for her maidenhood, to trap him into a lifetime commitment, was not her goal, but neither was she prepared to settle for anything less than this sorcery he evoked. So, given marriage no longer featured in her future... whatever her mother said...

"I am guilty of a similar inclination, but once we cross that threshold, there is no going back, and I am not referring to the door."

"Sapphira I l—"

She pressed a finger to his mouth. "No, do not say something in the heat of the moment, you are unable to retract. Even if 'tis true, what of it? I am leaving, you are staying. I cannot brave the burden which comes with that word, neither can you. Sufficient that it lingers in the air, undisclosed, yet implied."

She looked down at his hands, engulfing hers. Beautiful hands, the idea of them caressing her, adoring her was like a spark to tinder.

"Show me," she murmured.

"Show you...?" His question was more a sensual growl and a smile began to form.

"Show me how you would kiss me until my knees buckle,

divest me of my gown, uncover my body inch by — what was it? — *delectable* inch, and worship me until I am begging for mercy."

"Your wish is my command." He opened the door into a sun-drenched room, very masculine in its decor, but neat and tidy… everything in its place. Shutters pushed back, welcomed in the balmy breeze.

Underlying the fragrant air, Sapphira was sure she detected a trace of that same exotic scent, she had come to associate with Leo. More familiar to her now than her own home.

Taking Sapphira into the circle of his arms, Leofwin began his demonstration.

Sapphira kicked the door shut.

There was *nothing* lamentable about what followed.

Fate rubbed her hands together, gleefully. *Now… if the marquis would just heed her not so subtle hints…*

When Hester and Archer ventured onto the terrace that evening after a long yet profitable day at Pompeii, they were astounded to find Sapphira and Leofwin chatting as though the morning's contretemps had never happened.

"Have I gone back in time?" Hester appealed, baffled.

Sapphira could not help the rosy colour which suffused

her cheeks, but she maintained her poise, and replied gaily, "It transpired Lord Osmund's pique was more a case of wounded pride. The consequence of a misunderstanding which, as you know, all but blighted our accord.

"Thankfully, once deciphered, it was easily... errr... resolved, and I did not have to throw down the gauntlet in order to effect a reconciliation."

She sent Leofwin a wicked grin, amused to see a matching flush steal up his face.

"I never did," Hester flopped onto her favourite chair and scrutinised the couple, unknowingly echoing their words.

"Neither did we," they chorused.

"Please, let us put it behind us." Sapphira reached out to press Hester's hand, encompassing Archer in her plea. "It is done, forgotten. I do not want my last few days to be spent raking over coals already doused. Trust me, Leofwin's apology was sincere and from the heart."

Hester swung suspicious eyes between the two, recognising undercurrents, but preferred not to peel back the layers and examine them. Sometimes, ignorance was bliss.

By tacit agreement, Sapphira and Leofwin resumed their midnight promenades, along the beach. The only difference being that Leofwin did not leave Sapphira at her door.

While circumstance dictated, he return to his quarters before the household stirred — he was determined not to jeopardise Sapphira's reputation — their snatched hours of intimacy were worth the risk.

He *did* ensure she was in no doubt of his ardour, leaving her satiated and drowsy as the dawn broke.

Protected by the darkness, whispered endearments unveiled the truth in their hearts, only to be shrouded in the light of day.

CHAPTER TWENTY-FIVE

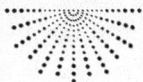

*R*omantic encounters aside, the quartet focused their attentions on Pompeii and in excavating as much as possible before the summer hiatus.

In the insulae where Sapphira had been working there were several tantalising hints of finds currently enduring the ponderous process of being removed from their long burial. Sketching every stage, she pinned her hopes on seeing them unearthed completely before she left.

Signore Fiorani had offered to escort them down to the cavern at Herculaneum, but Sapphira — despite her love of the ancient theatre — could not stomach the idea of a repeat visit. Hester and Archer, in no hurry since they were extending their stay, asked if they could postpone a second tour until later in the year... to which Signore Fiorani was quite agreeable.

Scamp turned up, punctually and often with two or three other strays in tow, every day as Sapphira was preparing to leave. His canine intuition told him this human was a soft touch. He was correct. Without fail, Sapphira had a pocket full of tasty morsels, which she distributed among the little group, whom she had named — to the good-natured despair of her comrades.

"What are we to do after you leave?" Signore Valana complained one afternoon, while Sapphira sat on a broken pillar and fed the dogs who sat in a polite queue, tails sweeping the dust.

"'Tis no hardship to feed them scraps you would otherwise throw away," she replied. "If not for Scamp here, we would have no idea who stole that mosaic and the other artefacts."

"If not for Scamp here, you would not have been injured," he countered, dryly.

"Maybe so, but they *are* here and why should they starve? They deserve life as much as the next person or creature," she reasoned.

"You are too tender-hearted." The supervisor shook his head tolerantly.

"You never know when they might return the favour," she said in all seriousness. "Now, you already know which one is Scamp. The black one is Augustus. The... errr..." she hesitated, scouring her brain for a polite term to describe the grubby off-white fur of the third creature, choosing... "flaxen one is Smudge. You see, he has that large smear going from his left eye up and around his ear, as though he rubbed his head in the coal scuttle. The little fluffy brown one is the only female among Scamp's gang. She's quite timid but getting braver every day. I named her Livia."

"You *named* them... Augustus, Livia...?" Signore Valana gawked at her. *These inglese and their animals... pazzoide... moonstruck.* He threw up his hands in benevolent resignation.

"They must have names," Sapphira maintained. "Otherwise, how do they know who you are talking to? Such beautiful faces…" she cooed at the four strays who bared their jowls in doggy grins.

"*Fantastico*," Signore Valana grumbled with gloomy sarcasm. "Every dog in the district will be on our doorstep."

"Pooh, such exaggeration." She patted his arm. "It takes nothing to be kind and I guarantee their loyalty will be worth their weight in treasures."

"Why argue with her?" Mr Fernsby joined in. "You know the lass is intractable when it comes to animals."

There were amiable nods from the cluster of experts with whom she spent the majority of her time. They had long given up telling her not to encourage the dogs and the odd cat who prowled the ruins.

"Thank you, Mr Fernsby." Sapphira dimpled. "I shall see you all on the morrow. *Ciao, a domani.*" She encompassed everyone in her farewell and sauntered along the streets to the amphitheatre.

Acknowledging she ought to take her parents a memento of her stay, Sapphira asked whether they might have one last trip to the local market due to be held the following day in a village a stone's throw from the ruins.

Already the proud owner of some daintily embroidered handkerchiefs and a collection of brightly painted pottery, she wanted to inspect the assortment of napkins and table runners. A set would make the perfect gift for her mother, while one of the ornately carved pipes she had spotted, would suit her Papa admirably.

The other three professed themselves amenable, and the next morning, a Saturday — taking the carriage so they had a way of conveying Sapphira's acquisitions — they rumbled into a bustling scene which rivalled the bazaars on Bond Street.

An hour later, laden with purchases, Sapphira was looking for Hester, when she spied a familiar profile. Confounded, she hesitated a moment too long and the object of her scrutiny turned.

By happenstance, the day was unseasonably dull. An overcast sky muted the hues of the usually verdant countryside, and a sea mist hung in the air. The sun, hidden by a layer of cloud, had resulted in a peculiar, almost ashen light.

"*You*," Nev gawked at her in shock.

Sapphira was wearing a silver-grey gown with matching spencer. A chill ran down his spine at the sight of her, silhouetted against the colourless backdrop. Was she real, or a figment of his alcohol fuelled imagination? Even her armful of packages did not convince him.

"Yer meant to be dead."

His words were heard by a number of marketgoers who spun in his direction, smelling a ruckus.

"Ha, you should check the body when you attempt to murder someone," Sapphira spat, and drawing herself up to her not inconsiderable height, strode towards him.

Hester, rounding a stall, noticed her friend bearing down on a white-faced individual, whose features she felt she ought to recognise. *Now, what was Sapphira doing?* Heaving a pained sigh, Hester pursed her lips together and gave a most unladylike whistle, waited a few seconds, then repeated the signal.

Engrossed in a debate about nothing of import, Archer

canted his head. Hester was summoning him; this couldn't be good.

"Osmund." He dropped his tankard on a little table, slapped Leofwin on the arm, and sprinted in the direction of the sound, his friend catching up as fast as his damaged leg allowed.

The market was not large, but the stalls were arranged haphazardly, and it took Archer a moment or two to locate his wife.

"Problem?" he asked, skidding to a halt beside her.

"What do you think?" She motioned towards Sapphira.

A small crowd had formed a loose circle around the two. Sapphira was announcing Nev's transgressions to anyone within hearing range, while Nev was endeavouring to appear as nothing more than an innocent bystander.

"Bad enough this *gentleman*," she sneered the word, "stole a number of artefacts from the ruins of Pompeii. He also nearly suffocated me."

Oooohs and ahhhhs rippled through the onlookers who edged closer so as not to miss any juicy gossip.

Sapphira nodded emphatically. "Yes, and that is not all. Adding injury to insult, his partner in crime, assuming me to be dead had the audacity to kick me as I lay helpless on the ground. Where is Walt by the way?" Pivoting slightly, Sapphira craned her neck to peer over the spectators. "Waaaalt, Waaaaaalt," she warbled.

"*Me*, yer accusing *me* of being a *thief*. That is a serious charge," Nev snarled. "Where's yer proof?"

"Would you like me to show everyone Walt's boot print? Because I shall." Sapphira retaliated.

The crowd leant closer still... *what an interesting morning.*

Stallholders, some in mid-transaction, had swivelled to face the disturbance.

Leofwin and Archer elbowed their way through to the centre.

"Sapphira, you cannot bare your leg for all the world to inspect," Leofwin cautioned under his breath as he grasped her arm.

"Oh, hello," she bestowed on him a dazzling smile, then wagged a finger at Nev. "Lord Osmund, I give you, your treasure hunter."

"Liar," Nev disputed.

"Villain," Sapphira retaliated.

"Interferin' trollop." Infuriated at being exposed and cornered, Nev glanced to his right for a suitable egress. A gap between two stalls looked promising. He was about to head that way when he felt a hand grip his collar and haul him backwards.

"Hey," Sapphira yelled when Nev disappeared. "Not so fast, you rogue." Forgetting she was the daughter of an earl, she barged through the crowd, catching sight of her quarry as he pelted out of the square. He was not alone. "Bloody Walt," she groused, and started to run.

Leofwin and Archer overtook Sapphira, who although a reasonably fast runner was no match for their longer stride.

"Stay with Hester," Leofwin ordered.

"Walt's with him," she shouted after them, "be careful." Relieved to see Leofwin wave an acknowledgement.

"Sapphira Beresford, what are you playing at?" Hester, hands on hips, demanded as she caught up in a much more sedate fashion.

"I could not let them walk away," Sapphira argued.

"Despite their actions the last time you encountered them? Honestly, my girl, your reckless disregard for your own safety will be the death of you, not to mention the rest of us."

"Eminently possible, but never mind that now, I must go after them. They will need all the help they can get."

"No. You are not putting yourself in harm's way again. What did you say about lightning never striking the same place twice? This is too close for comfort. Do be sensible." Hester appealed.

Her entreaty fell on deaf ears.

"Not a good idea for you to come with me. Here," Sapphira handed over her purchases, "take these to the carriage and wait there. We don't need to give Archer any more reason to be over-protective. If you see anyone we know, tell them which way we've gone." Leaving Hester no time to reply, she hitched her skirts and fled after the two men.

"Well... of all the..." Flabbergasted, Hester stared after Sapphira. Torn between wanting to follow her and staying put, prudence ordained she do as her friend bade... however galling. With a disgruntled huff, she wound her way back through the dispersing crowd to where they had left the carriage.

Sapphira might be a lady, but she had a younger brother whom she used to chase on many an occasion and, before long, had Leofwin and Archer in her sights. They were heading towards the ruin.

Obviously, Nev and Walt hoped to use the maze of streets and buildings to effect a getaway, insensible to their pursuers' familiarity with the site's layout.

She watched the earl and the marquis hurry through the *Porta di Nocera*, one of the more recently excavated gates. Directly in line with the ancient archway, she spied Vesuvius, its peak lost in the cloud, and paused to admire the beautiful juxtaposition of the man-made and the natural.

Shaking off her artistic musings, Sapphira made a beeline for the same entrance, relieved to see the two men had slowed their steps as they checked the buildings on either side of the street.

"Wait for me," she called, remembering to keep her voice low.

"Sapphi," Leofwin and Archer groaned in unison.

"You ought to have remained with Hester," Leofwin chided.

"You do not know me at all, do you?" She smiled sweetly, and linked arms with both men. "You forget, I know these two reprobates. You have caught but a glance, whereas I observed them for much longer."

"*You* forget, Dynham and I fought in the wars, where it was imperative you could retain someone's features in an instant. To know friend from foe was not always a matter of recognising the uniform." Leofwin countered.

"I am not leaving until we have detained the thieves." Sapphira's mutinous expression informed her companions that to dissuade her was an exercise in futility.

"Fine, but stay with us." He held her gaze. "I mean it Lady Sapphira. You dare to go off on your own and, when I find you, I shall put you over my knee and spank you like a naughty child."

Sapphira studied him, weighing up the pros and cons of his words. She ought to be scandalised at the notion of being spanked but, in truth, she was tempted to see whether he would make good his threat, and how severe it would be…

"*Sapphi,*"

Her name, spoken sharply brought her back to the moment. Flushing, she dipped her head. "As you wish." The gleam in her eyes at odds with her serene response.

Leofwin frowned, suspiciously. Time was of the essence, otherwise he might be tempted to question such uncustomary compliance. While he was the one giving the warning, he sensed it was she who held some, as yet undisclosed, advantage.

Putting it aside, he acceded with as much grace as he could muster. "If I cannot discourage you, *do* try to behave yourself. And no need to give me that look. You know you tend to act before you think."

About to reproach him, Sapphira saw the funny side and gave a chuckle. "Fair point."

The three carried on, peering into every exposed building, along every accessible street. Not a sign of either Walt or Nev. They reached the open rectangle of the Forum. There were several people about but, between them, Leofwin and Archer recognised all as being part of the legitimate workforce.

"I cannot imagine they would loiter in the ruin, knowing we are tracking them," Leofwin remarked.

"I concur," Archer replied. The two scanned the periphery of the Forum; nothing and no one was out of place.

"Would they be bold enough to attempt another theft?" Sapphira pondered out loud.

"They are treasure hunters, always on the lookout for easy pickings." Archer's tone, fatalistic.

"Then, mayhap they are hoping their jaunt into the site will garner them some easy pickings," she suggested. "All they have to do is follow the sounds of voices and tools to know which sections are under excavation. I doubt they would risk snatching something in broad daylight, but, if they are scouting around those areas, we might come across them."

The two men looked at each other.

"'Tis worth a quick look," Archer said.

"We have nothing to lose and the possibility of a very tidy gain," Leofwin agreed.

As the one most conversant with the site, Leofwin took the lead, and the three set off once more.

CHAPTER TWENTY-SIX

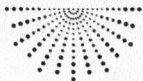

*W*ith the exception of a few hardy antiquarians, who Leofwin warned to be on the look-out, Pompeii appeared to be deserted.

There was not enough of the site uncovered to lose two people so thoroughly. The pair were more slippery than a couple of eels.

Disheartened, Sapphira had taken to kicking the stone strewn path with every step — uncaring that she was doing irreparable damage to her boots — and grumbling under her breath. Her face as miserable as the weather.

"Cheer up, lass," Mr Fernsby's comment made her jump.

"Oh, hello, I had not realised you would be here on a Saturday." She offered the semblance of a smile.

"You cannot keep me away, and Elena is visiting her mother." His droll expression suggested his presence was superfluous to requirements, which suited him just fine. "'Tis not like you to be forlorn. What happened?"

Sapphira provided a condensed version of the morning's encounter, leaving out her less than polite quarrel with Nev, concluding with, "We believe them to be somewhere in the ruins but, either they know we are hunting them and keep managing to avoid us, have decided to lay low until we quit, or, and the worst option, they are using this opportunity to steal more artefacts."

"Never mind, they will make a stupid mistake, vermin like that always do, and then we'll nab 'em," Mr Fernsby consoled.

"I just wanted them apprehended before I left," Sapphira replied. "To depart knowing they are at large and continuing their thievery galls me."

'Tis the way of the world, lass. Now, how about you come give me a hand with this 'ere plot?" He motioned his head towards a nearby doorway. "Let the gents do the looking, no point the three of you tramping around in circles." He addressed his friends, "Either of you have any problem with Miss Beresford assisting me briefly?"

Leofwin and Archer nodded distractedly, neither thinking to mention she should stay with Mr Fernsby until they came to find her. As the pair headed off, Sapphira followed Mr Fernsby into the building.

The generous proportions of the interior surprised her. Wide-eyed, she turned in the space. "Goodness, this is considerably larger than the buildings I've been working in thus far."

"Ay, this is a domus, not an insula. More like yon Osmund's villa," he flapped his hand in the general direction of the two men. "A home for wealthier families." He talked Sapphira through what they had excavated.

"This narrow passage is the vestibule and equates to the depth of the tabernae, the shops, which typically, occupy the front of most city residences," he began.

Sapphira backtracked to the entrance and glanced along the street. "So, these openings would have been shops?" she asked.

"Indeed, and although it might seem odd to us, it meant the houses were set back from the noise of the streets."

"Convenient too." She grinned.

"I imagine so. Here…" he pointed to a large sunken square in the centre of the atrium where they were standing. "…is the impluvium which is almost intact, an exciting discovery. Sadly, the roof did not withstand the weight of the pumice and collapsed…"

"That's the rain catchment pool, yes?" Sapphira asked.

"It is." He beamed. "Given the date of Vesuvius' eruption, we can say with some certainty that these were the bedchambers, or cubicula," indicating the openings at either side of the atrium, "because layouts differed over time. The lararium, the family shrine," he clarified at Sapphira's puzzled frown, "was probably tucked in there." He pointed to the left-hand corner of the atrium.

Nothing remained, but Sapphira found she could visualise it quite easily.

Here and there, she spied patches of the beautiful frescos which once adorned the walls. She stepped closer to study them; the detail and colour was extraordinary. "These are astonishing. I cannot believe they survived." She resisted the temptation to stroke the motifs, afraid of damaging the delicate paintings.

"Fortuna saw fit to favour us, and her generosity has afforded us the chance to pinpoint Roman artistic techniques. We know the date of the eruption, so when we uncover a style, we know it must have been practiced prior to AD 79, and thus provides a timeline."

Sapphira, intrigued to hear a man of science invoke the Roman goddess of luck, made do with, "How fascinating," as her response.

"It certainly is… this space was more public, a bit like a drawing room." Mr Fernsby led Sapphira through the tablinum — a study — to what would have been the peristyle courtyard. Broken pillars, now leaning at drunken angles, once supported an elegant colonnaded walkway, which surrounded a small garden, complete with shrubbery and possibly a fountain. The rooms off the garden consisted of the family's private sphere, and the domestic quarters.

"They knew how to live well, did they not?" Sapphira mused.

"The upper classes did, those less privileged lived cheek by jowl."

"Not much has changed," she reflected.

"Probably never will." He changed the subject. "Here is where we require a little help."

She greeted the two antiquarians, Penelope and Frank, whom she already knew, and who were kneeling on the ground digging out what appeared to be a brick square, its purpose lost on Sapphira. The husband-and-wife team nodded a hello, immediately returning to their task.

She looked around the room, the floor of which was higher than where she stood and sported several intriguing heaps of dirt.

"What was this room?"

"The culina..."

"Which was?"

"The kitchen."

The word tugged at something in Sapphira's brain, and she crowed, "Oh, please tell me that is the origin of culinary?"

"Correct, we'll make a Latin scholar of you yet," Mr Fernsby commended.

Sapphira blushed at his praise. "I have been reading some of Lord Osmund's history books. He owns one or two volumes in Greek and Latin with translations, and I like the challenge of working out the English stems. I confess it is less arduous to read Edward Gibbons' Decline and Fall of the Roman Empire."

"Goodness lass, that's a dry and dusty set of books to start with. Has he nothing lighter? Mind, it probably ensures you fall asleep." He chuckled.

Sapphira blushed fiery red, glad Mr Fernsby was not looking at her. Of late, sleep was sporadic at best. She focused on what he was saying.

"These piles cover caches of pottery shards. We are unearthing them layer by layer, hence the discrepancy in the floor levels. Frank and Penelope think they have located the stove," *that explained the squat shape.* "I'm hoping to get all these pieces logged by the end of the weekend. Much quicker if I excavate and you document." He eyed her hopefully.

"Then there is not a moment to waste." Sapphira stepped into the room.

Time had no meaning for Sapphira as she watched Mr Fernsby alternately brush and dig, brush and dig. For a man whose hands resembled spades, he worked with the finesse of a violinist. She sketched and scribbled as he tossed out information about the pottery.

The pieces of terracotta, darkened and stained from the soil which had protected them for so long, gradually came to light. Mr Fernsby laid them out, the different sizes becoming obvious, revealing that the larger ones, known as amphorae, usually held liquid such as garum, olive oil or wine and had a spiked base for ease of stacking.

"The smaller ones?"

"Dry goods, spices, grains." He shrugged. "It is all speculation. We have no definitive evidence, but logic plays a part, and we have mosaics and frescos along with written sources to help us make a reasonable determination."

"I wish I had known about this years ago," Sapphira sighed. "I am a complete novice and woefully uneducated."

"No lass, you are an enthusiastic beginner, with years ahead of you to finesse your knowledge," he placated.

Voices could be heard beyond the atrium.

"That is probably Lords Osmund and Dynham." Sapphira said. She leapt up, brushed the dust off her skirts — with minimal success — and hurried towards the entrance.

Engrossed, it took Mr Fernsby several minutes to register that Sapphira had not returned.

"Miss Beresford?" he called out.

The only sound was the scraping of the trowels and the murmured conversation between Frank and Penelope.

He frowned and rocked back on his haunches, listening intently, recollecting the reason she was at the site that day.

A faint unease badgered him. He pushed upright and sauntered through the ruined domus.

Of Sapphira there was no sign.

He went into the street where the sight which met his eyes brought him up short.

Two men, who Mr Fernsby recognised as Sapphira's thieves, had her in their clutches, and one held a blade to her throat.

Sheet white, Sapphira was rigid, but the condemnation spilling over her lips would have made lesser men quail.

At the same moment, Leofwin and Archer rounded the corner, instinctively removing their jackets, dropping them on the top of a broken wall.

"Come any nearer and I'll slice 'er throat." The man

holding the knife jabbed it menacingly before pressing the tip back against Sapphira's neck.

"Don't be a fool. Why add murder to your litany of crimes?" Leofwin reasoned, inching closer.

"Stay back, I have nothing to lose."

"Unhand me, Nev," Sapphira ordered, giving an experimental wriggle. Her demand revealing her captor's identity and, by extension, that of his accomplice.

"Hush your yapping," Nev barked, and tightened his grip.

"Lightning." Archer raised a brow at Sapphira pondering how on God's good earth, he was going to tell Hester.

Sapphira smiled sheepishly, grateful for his attempt to inject humour into a grave situation.

While Leofwin and Archer had Nev's attention, Mr Fernsby aimed to become one with the wall and slide along unnoticed. He got within a yard or two of Walt, and was contemplating rushing the thug, when his approach was detected.

"Back off old man," Walt snarled.

"Old man?" Mr Fernsby was insulted. "*Old man*. How old do you think I *am*?"

"Matters not, but one wrong move and I'll pound your face into the pavement." Walt threatened.

"I'd like to see you try."

"Walt, he's baiting you." A thought struck Nev. "What are you excavating in there?" He nodded at the doorway through which Sapphira and Mr Fernsby had exited. "Maybe we can barter."

"Barter? You would use me for leverage," Sapphira snapped, incensed. This was ridiculous. She stamped her foot in frustration, only to feel the cool bite of the blade under her left ear.

"There are things I could do to you, my pretty, if you would only learn to shut your mouth." Nev leered.

"There are things I could do to you too, you vile excuse of humanity, preferably involving rusty implements and a rack," she retaliated, fear making her reckless.

"Goading me, slattern?" he crooned and stroked the cool metal down her cheek.

"*Goad*? A lady does not goad." Sapphira lifted her chin. "She might trifle with, prevail upon, and perhaps, at a push," she twisted her head and all but purred into his ear, "arouse, but…" she instilled a superior note into her voice, "…never *ever* goad."

"Enough, witch, stop prevaricating. What is so important you are working on a Saturday?" He jerked his head toward the opening, addressing his question to Mr Fernsby.

"Nothing but a few shards of pottery," Mr Fernsby bit out, continuing to glower at Walt. "Certainly nothing your grubby paws or your grubbier masters would find worthy of appropriating."

"Perhaps I ought to be the judge of that." Without lowering the knife, Nev dragged Sapphira towards the doorway.

Resolved not to give Nev the upper hand in this debacle, Sapphira cast about for a way to force him to loosen his grip. She needed less than a second, her hopes dashed when she realised there was nothing within reach.

Despairing, a thought stuck her… what about herself? That she was behaving irrationally was insufficient reason to reject the notion. These men had to be stopped, by fair means or foul.

The former had been unsuccessful. Foul it was.

Sapphira gave another wiggle and shifted from foot to foot, causing Nev to adjust his grip.

"'Tis like you are asking for a beating," he snarled.

Her eyes locked with Leofwin's.

She lifted one foot and demonstrated her intent.

Leofwin knew, without a shadow of a doubt, what she planned to do. His hands were tied. To beg her not to, meant warning her captor, but keeping quiet left her more vulnerable if that was remotely possible. He had no time to ready himself, hoping his instincts, honed on the battlefield, would come to the fore.

"Watch her," he muttered to Archer from the corner of his mouth. "She is about to upset the applecart."

"The gap is too great," Archer replied, quick on the uptake.

He was right. If this went awry, Sapphira could be dead before they reached her.

He tried to reason with Nev again, to no avail.

"Enough. There is nothing to discuss. As far as I can see, this is a simple exchange. You give me something in return for your whore, and we all walk away... happy."

Even from several feet away, Leofwin saw the fury in Sapphira's green eyes.

He gave a silent groan. There was no chance this would end civilly.

For a long moment nothing happened.

Leofwin and Archer were poised, eyes fixed on Nev and Sapphira.

Mr Fernsby and Walt were sizing each other up like wild animals preparing to spring.

That Nev had the unmitigated insolence to call her a whore was the final straw for Sapphira.

With every ounce of strength she possessed, she rammed the heel of her boot into Nev's shin.

CHAPTER TWENTY-SEVEN

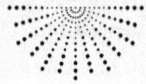

*S*hock made Nev relax his grip. Sapphira was out of his clutches and skidding across the cobblestones before he registered what she had done and meted out his punishment.

Bawling his agony, Nev slashed his knife in a vicious arc, aiming for Sapphira.

Walt spun around to aid his partner, only to find himself pitched into the dirt as Mr Fernsby launched his own assault. The two tumbled to the ground in a tangle of limbs.

Leofwin and Archer joined the fray. Archer hurried to assist Mr Fernsby, while Leofwin was intent on tackling Nev.

Eventually, the racket disturbed Frank and Penelope, normally deaf to whatever was going on around them, who rushed out of the domus, only to be warned off by Archer.

"Please track down one or more of the guards?" he puffed, in between grappling for Walt's hands. "Better that, than either of you getting hurt too."

The couple was not in their first flush of youth. Archer had no mind to place them at risk of injury, aware the guards

— burly characters one and all — were not afraid of a good brawl.

Pandemonium reigned.

Nev, his day going to hell, was not prepared to suffer the ignominy of capture. Despite Sapphira's attempt to divert his attention with her wild capers, he glimpsed Leofwin out of the corner of his eye.

Judging the distance correctly, and in an almost impossible feat of balance, he seemed to bend at the knees, then, rotating on the ball of his right foot, kicked out with his left, while jabbing the blade at the marquis.

Leofwin avoided the knife, but Nev's boot connected with his old injury causing him to stumble.

Nev gave an evil cackle. "Do yerself a favour and stay down."

"Leo." Seeing him fall sent a spasm of dread through Sapphira, alleviated somewhat when she noticed he was flexing his leg.

To give him time to get to his feet as well as to grant Archer and Mr Fernsby the best chance of overpowering Walt, she sought to draw Nev away from the skirmish.

Screeching like a banshee and hopping about in the manner of a raving lunatic, she hurled invective at Nev, all the time slowly backing away from the other four.

Ignoring the pain lancing through his shin, Nev circled ever closer, his blade glinting in the sunlight. The sneer on his face, malevolent.

"By the time I'm done with you, yer'll wish yer'd died the last time we met."

Sapphira's ear-splitting screams — loud enough to wake the long dead souls still buried under tons of rubble and volcanic ash — alerted a cluster of strays, foraging for scraps in the Forum.

As one, their heads shot up, ears pricked, and soft noses sniffed the air. Scamp in the lead, they padded swiftly and unerringly through the ruin in the direction of the cacophony.

Concentrating on separating Nev from the others, Sapphira had not thought to look behind her, inadvertently ending up jammed into a corner. Her only escape was around her pursuer. The cool from the slightly damp, lichen-covered stone, seeped through her spencer and into her gown. She pressed her palms against the immovable barrier and prayed for a miracle.

Mr Fernsby, straddling Walt's chest, dispatched Archer to find something suitable to bind the thief's wrists and ankles. Walt protested this mistreatment, declaring his innocence to anyone who cared to listen... which was no one.

Winded from his heavy fall, Leofwin was scrambling to his feet when his fingers scraped on a pile of loose dirt and gravel. His fist closed around it.

Several things happened at once.

Upright, Leofwin advanced as stealthily as he was able — given they were in a narrow street — the coarse grit in his palm forming a crumbly ball. He needed to get as close as possible because when he flung it, the dirt would scatter reducing any impact.

Nev seemed to have eyes in the back of his head, because he swivelled to halt Leofwin's progress. "What do you reckon the odds are of you getting to me, afore I get to 'er?" He stabbed the knife at the marquis.

Walt, determined not to be handed over to the authorities, gave a violent lurch, doing his damnedest to dislodge Mr Fernsby. Although unsuccessful, his ploy obliged the latter to focus all his attention on his captive.

Archer, after combing the domus for something to restrain Walt, had found nothing of use and re-emerged, yanking off his cravat.

For an instant no one moved or spoke, as though time itself was suspended.

A chorus of barks rent the curious hush as, in a flurry of fur, tails, and paws, four dogs seemed to materialise out of thin air.

Sensing the source of the danger, Scamp launched himself at Nev, teeth bared, a fierce growl rumbling in his throat. Augustus and Smudge were right behind him, jaws snapping.

Nev laboured to fend them off with his free fist and the knife, only to find little Livia — not to be left out — skipping around his ankles, nipping at his trouser leg.

"What the devil?" Nev tripped over the diminutive hound and staggered backwards. He managed to keep his footing, but his flailing hands came perilously close to inflicting some serious damage.

"Scamp, come here boy," Sapphira beseeched, terrified one of her precious strays would be injured.

A dog of courage and honour, Scamp trusted his instincts — which told him the cur could not be trusted — and ignored her plea.

To his detriment.

Leofwin could not get within two feet of Nev while the dogs circled him.

At any other time, the furore would have been comical, beating a Covent Garden farce into a cocked hat.

Not today.

Not with that knife in play.

Leofwin needed to disarm Nev, making them equal combatants.

He skirted the barking quartet, edging between them and his quarry, while evading gnashing jaws and Nev's boot.

Before he could reach Nev, a frantic Sapphira hurled herself into the melee.

Cursing, Leofwin gave up finessing his plan of attack and followed suit. The fistful of gravel, no longer a viable weapon, cascaded through his fingers.

His freedom on the line, Nev let fly. In a frenzy, he kicked out, the tip of his toe connecting with the soft underbelly of one of the dogs, flinging the creature across the ground.

A high-pitched yelp pealed around the ancient stones.

"Noooooo," Sapphira wailed as her protector made a valiant effort to rise, only to crumple, his body limp.

Wrath overrode alarm. "You sodden-witted, puke-stockinged, gut-griping, knotty-pated, plague-sore." Her recall of Shakespearian slurs bubbling for release. "You would harm an innocent animal. You... you... you... swag-bellied, onion-eyed, bat-fowling..."

"*Sapphi...*" Even amid the chaos, Archer felt he ought, at the very least, to discourage the volley of insults.

"...maggot pie," she spat. Without thought for the consequences, Sapphira flew at Nev, clawing his face and neck, drawing blood.

"Damn bitch," he roared, lashing out to deflect her onslaught. His knuckles bounced off her temple, sending her spinning, and throwing her off balance.

That gave Leofwin the opportunity he needed, and the two men clashed.

The combination of snarling dogs, puffed expletives, harsh grunts, and the sickening thunk of fists against flesh, produced a symphony of sorts — although, admittedly, somewhat discordant.

Preferring a less... grating melody, Sapphira tried to ignore it, her fear for the strays rapidly overtaken by her fear for Leofwin.

Powerless to render the marquis any aid, she went to check on Scamp. Running her hands over his fur, she probed for what she did not know. The creature did not flinch or whine under her gentle examination, leading her to believe he had avoided anything more serious than some bruising.

Scamp pushed his head into her hand, and she stroked him absently, her attention on the two men. They were evenly matched, but Leofwin was a gentleman, whereas his adversary most decidedly was not — something on which the thief capitalised.

All Nev cared about was absconding without losing a limb... or worse. If that meant inflicting a little damage on the opposition, so be it.

Two of the guards rounded the corner into the street at a run, Frank on their heels, flexing their knuckles in anticipation of a decent scuffle. Walt howled his support for Nev in between spewing abuse at Archer and Mr Fernsby.

"Be careful," Sapphira exhorted, as the pair edged closer. "He has a knife." She pointed at Nev.

"Makes it more fun." One of them, she thought his name was Matteo, grinned wolfishly. "Eh, Ruben?"

The second guard nodded, his sombre face warming slightly.

Now it was three against one, Sapphira's panic dissipated. Glad to be sitting on the ground — her legs didn't seem disposed to bear her weight — she registered that the side of her head hurt.

Gingerly, she traced the beginnings of a lump at her hairline. Generally peaceable, Sapphira was possessed with an unchristian impulse to darken Nev's daylights and hoped Leofwin would save her the trouble.

A muffled curse banished a creeping weariness, and propelled Sapphira to her feet. To her horror she spied a telltale red stain marring the sleeve of Leofwin's shirt, testament to Nev's desperation.

"Back off and I'll let yer live," Nev taunted, the knife whizzing close to Leofwin's throat.

"Ha, I've survived worse than you. Have you ever attended a ball in the London Season?" Leofwin jerked backwards and, pivoting on the balls of his feet, snagged Nev around the waist, dragging him to the ground. They rolled over and over, pummelling each other, mercilessly.

The knife flew out of Nev's hand and bounced across the stones to land harmlessly in the gutter.

The dogs — except Scamp, whose tail thumped the dirt in canine support — danced around the pair, barking madly, biting anything that came within reach, regardless of whether it was friend or foe.

Matteo and Ruben, their intervention foiled by the antics of the strays — one false step and they would be eating dirt — set about plucking the creatures out of the fracas.

Carried one by one to where Sapphira was sitting, each dog was set down and adjured to stay — an order, no one expected them to keep. Verified when — after a quick sniff at Scamp, and a cocked eye at Sapphira — they turned tail and, with a hauteur exceeding that of royalty, strutted back to the centre of the action.

Despite the gravity of the situation, the ridiculous scene struck Sapphira as extremely funny, and she convulsed with laughter. Not the most auspicious reaction in the circumstances, but hysteria may well have played a part.

Mistaking her merriment for mockery, Nev lost the last vestiges of his control. He attacked Leofwin with renewed vigour and, so focused were the observers on making sure the dogs did not suffer a wayward fist, or that Walt somehow evaded the clutches of his custodians, they failed to register Nev's intent.

Inch by inch, he guided his tussle with Leofwin closer to the knife. The knife everyone had forgotten about. The two guards were itching to participate, but the risk of hitting the wrong combatant and allowing the guilty party to evade capture was too great. They hoped as one tired they could step into the breach and finish it.

Leofwin's old war injury plagued him, draining his strength.

Nev, noticing his opponent was favouring his right leg, acted. He kicked Leofwin's foot out from under him. The marquis fell backwards, hitting his head on the unforgiving grey stone of the street.

He did not get up.

"Leofwin," Sapphira shrieked. "You've killed him, you murderous coward." White hot fury licked along her veins, as she drew herself up to her full height and faced Nev.

Before either Matteo or Ruben could blink, let alone stop her, Sapphira hitched her skirts, and started to run. Nev, his window of opportunity opened, grabbed the knife, and legged it.

"*Demente!* These *inglesi*, are all *demente*," Matteo groaned. Instructing Ruben to tend to Leofwin, Matteo bolted after them, three strays on his heels.

Boots, ankle-length gowns, and a foot chase do not mix,

and Sapphira quickly lost ground to Nev, but Matteo and the dogs had no such problem.

Anticipating Nev would aim for the *Porta Sarno* — currently, the least used of the gates — and being far more familiar with the layout of the site than the thief, Matteo predicted the likely path and opted for a short cut.

Sapphira trailing in his wake, the guard sped along the excavated streets, dodging debris, coming out onto Via dell'Abbondanza.

No sign of Nev. Frowning, Matteo listened, but all that met his ears was silence. The dogs congregated by his feet; heads cocked in anticipation of more games.

He heard an outraged and very unladylike bellow.

"*Oi*. Do not think you can get away with your crimes, you reprehensible…" there was a long pause then a spluttered, "…whoreson."

Matteo didn't know whether to be shocked or amused. It sounded as though Miss Beresford had scoured her brain for the worst epithet she could find and then wanted to say it as quickly as possible. He was impressed with her knowledge of colourful language. She could teach his mates a thing or two.

Chuckling, he tracked her outraged tones to a lane undergoing excavation, dogs trotting alongside. It was a dead end. More an alcove than a street, less than ten feet had been dug out and, since nothing of note had been uncovered to date, duly abandoned for the current season.

It meant Nev had nowhere to go, unless he removed the obstacle preventing his flight — which happened to be Sapphira.

Sapphira was wielding a large branch, goodness knew where she had found it, but she brandished it with determination.

"Go on, try it, you brigand," she taunted as Matteo loomed up alongside. "Oh, praise the good Lord you are here,

Matteo. Please remove this... this... this... rat to somewhere more fitting." She switched her gaze from Nev to Matteo, then saw the dogs. The branch dipped downwards. "Oh, you precious poppets." Her endearment eliciting a forest of wagging tails.

Like the snake he was, Nev slipped past them.

"You..." this time words failed Sapphira. In a fit of pique, she pitched the makeshift weapon against the wall of hard-packed lava, whereupon it disintegrated. "So much for that being any use," she complained. "That man could get through where a draught cannot. If this wasn't so serious, it would be hilarious."

She wafted her hands. "Go, go, we are wasting daylight."

CHAPTER TWENTY-EIGHT

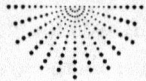

The motley gang — consisting of guard, lady, and three strays — hightailed it after Nev who looked as though he was doubling back to the original scene.

An illogical option, but since nothing pertaining to this chase was logical, neither Sapphira nor Matteo questioned it.

On their approach, Matteo gave a sharp whistle of warning and barrelled into the street, coming to a stop so suddenly, Sapphira collided with his very solid frame.

"Ooof," she panted and peered around him.

Leofwin was on his knees, his body angled over Nev, who lay in front of him, the hilt of a knife protruding from his stomach. Ruben was standing alongside, raking a hand through his shaggy hair.

Panic stricken, and with no regard to the danger, Sapphira dodged around Matteo, only to be halted when large hands spanned her waist.

"No, signorina, wait here." Uncaring how inappropriate it was, Matteo hoisted her bodily, swung her around, stood her on the raised path next to an open-mouthed Frank and Penelope, and strode forward.

Augustus, Smudge, and Livia whined, pacing restlessly. Scamp, comfortable where he lay, woofed, his feathery tail swishing back and forth.

Sapphira gave the huddle of people in the middle of the street a wide berth to check on her furry champion who, she was certain, grinned a salutation.

Sitting on the edge of the path, which was high enough that her feet didn't reach the road, she strained to distinguish who was speaking.

In between spewing profanities, Walt was begging his partner to get up.

Archer and Mr Fernsby suggested he ought to shut his damned mouth, or they might feel moved to shut it for him — a threat which fell on deaf ears.

Ruben helped Leofwin to his feet. As he straightened up, more slowly than Sapphira would have liked, it appeared he had suffered a grievous injury.

A long tear in his sleeve exposed a cut from which blood oozed to trickle down his arm and drip off his fingertips, but that was minor compared with the blood congealing on the breast of his shirt.

"Leofwin. What the *hell?*" Sapphira screeched the oath.

Hearing the fright in her voice, Leofwin glanced down. "Not all mine, I'm pleased to say," he smiled wearily.

She flew over to fling her arms around him. "Leo you could have been…"

"But I wasn't." He hugged her close, dropping a kiss on her dishevelled hair.

A ghastly gurgle interrupted them, and a hand reached out to grip Sapphira's ankle.

Shuddering, she jerked her foot away. "Release me, you cad." She glared at the dying man. "You have a blade in your belly, how are you still breathing?" Putting her thoughts into words before she realised. "Oh, that was cruel." She clapped a hand over her mouth.

Nev laughed, a sound devoid of mirth. "Seems like me luck's run out."

Sapphira stared down at him.

By rights, she ought to be shocked, terrified, be overcome by a fit of the vapours but she had nothing left. Later… later when the full ramifications of the event registered, she would probably suffer a glut of nightmares, but all she felt right at this moment was hollow.

She possessed no medical knowledge but to her untrained eye, the gaping wound looked devastating. Blood pooled round Nev's body, draining away along the groves between the large grey cobbles, the pattern reminiscent of a huge and gruesome spider's web.

"Is there anything we can do?" she asked Leofwin in undertones.

He shook his head. "If I was feeling generous, we could make him comfortable, but he forfeited that privilege weeks ago." His expression, inscrutable.

It sounded brutal, but Sapphira conceded it was nothing more than Nev deserved. He would have injured or killed all of them without compunction to keep his freedom. Her head fought with her heart, as everything Nev had done careened through her brain.

His perfidy was indefensible, and her wrath simmered, yet her innate sense of honour refused to condone turning her back on a dying man.

Nettled by how easily she permitted sympathy to overtake ire, Sapphira gave a resigned tut. She knelt on the cold stones, as Ruben placed a neatly folded piece of thick cloth over the wound to staunch the bleeding. Frank appeared at the other side of Nev holding a cup of what smelt like the local wine.

Carefully, she elevated Nev's head to offer him the cup. Frowning in confusion at this act of kindness, he took a sip but, when he swallowed, it bubbled back up mingled with dark red blood to spill over his lips.

He grunted. "Nothing doin'," he husked.

Sapphira caught Archer's eye and nodded to the jackets still draped over the wall a little further down the street. Interpreting her gesture correctly, he collected both and bundled them into a pillow. Sapphira eased them under Nev's head.

"Gawd but you are the most unpredictable chit, I've ever 'ad the misfortune to meet," he griped. "Now I am in your bloody debt."

The disgust on Nev's face pulled a weak chuckle from Sapphira. "If you like I can make us even, by helping you on your way?" she teased. "A quick twist of that knife and you'll be sailing across the Styx."

"The Styx?"

"Yes, the river across which Charon ferries you to reach the Underworld. What?" At Nev's grimace, "You think you have any chance of being welcomed into heaven? Tsk, I can hear the hilarity of the angels from here. Hades will be rubbing his hands with glee knowing such a scoundrel is about to enter his realm." Sapphira mustered up a wicked twinkle.

"Better'an all them do-gooders, I s'pose," he strove to sound cheery, but his voice was failing along with his life.

The cloth covering his wound had turned dark red and blood oozed out from underneath the folds. Unwilling to cause Nev any more pain, Sapphira let it be. She closed her

261

eyes briefly, amazed he was still talking, not suspecting it was fear making him loquacious.

To stop speaking gave death a foothold, and he wasn't ready.

She took his hand and squeezed lightly. "Let go, Nev, shut your eyes and let go. I know you are scared but, on my honour, I will hold your hand until your spirit is free."

Even Walt had fallen silent. All eyes were fixed on the man and woman in the middle of an ancient street. Two people from opposite ends of society, forever bound by one moment of madness.

"I want to curse you up and down this ruin for the distress you caused me," Sapphira murmured contemplatively. "Never mind *my* physical injuries, you and your kind are doing untold damage to places like Pompeii. You are destroying wonders of immeasurable magnitude for what? A few silver coins? You are no better than Judas."

"If this is your idea of distracting me, you need a few more lessons." Nev coughed and scarlet droplets sprayed Sapphira's gown.

"Just making sure you are listening," she countered, dryly.

"Please, my lady, do go on." His rueful smirk softening the lines of pain etched on his face.

"Why, thank you." She pretended to curtsy. "I was about to say, while I *want* to curse you, I cannot. Your life is wasted, and you cannot take your coin with you. What was the point? You would have been better employed applying your acuity to honest work. Think on that. I am saddened by the futility of it all, which leaves me unable to condemn you... an eternity in hell will do that for me."

While she was speaking, she noticed his skin, already waxen was turning a sickly, ash grey, his breathing — hoarse and shallow. Sapphira shot a pleading glance at those around her, their expressions told her what was about to happen.

Leofwin took a step, as though to join her, but she shook her head. This was between Nev and her.

Sapphira, who although unquestionably spirited and courageous, was also sheltered. She had never seen a dead body, let alone held the hand of a person who was dying. Half of her wanted to scream and run, while the other half was secretly proud, she hadn't.

Plastering a smile on her face, she kept up a flow of bright chatter about anything and nothing.

The sombre grey of the day matched the pervading mood of the assembly. The very air around them seemed imbued with melancholy, not a bird sang, nor a dog whined. The four strays were curled up together, surveying the tableau with watchful eyes.

Nobody moved. Like the ruins they were among, they had become a scene frozen in time.

After what seemed an age, though it was less than half an hour, Nev's breathing changed to an odd wheezing rattle. His lids fluttered open, and he met Sapphira's calm gaze.

No words were necessary.

Sapphira reached out to twitch a few strands of hair off Nev's forehead and heard a faint rasp.

"Yer not bad for a lady."

She chuckled. "You're not bad for a blackguard."

His grip slackened. A flash of abject terror contorted his features, then his gaze dimmed, and his head lolled to one side.

"Sleep well, Nev. I hope the underworld appreciates the calibre of its newest guest."

With nary a sigh, he died.

As one the dogs lifted their heads and howled. A

mournful lament, which — Sapphira mused, less than rationally — conveyed Nev's spirit to its final destination.

The next instant, Leofwin was at Sapphira's side, helping her to her feet. Her legs ached from kneeling on the hard stones, and tears spilled down her face like a spring deluge. A distress she could not fathom rent her heart.

Nev was no angel, he was a corrupt villain who would have done anything to avoid capture, but she was positive she had spied something in those last moments, a minuscule pinprick of humanity.

Losing his life before he had a chance to redeem himself was, to Sapphira, a life squandered. Then again, he hadn't apologised or given any sign of regret. In fact, she mused cynically, galled his activities had been disrupted seemed to be Nev's overriding emotion.

As Leofwin bore her away, she glanced over her shoulder. Matteo and Ruben blocked her view as they began the task of removing Nev's body. Archer and Mr Fernsby were dealing with Walt, while Penelope and Frank just stared.

The enormity of the situation hit her.

"Leo…" the world teetered and, to her everlasting mortification, Sapphira succumbed to the darkness of oblivion.

Sapphira had no awareness of the ensuing bustle of activity, which began so suddenly it was as though everyone had woken from a trance.

Ruben disappeared to locate a suitable method of transportation, while Matteo hunted down something in which to wrap the corpse.

Archer hastened to find Hester and their carriage. Mr Fernsby dragged Walt... who bemoaned his woes to anyone prepared to listen — still no one... upright, then helped Frank fill buckets at one of the water fountains dotted around the site, incredibly, operational after centuries buried under tons of lava, to swill the street.

Penelope, normally absent minded about matters pertaining to anything beyond the confines of Pompeii, sat with Sapphira and Leofwin. Conceding it was like shutting the stable door after the horse had bolted, she was unwilling for Sapphira's reputation to suffer irreparable damage. Rumours had a habit of crossing oceans faster than the westerly winds.

Four dogs whose intuition told them the danger had passed, stretched out in the sun, and dozed, although Scamp kept one leery eye on proceedings.

A voice close to her ear and a cool hand on her cheek, pierced Sapphira's consciousness. She grumbled incoherently about sleeping, but the speaker persisted. Swimming up through what felt like layers of fog, she prised open her eyes, to meet Hester's anxious gaze.

"Hester?" she mumbled, although it sounded more like, "Hermumphr?" Her lids drifting closed.

"Seems you cannot be trusted not to find trouble, even when under the protection of two esteemed gentleman," She heard Hester chide, wryly.

"Sorry, so sorry." She forced her eyes open. "Tired."

"How about we get you home and you can take a nap?" Hester spoke soothingly, as though to a crotchety child.

"Home, how nice." Sapphira allowed herself to be drawn upright, unable to shake off the lethargy which swamped her. "Leo..."

"Is right here, come on, let's find the carriage," Hester coaxed.

Blindly, Sapphira took a few steps, desperately wishing she was already in bed. A breeze swirled along the street. Its cool edge with a hint of rain expelled the lingering daze, and her head cleared.

"Oh," tilting her face upwards, she savoured the damp, refreshing air. "That's better. Goodness, what a pitiful excuse for a lady I am being."

"Do not denigrate yourself, Sapphi. Your fortitude in execrable circumstances was remarkable." Leofwin spoke from her other side.

She turned to look at him. "You were hurt. You need... Hester, he needs..."

"Amalia will tend to my scratches at home," he assured. "Stop fretting." He snuck a kiss to her cheek, ignoring Hester's knitted brows.

"What will happen to the bod... Nev," she asked.

"He will be removed from the site and buried quietly."

"How...?" She had no need to spell it out.

"When Nev charged into the street, Archer stepped out to intercept him. He, Nev, swerved coming within my reach. I got a hold of his jacket but, somehow, he squirmed out of it, flailing his knife, which is how I got this," he nodded at his bloodied shirt, "and threatened Mr Fernsby with a gruesome death if he didn't release Walt."

And explained why he came back this way, Sapphira thought.

"Needless to state we were not prepared to accede to his demands, which displeased him..."

Sapphira's lips quirked. *Understatement of the decade.*

"...he spun around and tripped over an uneven cobble. He staggered, then toppled over, although how he managed to stab himself is beyond me, it didn't seem possible. The whole thing was over almost before it had begun. Freak accident, or divine intervention."

Leofwin fell silent, his gaze fixed on the dark stain.

It was what it was. Nev's death was self-inflicted. No one would be blamed or held accountable; a fact, which came as some relief to those involved. Taking a life left its mark, whatever the circumstances and however justifiable.

"And Walt?" Sapphira pressed after a moment of quiet.

"That is for the local magistrate to decide." Leofwin pursed his lips. "Bearing in mind his actions resulted in injury to two members of the British nobility, one of whom is a lady, the penalty ought to be stringent, but the decision is out of our hands.

"The wheels of justice grind exceedingly slow here, crime is rare. You will be safely home on English soil by the time any hearing is convened. Perhaps if you were prepared to write a statement concerning your part in the matter, it could be submitted among the other evidence."

"You think there is a chance he might evade confinement?" Sapphira fumed.

Leofwin shrugged his shoulders philosophically. "Many do, but this is different. A fatality is not as easily swept under the carpet as a robbery."

The *Porta Nocera* came into view. Sapphira paused and stared down the ancient road to the gate before swivelling around to admire Vesuvius, the cloud dispersing.

In her heart, she acknowledged this was her last visit to the ruin. Glad to have been instrumental in thwarting a thieving duo, that her final memory of this awe-inspiring place was marred by death, left her disconsolate.

Mayhap it was fitting — given Pompeii's history.

CHAPTER TWENTY-NINE

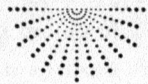

*I*n the immediate aftermath, Sapphira struggled to regain her equilibrium, which irritated her; she had suffered nothing more than a sore head.

The slightest noise made her jump and, for a day or two, she was subdued. Nightmares disturbed her rest, not even Leofwin's embrace was sufficient to extinguish them, leaving her peevish.

The tranquillity of the villa, combined with restorative walks along the shore, worked their magic.

Her natural resilience revived, and her vivacity resurfaced — possibly boosted when Mr Fernsby turned up with four inquisitive strays, who took up residence around the villa as though born to do so.

At Hester's insistence, Dr Guarino was summoned.

"The inhabitants of the Villa dei Fiore seem destined to attract disaster," the affable medic muttered while he inspected Sapphira's head.

"Young lady, the knock to your temple has not caused any lasting damage. The odd headache ought to be the worst of it and should subside in a day or two. If they do not, send for me. Perhaps this is a lesson not to catapult yourself into dire situations."

Apprised of the circumstances behind his patients' injuries, he studied Sapphira over the rims of his spectacles until she reddened and nodded sheepishly.

"I promise to do my best," she offered, with which Dr Guarino had to be satisfied.

He gave a resigned grunt and bustled Leofwin to the privacy of his chambers. A thorough examination revealed more scrapes and contusions than the doctor could count, but Leofwin's leg had survived, almost intact, and the lacerations to his chest and arm, although nasty to look at were, thankfully, not deep.

The advice was to rest.

"It is the quickest cure. Short walks to avoid your muscles seizing up, maybe even an occasional swim, but no more. Apply this salve regularly, it contains arnica and will help reduce the discolouration and soreness. Rest and time, Osmund. Rest and time." Dr Guarino handed Leofwin a pot which had a subtle sage-like fragrance.

Given he resembled a walking or rather hobbling mass of bruises and various aches, Leofwin complied. He *was* heard to grumble that with all these bloody unctions, he would smell like a damned brothel. Nobody took any notice.

The four friends dissected the affair in detail, and at length. While not something they could forget, they relegated the incident to the far reaches of their minds.

Granting the dreadful episode, the luxury of dominating their thoughts attributed a power unmerited and, neither Nev nor Walt deserved that degree of attention.

They *did* return to Pompeii. Leofwin deemed it imperative Sapphira walk the site unhindered by unnerving undercurrents incited by the thieves.

It afforded Sapphira the opportunity to extend her gratitude to Signores Fiorani and Valana, and Mr Fernsby, as well as everyone else who had guided and taught her during her stay. It was a bittersweet day, but one she cherished all the same.

"We'll see you soon," Mr Fernsby said when they farewelled each other.

"You sound very confident," Sapphira smiled at the conviction in his tone.

"That I am." He bowed. "Before the year's out I reckon."

Sapphira grasped his hand. "Thank you for everything," she whispered. "I wish I had your confidence."

"Fortuna does not sit idle," came Mr Fernsby's considered response. "I'll hark back to this conversation when next we meet."

"Should I be so lucky, I shall be glad to be reminded." Sapphira chuckled.

Now it was the night before her departure.

To Hester's consternation, Sapphira had begged that only the grooms who would bring the coach back, accompany the meagre entourage to Naples.

The parting would be hard enough, to say goodbye on a dockside was more than she could bear. As she was leaving early in the morning, rather than disturb the household, Sapphira had farewelled her friends amid tears and avowals to write as often as possible.

Her final good-bye would be private.

There was just one small task she wanted to complete first.

Sapphira leant on the railing of *The Trident*, the same ship which had brought her here to Naples. It was nearing midday, and she was thankful some of the sails were being unfurled in readiness, throwing her portion of the deck into shade.

The sun blazed down from a cloudless sky whose dazzling cerulean hue matched the glistening water below. From her vantage point, Vesuvius towered in majestic splendour like a queen.

The distant mountain ranges, floating ethereally in the hazy summer light — her courtiers. The colours seemed especially vibrant, as though putting on a show to ensure she would never forget... as if there was the slightest chance.

It took everything she had to remain on board. The urge to dart down the gangplank and chase after the Osmund carriage was almost irresistible.

The travellers had left the villa in the cool of the dawn. Determined not to weep, Sapphira had clamped her lips together, and fixed a stoic gaze on the dearly familiar countryside, letting Sarah's nervous chatter flow over her.

The farther they rode, the more her heart cracked.

Her mind wandered to the previous night. It had been everything she desired and more. At once the seduced and the seducer, Sapphira poured her love into every touch, every kiss, as Leofwin transported her to the heavens again and again, before she returned the favour with relish.

They fell asleep entangled together, but Sapphira had woken in the early hours and slumber eluded her. Carefully levering herself up onto one elbow, she had studied Leofwin in the light of the waning moon.

He had asked her to stay, his methods of persuasion able

to spark delectable shivers even now. Save a minuscule — and to some unimportant, admission — Sapphira would have assented in a heartbeat.

Three words neither of them had uttered, not even in the throes of passion. Three words which had remained stubbornly elusive.

I love you.

She believed Leofwin's affection mirrored hers, and so many times the declaration almost flew off her tongue, yet she always held back.

They had made a deal.

That their *agreement*, negotiated on a moonlit beach weeks ago, had stepped out of a dream and into reality was immaterial. The admission was *not* part of that deal, however profound and immutable.

She heard the captain sound an order.

It was time to wake up.

Leofwin stirred, unsure what had roused him. The sun through his open window told him he had overslept. He rolled over to kiss Sapphira, to find her gone.

Dammit, when did she leave? He wanted to try one last time to convince her to stay. He had done everything in his power last night to demonstrate the depth of his feelings.

Not quite everything, his inner voice taunted.

With a groan, he flung back the covers and hopped out of bed. Throwing on his banyan, he rushed to the door, only to be halted by a sheet of paper bearing his name, propped on his chest of drawers. Frowning, he unfolded and scanned it quickly, before sinking onto the adjacent chair to read it properly.

My darling, Leofwin,

He was her darling? A warm tingle began to uncoil from the tips of his toes

'Tis time to go, and there is much left unsaid. To pen my thoughts might seem spineless, but a letter affords me the chance to express what is in my heart, unhindered by etiquette.
I was poised, quill in hand when all my fine words, the perfect balance of erudite and entertaining, deserted me, along with coherence. So, permit me to crave your indulgence.

When I set sail from England, I could not imagine what Fate had in store. Two, potentially onerous, months in a far-off land, turned out to be extraordinary, and opened my eyes to more than just a ruined site. Two months of spirited debate, quiet conversation, and fiery dissension. Two months of expanding my knowledge about all things ancient, of challenges, and new experiences... and, perhaps, a fraction more excitement than is healthy.

He heard her wry tone, and his lips twitched.

Two months when misjudgements and misconceptions nearly destroyed a blossoming romance. Two months of laughter, joy, and fun. Utterly liberating.
Of all these incredible moments, my most cherished were those spent with you. Secret hours just being together, learning about each other, discovering why we are who we are. Nights of unbridled desire, sharing a passion which exceeded my wildest dreams.

'Tis time to go.
Our hello was easy, not so our goodbye.

Farewell. A simple word yet loaded with meaning. On the surface,
'tis a wish of happiness upon parting, but delve deeper and you find
it is also hope, gratitude, an end, and a beginning, and... for me... a
heartbreak.
Shakespeare expresses it perfectly... parting is such sweet sorrow.
An ache, time and distance will never erase, makes me brave
enough to bare my soul.

You are the most exasperating, infuriating, and obdurate man I
have ever met, but you are also tender, compassionate, and kind.
You derive gleeful delight in upsetting my equilibrium or driving
me to distraction, yet you are also the one who took me to paradise.

You are unique among men, Leofwin Colleville, Marquis of
Osmund, and I love you, with a love imperishable.

Simply put, I would walk the world with you.
Sapphi

He gripped the paper, her words cascading through his head. She loved him. Sapphira loved him, and he had let her go.

"Fool," he castigated himself. "She's gone because you are a lily-livered paltroon. All you had to do was tell her you love her. Did you? No, not once, even though you do, indelibly. You knew she felt the same. No lady gives herself to a man, the way Sapphira gave herself to you, on a whim. Yes, she knew the consequences, but so did you. A gentleman would have curbed his ardour or proposed."

The memory of Sapphira's touch sent a surge of infinitesimal vibrations undulating through him. *How could I have been so stupid as to let her go?*

He palmed his forehead, and barged out of the room, yelling for Nuncio.

A rumpled Archer appeared, asking what all the fuss was about. Listening to Leofwin's abridged version, he folded his arms and studied his friend.

"Fool."

"Yes, thank you. Tell me something I don't know," Leofwin grunted.

"Go get her."

"Beg pardon?"

"You heard. Go on, saddle up. Fortuna might be feeling generous. The ship sails on the tide. I think around noon.

Leofwin glanced at the grandfather clock in the corner. It was nearly eleven.

"Stop thinking and act." Archer shooed Leofwin out of the salon and into his bedchamber. "Wash, dress, ride. Food can wait."

Without waiting for Leofwin's response, he traipsed back down the steps, to find Hester leaning on their bedroom door. She crooked an eyebrow in greeting.

"Leo," he said.

"About time."

Following the route Sapphira had taken hours earlier, Leofwin rode like a man possessed, crossing paths with his own carriage halfway there. Precious moments wasted while he reined in Vulcan to speak to his grooms, then he was off again.

The stallion slowed as they traversed the port, looking for *The Trident's* berth. One of the longshoremen directed Leofwin to the huge L-shaped pier and, ignoring aggrieved shouts from the dockhands berating his behaviour in so risky a place, Leofwin coaxed Vulcan into a canter.

Horse and rider slithered to an ungainly halt at the end of the wharf to see the ship carrying Sapphira, gliding away, the mainsails unfurling to billow in great curves of white canvas. His head bowed in defeat. He had missed her.

"**Sapphira**," he bellowed.

A handful of seagulls rose from their perches on the wooden stanchions, admonishing him with an irate flapping of wings and raucous squawks.

A bonneted figure appeared at the rail.

Leofwin watched Sapphira's hand shade her eyes then her body lifted on tiptoe as she waved frantically, her dress whipping around her in the breeze. A grudging grin softened his rugged features. She never did anything by halves.

For a split-second, he was tempted to dive into the bay to swim after the ship, immediately discounting the inclination — *The Trident* was sailing too fast for him to catch up. He made do with waving back until he doubted, she could distinguish him among the crowds of people milling about the wharf.

Even then he did not move, remaining where he was until the ship was naught but a speck on the horizon.

Vulcan whinnied and tossed his head, whether in sympathy or boredom, Leofwin could not decide, choosing to believe it was the former.

"Sorry, boy," he patted the faithful stallion's neck. "Let's go home. I need to make a plan."

Sapphira gazed out over the endless ocean with unseeing eyes, long after the coastline had receded to a shadowy smudge. That he had followed her, warmed her shattered heart and she speculated over what he might have said, had time and tide not conspired to keep them apart.

Perhaps Fate had decreed theirs was to be naught but a fleeting encounter. A love for a season not a lifetime.

Regrettably, Fate did not think to warn Sapphira, and now it was too late.

Fate swallowed a frustrated curse. *Serves me right for resting on my laurels. Why did humans have to be so maddening?*

CHAPTER THIRTY

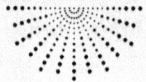

SEPTEMBER 1818

*L*eofwin Colleville approached the old pergola, coming to a halt at the sound of voices. He frowned, recognising Sapphira, but was at a loss as to the identity of her companion.

Unwilling to interrupt, he hesitated. Given the debacle that had resulted from the last time he had overheard a conversation, he was loath to repeat the experience.

He glanced around, there was no sign of a chaperone, which deepened his frown. Perhaps this was a new suitor, and they were enjoying a moment's privacy.

The notion wrenched at his soul, but he forced it aside. If she had moved on, he had only himself to blame. He should have told her he loved her before she boarded that damned ship, before she left the villa, on one of their countless walks, when he taught her to swim, when they lay wrapped in each other's arms… innumerable opportunities wasted.

Their unspoken understanding of so profound an emotion, while a tacit accord, was not sufficient, it would never be sufficient. The moment she had placed her finger on his lips to prevent his admission was indelibly imprinted in his mind. He knew it was because she didn't want to hear the words, aware their romance was finite, and their time together was running out.

He should have trusted his instincts and declared his love anyway, despite their mutual wariness of what accompanied such an avowal. It might have made all the difference.

What if I am too late?

About to retreat, her outraged, "Unhand me, sir. How dare you?" quashed his equivocation along with any niggling doubts about the wisdom of chasing the woman he loved halfway around Europe.

He rounded the corner to see Sapphira, fair spitting with rage and shoving a tall gentleman away from her side.

Sapphira was appalled and somewhat unnerved by Jeremy's recent behaviour, which was tantamount to stalking. Gone was the amiable boy, whom once she thought she loved, in his place a belligerent egotist.

Prior to last week, she had not seen the newlyweds since her return but, from the moment the couple arrived at The Towers, unannounced, it was obvious all was not rosy.

Give Gisela her due, almost the instant she stepped down from the carriage, she sought out her sister to ask forgiveness. Sapphira, disposed to scorn the apology and reject it outright, found she could not. In truth, Gisela had done her a favour.

Over the next few days, the sisters made the most of the idyllic late summer weather, and disappeared into the wilds of the estate for hours, rediscovering a neglected friendship. Their candid discussions revived a closeness they had not enjoyed for longer than either could recall.

Gisela avoided any mention of the state of her marriage,

but Sapphira was neither blind nor deaf and, while she acknowledged her sister must shoulder some of the blame, Jeremy was the one who needed some sense slapping into him.

Not that it was her business. People's relationships were private, but Gisela was dreadfully unhappy, with no idea how to solve the problem.

Sapphira broached the matter with her father for his perspective, already anticipating his advice not to meddle.

"Getting involved will more likely backfire than benefit," he cautioned.

"I cannot stand by and watch my sister unravel," Sapphira countered.

"On your head be it. What goes on in a marriage is between husband and wife. Those who dare interfere, however good their intentions usually end up being labelled mischief-making busybodies."

"I appreciate your concern, Papa, but I would rather that, than witness Gisela suffer this way. Regardless of what they did to me, Jeremy's behaviour is unreasonable and unnecessary. She might be heedless, but she loves him, not that he deserves her. If the opportunity presents itself, I cannot and will not ignore it."

Her father smiled, benignly. "Sapphira, my dear, you might be an adult, who has experienced more in two months than I will in my whole lifetime but, to me, you remain a wilful child. Follow your heart but do so with care."

Thank you, Papa." She kissed his whiskered cheek and changed the subject.

A light shawl around her shoulders, Sapphira had slipped out of the house hoping for an hour's peace and quiet. A hope dashed when her tranquil walk was disturbed by Jeremy, who refused to respect her quietly voiced assertion she did not require company.

Eventually, she lost her temper.

"How many more times do I have to tell you? I am not interested. You jilted me without compunction. You wanted Gisela, the younger, prettier, more vivacious daughter. Then, when you realised marriage is more than a piece of paper, that it requires dedication, attention, and is a continual work in progress, you gave up.

"Adding to your insolence, you have the temerity to send me a letter, *behind my sister's back*, in which you presumed I would fall into your lap like some spineless milksop, willing to accept whatever soupçon of affection you could offer, *while you are married to her.*

"What kind of sister do you think I am? Regardless of what happened, I love Gisela and for you to imagine I would hurt her in so malicious a fashion is beneath contempt.

"You sir are a bounder and a boor, and I would prefer not to clap eyes on you again, but you are a member of our family now. Instead of pestering me, you would do well to go back to Gisela, fall on your knees and grovel for her forgiveness.

"Your elopement was no spur of the moment decision, you had been courting her for months. You loved Gisela so much you risked everything for her. Where is that senti-ment? Where is your integrity? Prove to her you are the man she believes you to be.

"What I felt for you was a gentle affection and had we married, doubtless we would have muddled along amicably, but it was not love. True love binds you to a person for life whether you want it to or not. It is seared into your very essence like a brand. It is passion, emotion, sensation, trust, respect, and fidelity.

"You want nothing more than for that person to be happy for the rest of their lives. It is not selfish, guarded, or unkind. One does not own the other — whatever the law states — it is a partnership, one of shared joys and sorrows, of highs and lows."

She paused, her feelings for Leofwin crowding her head, tripping her tongue.

"You have experienced such affection?" Jeremy's question held a trace of sadness mixed with disbelief.

"Yes, I have had that privilege."

She did not elaborate. It was still too raw, too personal. Leofwin's face took shape in her mind. His grey eyes, brimming with love, fiery ardour, and perhaps a tinge of tender amusement, ensnaring her. His sculpted body, his touch… a frisson skated down her spine. Nigh on two months since they had parted, the image remained so strong, it was as though he was standing next to her.

"But I am here, and he is not." Jeremy's confidence in her capitulation, died hard.

Sapphira's hand shot up, palm out. "Lord Brunswick, enough of this nonsense. I wager if you are sincere, behave like a gentleman and less like a whiny child, Gisela will meet you halfway. All your lives the pair of you have had your every whim pandered to, but now it is time to stand on your own two feet. You are an earl, Jeremy. It is a quality not just a title."

"Sapphira," Jeremy grasped her hand, not quite ready to accept defeat.

Leofwin stepped into the sunlight.

"I think the lady has made her opinion plain. 'Tis time you took your leave." His deep voice reverberated around the crumbling folly.

Jeremy dropped Sapphira's hand as though it burnt him and glared at the newcomer. *Who was this stranger who had the impudence to interrupt?*

Transfixed, Sapphira gaped, slack jawed. He was a figment of her imagination; a manifestation of her dreams, the ones which recurred every single night. She screwed her eyes shut, opening them to find he was still there.

She repeated the action.

He was no fantasy.

Her heart stuttered and her breathing caught.

He is here, in England, in my garden.

The tiny spark she had nurtured without faith it would become a flame, flared.

"Leo…" his name an invocation.

He closed the gap and, clasping her hand, grazed a kiss to her knuckles. "My apologies for the intrusion, but I could not wait another moment. The greatest mistake of my life was letting you go.

"Foolishly, I thought my life was complete. I have a comfortable home, loyal staff, and a job to occupy me until I am old and grey. Why would I allow such freedom to be complicated by a wife, and *love*… as far as I could tell, love was an emotion that curdled the brain. I wanted no part of it. Better to remain unfettered than to be shackled.

"Then you burst into my life. I tried, I tried so hard to keep you at arms' length, when what I should have done was enfold you so tightly within them you could never escape. Sapphi, you have tipped my world upside down, you challenge me at every turn.

"You are one of the most exasperatingly intransigent people I have ever met, but you also enchant, beguile, and delight me. I miss our debates, our moonlight walks. I miss your inquiring mind. I miss the joy of being near you. The idea I might never kiss you again, hold you again, leaves me broken.

"I do not want to tame or rule you. I adore your free spirit; it is what catapulted me out of an apathy I did not realise I had sunk into and is to be cherished. You consume my waking moments and haunt my dreams. Without you, I barely exist. With you, I am alive.

"Sapphira Beresford, I love you with every fibre of my being. Might you take a gamble on a grumpy marquis? I promise to spend the rest of my days demonstrating the depth of my affection," his pause was deliberate.

"I would be honoured to walk the world with you."

Sapphira gulped. As declarations went this was utter perfection. She opened her mouth to speak, but all she managed was a rasp. Swallowing, she coerced her brain into forming a coherent reply.

"Leo..." *Really? That's it? His name. The man has just proclaimed his undying devotion and all you can say is 'Leo'? Sapphira Beresford, pull yourself together.*

She held his gaze, his beautiful smoky gaze, seeing not only herself reflected there but also a wariness. That hint of vulnerability spoke volumes. She squeezed his fingers, a delicious tingle undulating through her when he reciprocated. The spark smouldered and the flame took hold.

"I love you, Leofwin Colleville. You are irascible, obstinate, opinionated, and can be frustratingly oblivious to what is right in front of your nose. Yet you are honest, compassionate, and kind. You bring out the best and the worst in me..." unknowingly echoing his remarks to Hester on the day when everything changed. "...but there is nothing I would rather do than spar with you every day of my life."

Leofwin's face creased into a smile of unadulterated happiness. Ignoring Jeremy, he drew Sapphira into his embrace and stole her lips in a kiss which sealed their love, entwined their hearts, fused their souls, and cemented their future.

Fate huffed a relieved sigh. *I need a holiday*!

EPILOGUE

POMPEII - MAY 1826

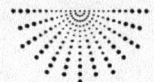

A solitary figure stood on the upper level of the amphitheatre and surveyed the ruins of Pompeii.

The emotion flooding the woman equalled that which she had experienced two days prior upon their return to Campania after a protracted sojourn in England.

She removed her hated bonnet, let the breeze blow through her hair and filled her lungs with the fragrant spring air. She was home.

Soaking it all in, Sapphira Colleville let her thoughts roam.

Her gaze fell on the stable — larger and better equipped now — where everything began.

Memories crowded in.

Following Leofwin's dramatic interruption eight years ago, she had dispatched Jeremy with a flea in his ear, suggesting he throw his energies into reconciling with Gisela, and pray she was in a receptive mood. After which, Sapphira spent a delightful afternoon reconciling with Leofwin.

In between sinfully swoon-worthy kisses, she discovered he had secured passage to England a mere week after she had departed, hence his expeditious advent. By the time she led Leofwin into the library where her parents waited impatiently, he had proposed formally and Sapphira, of course, accepted with alacrity.

Her mother, informed of the arrival of a marquis, expected to meet a sober gentleman. By sheer force of will, she concealed her astonishment when the tall, tanned stranger with the vaguely piratical demeanour who looked at her daughter with unabashed ardour, entered the room.

Her father, with whom Leofwin had already spoken, took Sapphira aside and whispered his approval.

The couple married a month later, and a month after that walked back into Villa dei Fiori to a tumultuous welcome. They returned to England only when circumstance necessitated, but both families visited periodically.

Hester — who took gleeful delight in reminding Sapphira of a certain conversation they shared in the amphitheatre so many months ago — and Archer had decided, after the birth of their first child, a son, to make Campania their home, purchasing the villa which had been their temporary abode.

Two daughters came along in quick succession — Leofwin and Sapphira embracing their role of honorary aunt and uncle with insouciant aplomb.

Marriage to Leofwin was a wonderful adventure. That is *not* to say it was all smooth sailing. Passionate, headstrong personalities do not make for a tranquil life and the couple continued to spar, although Sapphira insisted they were more akin to healthy debates.

Definitions aside, they savoured the banter which, as the years passed, became less heated, and was usually curtailed when one or the other employed their seductive wiles. Not even the advent of their own children along the way had changed that.

Twins, Leandra and Luca, aged six, along with their younger sister, Maud — a precocious four-year-old — kept their adoring parents very much on their toes.

Interestingly, rambunctious though the trio could be at home, their hoydenish tendencies vanished the moment they walked into the site. Somehow, the reverence Pompeii evoked in the adults had transferred to their children.

In the shade of the wall delineating the huge circular arena from the elevated terraced seats, three dogs feigned boredom. Scamp was never far from Sapphira.

He had proclaimed his delight at her return to the Villa dei Fiore with a lengthy refrain of ecstatic howls, to the canine accompaniment of his faithful cohort.

Little Livia was too old to come to the site anymore, and stayed at the villa, basking in blissful comfort, while her devoted slaves pandered to her every need.

A chorus of treble voices interrupted Sapphira's reverie. A tall man and three small children stepped into the sunlight from the dim entrance tunnel, rousing the dogs, who bounced around them joyfully.

Her lips twitched at the babble, and she watched her husband crouch to attempt, she suspected, to explain gladiatorial combat. Maud, her attention wandering, gazed around and spotted her mother high above her.

"Mama," her shriek resounded off the walls, prompting the other three to look up.

"Care to join us?" Leofwin didn't have to shout, the acoustics in the amphitheatre lifting the rich timbre of his voice to her ears like a caress.

Sapphira beamed and nodded, retracing her steps to the external staircase which she descended with unprecedented caution. They congregated at the bottom, her children gabbling nonstop, the dogs waiting expectantly for the next game.

Over the tops of their collective heads, her merry gaze met that of Leofwin, who winked.

Sapphira's heart swelled, at the same moment as she felt her husband entwine their fingers.

"Ought you to be climbing those stairs?" Leofwin's concern evident in his tone.

"I'm not infirm, my love..." Sapphira replied, "...and you know Dr Guarino believes exercise is beneficial."

"I think a stroll along the beach was what he had in mind at this stage, not a hike to the top of a ruined edifice. 'Tis not the height per se, but your woeful lack of coordination," he countered drily.

"Pooh, you are an old worrywart," she teased, then stretched up on tiptoe to kiss his cheek, "and I love you for it."

"Less of the old," Leofwin complained. "I am in my prime."

"Hester said they would meet us at the Forum." Sapphira changed the subject. During every pregnancy, Leofwin wanted to wrap her in a veritable cocoon of blankets, which she both adored and chafed against. Not surprisingly, they butted heads on the matter frequently.

"Then, the Forum it is. Luca, lead on." Leofwin accepted the topic was closed, for now, and ruffled his son's hair.

Luca marched off at a smart pace, flanked by the dogs, leaving his siblings trailing in his wake, demanding he slow down. To little effect it must be admitted.

Capitalising on a moment alone, Leofwin caught his wife to him. Uncaring that they were in full view of anyone who happened by, not to mention their children — who were used to random displays of affection anyway — he kissed her into a dizzy spiral.

"Oh my, Lord Osmund." Sapphira fluttered her hand parodying a fan. "To think I once imagined you to be a stuffy academic."

"Old worrywart? Stuffy academic? Lady Osmund, you wound me." Leofwin clutched his chest dramatically.

Sapphira burst out laughing. "Come on, you reprobate, we ought not tarry. You know what ruffians our children can be if left to their own devices. Perhaps when we are home…" she batted her eyelids, her fingers dancing down his jacket.

"I shall hold you to that, madam." He chuckled, grabbed her wandering hands and, tucking them around her back, gathered her flush to his body.

A cheeky response on her lips, she tilted her head, to be entranced by the boundless love radiating from the captivating grey of her husband's eyes.

Everything stilled.

Words were unnecessary.

A sharp yip broke the spell, as Scamp bounded up to weave around their legs.

"Jealous?" Sapphira crooned and bent to pat his wiry head, receiving a lick on the underside of her wrist for her troubles. "Ewww, you servile wretch," she admonished.

Scamp gave a doggy grin and trotted off, looking over his shoulder to make sure they did not lag.

Arm in arm, Sapphira and Leofwin followed him along the ancient road through the ruin, their conversation, as ever, becoming less about each other and more about the latest excavations.

Their voices faded and Pompeii, once the centre of a cataclysmic event, could be pardoned for taking credit for another — *significantly* less destructive but no less enduring — when two people, whose elusive hearts fought an indefinable attraction neither one looked for nor desired — dared to dream.

Fate smiled smugly, righteously proud of her efforts. *Now* she could rest on her laurels.

ABOUT THE AUTHOR

Rosie Chapel lives in Perth, Australia with her hubby and three furkids. When not writing, she loves catching up with friends, burying herself in a book (or three), discovering the wonders of Western Australia, or — and the best — a quiet evening at home with her husband, enjoying a glass of wine and a movie.

Website: www.rosiechapel.com

ABOUT THE AUTHOR

OTHER BOOKS BY ROSIE CHAPEL

<u>Historical Fiction</u>

The Hannah's Heirloom Sequence
The Pomegranate Tree - Book One
Echoes of Stone and Fire - Book Two
Embers of Destiny - Book Three
Etched in Starlight - Prequel
Hannah's Heirloom Trilogy - Compilation — e-book only

Prelude to Fate
Legacy of Flame and Ash

<u>Regency Romances</u>
The Linen and Lace Series
Once Upon An Earl - Book One
To Unlock Her Heart - Book Two
Love on a Winter's Tide - Book Three
A Love Unquenchable - Book Four
A Hidden Rose — Book Five

The Daffodil Garden
The Unconventional Duchess
Rescuing Her Knight

His Fiery Hoyden
A Regency Duet

A Regency Christmas Double

Fate is Curious

A Christmas Prayer *with Ashlee Shades*

The Lady's Wager

Winning Emma

A Love Impossible

Unravelling Roana

Love Kindled

Fairy Tale Romance

Chasing Bluebells

Contemporary Romances

Of Ruins and Romance

All At Once It's You

Cobweb Dreams

Just One Step

His Heart's Second Sigh

Dystopian Romance

Echoes & Illusions *with Rori Bleu*

HISTORICAL FICTION

The Pomegranate Tree

Hannah's Heirloom - Book One

Hoping to trace the origins of an ancient ruby clasp, a gift from her long dead grandmother, Hannah Wilson travels to the fortress of Masada with her best friend, Max. Strange dreams concerning a rebel ambush begin to haunt Hannah and following a tragic accident, she slips into the world of Ancient Masada.

A woman out of time, Hannah must rely on her instincts and her knowledge of what will befall this citadel to survive. Will she escape, or is she doomed to die along with hundreds of others as Masada falls — and what does any of this have to do with an ancient ruby clasp?

Echoes of Stone and Fire

Hannah's Heirloom - Book Two

Pompeii - a vibrant city lost in time following the AD79 eruption of Vesuvius. Now rediscovered, archaeologists yearn for an opportunity to uncover the town's past. Some things, however, are best left alone - revealing the secrets hidden beneath the stones could prove perilous. Hannah and Max are brought to Pompeii by a surprise invitation to join an excavation team who are trying to uncover the city's long history.

After entering an excavated house that bears a Hebrew inscription, Hannah's two worlds collide, and she falls back through time to ancient Pompeii. A place where her ancestor is a physician to gladiators engaged in mortal combat, where riotous mobs run amok and where a ghost from the past returns to haunt her.

Will Hannah and her loved ones manage to escape the devastation she knows is coming, before the town is engulfed in volcanic ash? Will she ever find her way back to Max the love of her life, waiting not so patiently millennia away? Or will echoes be all that remain?

Embers of Destiny

Hannah's Heirloom - Book Three

AD80 - Hannah and Maxentius must embark on a new journey to Northern Britannia. This harsh frontier is far from the comforts of Rome and danger lurks where least expected; a garrison of soldiers, some unhappy with their isolated posting; local tribes, outwardly accepting of their Roman occupier, but who may still resent the seizure of their lands.

Millennia away, Hannah Vallier finds a familiar item while working in a museum near Hadrian's Wall. It is the pomegranate; carved by Maxentius on Masada. Before Hannah can discuss it with Max, disaster strikes! Believing her husband has been killed, Hannah retreats into the past, her soul melding with that of her ancestor, but with little idea of what they could face. Is the risk from the conquered tribes, or much closer to home?

As rebellion threatens to shatter a fragile peace, Hannah's heart whispers that just maybe Max isn't dead and that he is calling her home. Can she trust her heart, or will she remain caught out of time, her destiny floating away like embers on a breeze?

Etched in Starlight

Hannah's Heirloom - Prequel

Maxentius - a Roman soldier fresh from the battlefields of Armenia, arrives to take command of the military outpost of Masada, Herod's isolated citadel in the Judaean desert. A seemingly mundane posting after years of warfare, Maxentius finds it more challenging to maintain a focused garrison than to face the wrath of the Parthians across a disputed frontier.

Hannah - a young Hebrew physician spends her days dealing with injuries from street brawls, deprivation, disease and loss. As her beloved Jerusalem plunges into chaos, her brother — who belongs to a band of rebels determined to drive out their Roman occupiers — tells her of their plans to storm a desert fortress and steal the weapons stored there, persuading his reluctant sister to go with him.

Masada - following the ambush, Hannah finds and treats three badly wounded Roman soldiers. In the aftermath and against impossible odds, Hannah and Maxentius realise that they are more than healer and captive, their fate already etched in starlight.

Prelude to Fate

For Lucia, staring into the jaws of an horrific death, escape seems impossible.

Rufius Atellus, a veteran Roman soldier, is appalled when he recognises one of the victims about to be executed. Surely this is a ghastly mistake?

A ferocious she-wolf, anticipating a tasty meal, suddenly finds herself under a human's control.

In an unexpected twist, and as danger threatens, the lives of all three become inextricably entwined.

Was it chance brought them together in that theatre of bloodshed, or simply a prelude to fate?

Legacy of Flame and Ash

A Hannah's Heirloom Story

An unremarkable family ring — lost when its owner was killed in the catastrophic eruption of Vesuvius — is excavated after nearly two millennia buried under tons of pumice and ash, setting off an extraordinary sequence of events.

A brazen robbery, and the ring is lost again. The theft and subsequent investigation, inspire twelve-year-old Cristiano Rossi to dedicate his life to the search and recovery of stolen artefacts.

Fast forward twenty years. Whispers of a rare item being offered for sale on the black market, initiates a joint operation between the Italian and British branches of the, colloquially named, Art Squad.

Hannah Vallier and her tech savvy assistant, Bryony Emerson — whose abilities to track down the untraceable, led to them assisting the UK Art and Antiquities Unit — have unearthed an intriguing thread. Reluctantly, Cristiano agrees to team up with the pair to thwart the traffickers, retrieve the artefact and, hopefully, dismantle the site.

What ought to be a routine assignment is complicated by a rogue operative, an unexpected romance, an ancient connection, and a *very* angry ghost!

REGENCY ROMANCE

Once Upon An Earl

Linen and Lace - Book One

When Fate saw fit to intervene in the life of Giles Trevallier, the very respectable Earl of Winchester, by dropping a female — soaked to the skin and with no memory of who she is or how she came to be there — literally at his feet, no one could have predicted the outcome.

While uncovering her identity, Giles realises he is falling hopelessly in love with his mystery guest, who unbeknownst to him, is succumbing to similar emotions; but, when the heart is involved, a thoughtless word or gesture can thwart even Fate's best-laid plans.

Faced with misunderstandings, whispers of scandal, secret documents and foreign agents, their chance at a happy ever after seems elusive, but fairy tales often happen when least expected, and love — however inconvenient — usually finds a way to conquer all.

To Unlock Her Heart

Linen and Lace - Book Two

Abused by a duke, and shunned by Society, relief seems at hand when Grace Aldeburgh is bequeathed a house in a small village, far from malicious gossips.

Once there, a tentative friendship blooms between Grace and Theo Elliott, the local doctor, who has already resolved to be the man to unlock her heart.

Just when happiness appears to be within her grasp, her erstwhile tormentor once again stalks Grace. After a failed kidnap attempt, the duke's quest culminates in an acrimonious confrontation, and the reason for his venal pursuit becomes agonisingly clear.

Love on a Winter's Tide

Linen and Lace - Book Three

Every day, Helena disappears into a world few acknowledge, helping the poor, downtrodden, and abused. A husband is the last thing she can be bothered with.

Busy managing his shipping line, Hugh Drummond sees no need for a wife, whose only joy is dancing and frivolity. If — and it was a huge if — he ever married, it would be to a woman as capable as he, not some giddy society Miss.

Then, Hugh meets Helena and despite their resolve, fate, it seems, has other ideas. As their attraction deepens however, treachery threatens to tear them apart. Will they uncover the perpetrator in time, or will their love be swept away, lost forever on a winter's tide?

A Love Unquenchable

Linen and Lace - Book Four

Jessica Drummond, a bright and cheerful young woman, rarely gives romance, let alone love, a thought. Long hours working in her brother's shipping office affords little chance of her ever meeting an eligible bachelor.

Duncan Barrington, veteran of the Napoleonic Wars, believes himself wounded in both body and soul. He has no intention of inflicting his demons on anyone, certainly not a beautiful and, in his opinion, irresponsible city lady.

One cold and snowy morning, the plight of a bedraggled puppy throws Jessica and Duncan together and, as a spark of something indefinable yet wholly unquenchable begins to burn, it is unclear who rescued whom.

A Hidden Rose

After witnessing his mother's grief at the loss of his father, Nick Drummond resolved never to cause someone he loved such distress. Even the happiness of his siblings would not sway him — until he met Rose.

Rose Archer was almost content assisting her doctor father in a tiny fishing village in the north of Yorkshire. To experience the world beyond, a tantalising dream — until she met Nick.

Unexpectedly, the impossible becomes possible, and the renounced — desired above all things, but the shipwreck that brought them together, may yet tear them apart. Will Nick learn to trust his heart, or will his love for Rose remain forever hidden

The Daffodil Garden

Horrifically scarred during the war, William Harcourt - Marquis of Blackthorne - prefers to spend his days in the quiet of his daffodil garden; plants do not pity, turn away, or judge.

Lucy Truscott, whose life is far removed from that of the *ton*, has no idea that by saving the life of a young woman, to whom she bears an uncanny resemblance, her own will be placed in mortal danger.

A chance encounter leads to something more. William begins to trust that Lucy sees the man beneath the scars, while Lucy is persuaded that love might actually transcend status.

Unfortunately, before their courtship has really begun, someone has every intention of ending it - permanently.

The Unconventional Duchess

Refusing to suffer the humiliation of her husband flaunting his mistress at Society events, the newly married Duchess of Wallingstead, Ella Lennox, takes control of her life. She leaves London for the family's country seat in remote Yorkshire.

A woman alone, Ella spends the next four years turning a cold, grim house into a home, and transforming the fortunes of the estate. Not afraid of hard work, she soon earns the respect of those around her with her determination and unconventional attitude.

Out of the blue, the duke arrives. Resigned to another arduous visit, Ella is stunned when it seems he is attempting to court her.

Impossible!

Could her dream of a happy marriage be about to come true?

Everything hangs on a snowstorm, a herd of cows and an uninvited guest!

Rescuing Her Knight

The *de Wiltons* — Book One

A story, invented to keep a little girl distracted, marks the beginning of another tale. One destined to remain unfinished for twenty years.

At thirteen, Adam Marchmain became Kitty de Wilton's 'Knight of the Garden' — a title bestowed following an accident which resulted in six-year-old Kitty having her knee sutured. Kitty never forgot his gallantry, but pledges made as children rarely survive into adulthood.

Their paths separated until Fate decreed, they meet again.

Widowed, badly disfigured and his sight ruined, Adam returns to his family home, a shadow of his former self.

Similarly afflicted, although her scars are invisible, Kitty — against her better judgement — is persuaded to help Adam banish his demons. This requires a subterfuge which, if discovered, might shatter more than the bonds of friendship forged two decades previously.

To Kitty, determined to break through the shield Adam has erected, the risk is worth it.

To see his smile and hear his laughter.

To rescue the knight of her childhood.

Just when a fairy tale ending is within her grasp, Kitty is threatened by the man who murdered her husband. In a cruel twist the tables are turned, and Kitty is the one who needs rescuing.

His Fiery Hoyden

A Novella

Livvy has no respect for the nobility; they let her down when she most needed them. Why should she accede to their demands now?

Philip, Lord Harrington, is stunned to discover the young heir to the dukedom lives a stone's throw away in a ramshackle cottage, and resolves to restore the child to his birthright.

They meet in a clash of wills, but just when it seems Livvy might surrender, the victory Philip desires, may not taste all that sweet.

A Regency Duet

Luck be a Pirate

Luck wasn't something retired pirate Kennet Alexson believed in — good or bad. However, even he had to concede that landing a job at Trentams shipyard, and meeting Lynette Collins, was more than coincidence.

Fortune it seemed, was smiling on him for once.

As Kennet adjusts to life on dry land, his friendship with Lynette deepens into something far more enduring, and what once seemed elusive now becomes possible.

Unfortunately, fate has other plans, and Kennet's good luck is about to run out.

The Highwayman's Kiss

Surrendered Hearts — Book One

Nothing exciting had ever happened to Juliette St Clair. Her days were spent assisting her father or calling on friends, wandering art galleries, taking constitutionals or, and more preferably, escaping into her books. Her evenings her evenings — an endless round of balls, where she preferred to remain invisible.

Until the day she was robbed by a highwayman.

A Regency Christmas Double

Heart Rescued

Four years since Jasper lost the woman he was hoping to marry. Four years since he closed his heart and withdrew from Society. He has no idea his reclusive existence is about to be shattered.

Enter his sister's best friend, Harriet, a flame haired beauty, who needs his help.

Reluctantly he agrees and as they spend time together, it is clear their feelings run deep. Although Harriet affects Jasper in a way no woman ever has, he believes her to be out of his league ~ but it's Christmas and she might just be the one to melt his frozen heart

Catch a Snowflake

Romance often blossoms in the most unlikely of places - but in a ward full of wounded soldiers - surely not?

When Lucas Withers comes face to face with Jemima Parsons - a young woman who blames him for her brother's injury - falling in love is the last thing on their minds. What neither of them anticipated, was the magic of snowflakes.

Fate is Curious

A Novella

Happily, ever after? No such thing! Bereft, following her beloved husband's sudden death, Lady Charlotte Sherbrooke has lost her belief in romantic nonsense.

Successful shipping merchant, Zacharie Romain, is no stranger to loss; his business can be hazardous. Moreover, his wife died in childbirth and even though it happened a decade ago, he has no mind to expose himself to such sorrow again.

They meet in less than joyful circumstances but, as the year turns and grief diminishes, the woes of a small boy become the catalyst for something wholly unexpected. Can Charlotte and Zacharie trust what Fate has in store or will past heartbreak prevent them from taking a chance on love?

A Christmas Prayer

with Ashlee Shades

A Short Story

An entreaty from a frightened child.

Orphaned and only nine, Caroline Thorne has to grow up before her time. She is doing everything she can to keep what is left of her family together and out of the workhouse but is terrified her prayers are not being heard. Or maybe they are…

A petition from a woman desperate for a family.

A chance meeting with three orphaned siblings, tugs at Elizabeth Barrington's heart strings. Thus far, she and her husband have not been blessed with children and, as Christmas approaches, a plan begins to form - one which might just be the answer to her prayers.

Two Christmas prayers, as different as they are the same.

Will they hear and, more importantly, heed the answer?

The Lady's Wager

Surrendered Hearts- Book Two

A Novelette

Ged Mowbray will do anything to avoid being married off to the suitable prospects his parents insist on parading in front of him.

Melissa Bouchard is under no illusion her sizeable dowry is the attraction to suitors, not her.

An overheard conversation leads to an offer too good to refuse, but what happens when a lady's wager, becomes a gamble on the happily ever after, you did not even realise you wanted?

Winning Emma

Surrendered Hearts - Book Three

A Novelette

Randolph Craythorpe — earl, covert operative, and occasional highwayman — believed his dalliance with Lady Felicity Hartwich would lead to marriage. It did, but not to him! The arrival of an unwelcome guest, however, provides the perfect opportunity to indulge in a little retaliation.

Emma Newbury accompanies her cousin, Lady Charity Anscombe, to London for the Christmas season. Once there, she comes face to face with the three men who witnessed the humiliating aftermath of her father's disgrace — one of whom, to her irritation, has taken up residence in her dreams.

Their infrequent encounters only serve to confuse but, while winter tightens its grip on the city, what was inconceivable becomes the one thing for which they both yearn, yet bound by Society's rules, cannot admit.

As the snow falls, Randolph begins to understand that to win Emma, he will have to surrender.

A Love Impossible

A Regency M/M Novelette

Tasked with investigating a heinous crime, Edward Lindsay travels from London to Dublin — a city which holds too many memories — in the guise of guardian to his sister. He knew it could be hazardous, and relished the challenge, but that wasn't what caused his stomach to tighten as they approached landfall.

Dublin held more than just a murderer.

There was also Aidan.

While attending a party, Aidan Griffen is astonished when he comes face to face with a man who fled Dublin two years previously. A man he has desperately tried to forget.

As Edward closes in on his quarry, a fire, deliberately extinguished, is rekindled. But what of it? Edward and Aidan share a love impossible, and to acknowledge their feelings — more dangerous than confronting a killer.

Is there any hope of a happily ever after?

Unravelling Roana

A Regency Novelette

Tired of being ignored by her husband, Roana Dumont, Countess of Brooketon does the one thing guaranteed to get his attention. She runs away… to Venice, leaving behind a set of riddles for him to solve… *if* he feels their marriage is worth saving.

Gideon Dumont, 6th Earl of Brooketon is flabbergasted when he discovers his wife has apparently vanished off the face of the earth. A series of puzzles, the only clue as to her whereabouts.

The question is… will he unravel them?

Love Kindled

A Regency Novelette

Recently widowed, Amelia Ingram - Countess of Gresham, decides to shake off the fetters from her arranged and loveless marriage. Exploiting her new-found independence, Amelia indulges her yearning to explore - incognito.

Her ploy works so well, she receives an offer of employment from the dangerously handsome, Rupert Latimer - Earl of Badlesmere. On impulse, she accepts and finds herself governess to Cate, a delightful scamp of a child. What began as a bit of a game on Amelia's part, evolves into something far more profound, and a flame she presumed impossible to ignite, is kindled.

An unexpected turn of events leads to yet another offer. This time there is far more at stake and, determined history not repeat itself, Amelia confesses her ruse.

Rupert has been burnt once. Will he douse the spark, or take a risk and trust his heart?

FAIRY TALE ROMANCE

Chasing Bluebells

A Fairy Tale Novella

Once upon a time, somewhere in France, there was a man whose
reckless obsession led him down a dark path — one which,
ultimately, cost him his life. That ought to have been the end of it.
Regrettably, as is so often the case, those who least deserve it, suffer
for the actions of others.

A decade after being sent away, Sebastien Daviau returns to the little
village where everything began. Hoping to lay the ghosts of his
childhood to rest, he studiously ignores the possibility, he might run
into Charlotte de Montbeliard.

As luck would have it, Charlotte is the one who runs into him…
well, his horse… and although the brief encounter leaves a lasting
impression, neither recognises the other.

A name revealed causes a freak accident, catapulting Sebastien's past
into his present, and bringing him face to face with a man whose
reputation would intimidate the most ardent of suitors.

Can whatever is blossoming between Charlotte and Sebastien
survive the challenge imposed, or is their happily ever after about to
fade as quickly as the bluebells they loved to chase?

CONTEMPORARY ROMANCE

Of Ruins and Romance

Kassandra Winters has intrigued Gabriel St Germain since he accidentally knocked her flying outside her university professor's office. Her face haunts his dreams, yet he never expected to see her again. So, he is surprised when she appears, as though destined to do so, in the middle of a ruin, and he concocts a plan to win her heart.

Gabriel's old-fashioned courtship touches something deep inside Kassie and, although struggling to believe someone as handsome as Gabriel could possibly be interested in her, she soon realises she has fallen irrevocably in love with him. However, just as Kassie shares everything of herself with Gabriel, her world comes crashing down.

Can their romance survive, or will it fall in ruins, like the relics of antiquity that brought them together?

All At Once It's You

When Alex arrives in the small village of Rosedale Abbey, to take up a position as a research assistant for a renowned archaeologist, the last thing she is looking for, or expects to find, is love.

Jake was perfectly happy with the status quo. When it came to relationships, he didn't do committed or long term. He called the shots, and if his current flame didn't like it, she knew what to do. A philosophy, which served him well - until he met Alex.

Romance blooms, but even as the untamed wilderness of the North Yorkshire moors weaves its spell, a long-buried secret might yet jeopardise their happily ever after.

Cobweb Dreams

A Novella

A holiday on the Scottish isle of Mull was just the break Chloe Shepherd needed, an escape from her boring office job and her complete lack of anything resembling a social life. Romance, it seems, isn't on the cards and, although Chloe dreams of finding her soulmate she is beginning to believe love is like cobwebs — spun overnight, only to vanish in the early morning breeze.

Under sufferance, Dominic Winters makes a flying visit to Mull to check on a rental property owned by his family. He hasn't got time for this — so indulging in a holiday fling is the last thing on his mind.

A lamb stuck in a bog proves a most unexpected matchmaker and, while Mull weaves its magic, Chloe wonders whether those fragile cobwebs might be far more stubborn than she thought.

Just One Step

A Short Story

In the aftermath of an horrific car accident, Daisy Forrester travels to Italy - hoping, so far from her memories, she might begin to heal.

Archaeologist, and single father, Adam Willoughby is too busy looking after his young daughter to give romance let alone love, a thought.

Neither expects a chance encounter in an ancient ruin to be anything more, but sometimes, that's all it takes.

His Heart's Second Sigh

A Novella

Reuben Faulkner and Paige Latimer are two happily single people, who have no desire to upset the status quo.

Unexpectedly, they are thrown together, only to discover both want far more than a casual friendship.

Just when things take an interesting turn, Reuben's past catches up with them, and threatens to derail their blossoming romance before it has chance to start.

DYSTOPIAN ROMANCE

Echoes & Illusions

The Hunters - Book 1

Twenty years after a global plague, the remnants of civilisation struggle to eke out an existence in a world where humanity is secondary to survival.

On the outskirts of a once vibrant Rome, Gabriel tends his vineyard. From dawn to dusk, he strives to carve out a living, while caring for Bianca, his heavily pregnant wife.

Life might be tough, but at least he had an income, meagre though it was. Trouble seemed a distant memory, until the day he notices their neighbours are not at work in the adjacent fields.

A gruesome discovery sparks a chain of events to rival the conflicts Rome witnessed at the height of its power. Gabriel and Bianca must pit their wits and their lives against a formidable opponent, in an attempt prevent an atrocity none could have predicted.

A bond, forged in a snowy field and strengthened in a city under siege, is put to the ultimate test.

In a world of echoes and illusions, is their love strong enough to surmount the odds, or will it crumble to dust like the empire their enemies are striving to replicate?